# WINNER KILLS ALL

# RJ BAILEY

**SIMON &
SCHUSTER**

London · New York · Sydney · Toronto · New Delhi

A CBS COMPANY

First published in Great Britain by Simon & Schuster UK Ltd, 2019
A CBS COMPANY

1 3 5 7 9 10 8 6 4 2

Simon & Schuster UK Ltd
1st Floor
222 Gray's Inn Road
London WC1X 8HB

Simon & Schuster Australia, Sydney
Simon & Schuster India, New Delhi

www.simonandschuster.co.uk
www.simonandschuster.com.au
www.simonandschuster.co.in

A CIP catalogue record for this book
is available from the British Library

Paperback ISBN: 978-1-4711-7398-1
eBook ISBN: 978-1-4711-7399-8

Typeset in Sabon by M Rules
Printed and bound by CPI Group (UK) Ltd, Croydon, CR0 4YY

Simon & Schuster UK Ltd are committed to sourcing paper
that is made from wood grown in sustainable forests and support the Forest
Stewardship Council, the leading international forest certification organisation.
Our books displaying the FSC logo are printed on FSC certified paper.

*For Sarah & Tris.*
*Our kind of trouble*

# PROLOGUE

*How far would you go to save a loved one? Your own flesh and blood?*

This far, I think, as I ease open one of the art nouveau panelled doors and step inside the ruined building. This is journey far enough into darkness for any rational human being. Except, I can probably delete 'rational' from that. I am driven by something that lies much, much deeper in my brain, far removed from the civilised centres.

My rubber soles make the merest squeak on the stained terrazzo floor. The interior reminds me of a cathedral: a great soaring dome, supported by once-gilded ribs, now cracked and denuded of decoration. At some point, it must have rivalled the great casinos of Europe in grandeur. In fact, it would have made Monte Carlo look like a branch of Betfred. I can almost hear the laughter and the chink of glasses from the *fin de siècle beau monde*.

Almost.

The ghosts are drowned out by the squelch of fresh

pigeon droppings underfoot. I glance upwards and one of the perpetrators sets flight, the flapping filling the cavernous space above my head, echoing around the balconies and balustrades.

I stop and listen as the bird finds a new perch and coos appreciatively. A few of his feathered companions join in, but silence quickly resumes. I listen for any further disturbances in the air. Apart from the drip of water from a breach in the roof and the occasional hiss of waves on the promenade outside, it is eerily quiet.

Wherever they are, the men I am looking for aren't in the building. At least, not this part.

Why would they be? It might be out of season, but the roof leaks, the pigeons shit and there's always the chance of an idle tourist wandering in. A tourist who would find themselves with a hole in the skull quicker than they could think: 'Oops, wrong turn!'

No, if I have guessed correctly, the gathering of men must be below my feet, in the cellars – *catacombs?* – of this derelict building. The Void, as it is known. I have to go down there. I can hear my partner Freddie's voice in my head: *Wait for back-up, Sam Wylde.*

But there is no back-up. My back-up is either dead or damaged.

I'm on my own. Not even Freddie at my side.

I place the holdall I have been carrying onto the floor and crouch next to it. With gloved hands I pull the zip. It comes smoothly. Always lubricate your zips – I've watched people die because they couldn't open a zipped pocket to pull out a weapon in time.

I peel the sides apart so that the bag gapes at me. From within I take out a gun. It's the kind of gun that would get me a hefty prison sentence if I were to even possess it in the UK. If they knew what I intended to do with it, what hate was eating up my heart, they'd lock me up and throw away the proverbial key.

I began this part of my life as a bodyguard: *Sam Wylde, Personal Protection Officer*. Now, I have moved on to something much more proactive.

I am here, if necessary, to kill.

I stand and check over the FN P-90 in the thin light that is streaming through the grimy and broken windows in the hall. It's a weird-looking weapon, all right. Made of polymer, it could pass as a ray gun in a 1950s science-fiction film. Or a device for vacuuming the interior of a car. But it can be fired one-handed, can penetrate body armour at one hundred metres and its magazine carries an impressive fifty rounds.

But even fifty rounds won't last long on full automatic.

I stuff two extra mags behind my own body armour and switch on the laser-dot system. As I move the weapon, the glowing spot dances on the far wall, over the scabrous rococo plasterwork. I imagine it exploding into dust.

I make sure the safety is on, just in case instinct – or rage – takes over.

As I look up and scan the higher floors, I notice a circular space where perhaps an internal window once sat. It is empty now; any decorative glass long gone. I draw the laser over it. It reminds me of the 'murder holes' the Taliban favoured in Afghanistan; small gaps in the walls of the compounds through which they would lay lethal fire on our patrols before disappearing into a warren of houses behind them. Shoot and scoot, as it was known. But the dot is lost in empty space. Nobody is up there getting a sighting on me.

I kill the laser, take out a Glock and put it in my belt, tucked down against my arse. I don't feel its polymer body because of the thin neoprene wetsuit I'm wearing under my clothes. I have a few other bits and pieces to conceal around myself, but most of the items I will need – including a second Glock – are in the small black rucksack I thread my arms through. I put on a head torch, but leave it switched off. Same with the throat mic assembly.

I hear Freddie again, using my army nickname; a phantom crackle in an imaginary earpiece.

*Ready, Buster?*

Ready.

Satisfied I am done, I slide the holdall into a corner, then check everything is tight, from bootlaces to bra straps.

It is.

I'm ready to go.

As I head for the stairs, limping to ease the residual pain in my left knee, I try to recall how all this started; how I ended up looking for the men I might have to hurt. Correction: *want* to hurt. The answer is always the same.

Albania.

Albania, a man named Adam and a nagging question: *How did I know it was a hit?*

# PART ONE

*'Suppressed grief suffocates, it rages within the breast, and is forced to multiply its strength'*

# ONE

'Albania? And you said *yes*?'

The sentence, with its imaginary accusatory finger, hung between them. Kath opened the fridge, took out the milk and slammed the door shut. Adam heard the various half-full condiment bottles racked inside rattle together nervously, as if they knew what was coming. He braced himself as he sat at the kitchen table.

The water hissed from the fancy boiling-water tap into the teapot. It was the latest toy in the house. Cut out the middleman: lose the kettle, scald yourself direct from the tap instead. Adam thought the water came out a degree or two below the ideal temperature for a decent cup of tea. Kath accused him of being 'too anally Yorkshire', even though it was many years since he had left Leeds.

As she fussed with making the tea, Adam looked beyond his wife, through the window, to the rain sweeping across the South Downs. A glorious landscape most of the time, it looked less than inviting with a wind-blown downpour billowing in curtains across the low hills. There was a point in his life when he would have been out there, swathed in Craghoppers or The North Face, head down against the squall, walking the dog. But their flat-coated retriever had expired before its allotted time, thanks to some inbred genetic predisposition to cancer. Six months had passed since the poor animal had been put down. They had recently started to talk about a successor, but only tentatively. In truth, there was a sense of freedom that came with not having to worry about daily walks or who would look after it while they were on holiday.

Still, right at that moment, he'd rather be out there braving needle-sharp rain on his face than waiting for Kath to blow.

He glanced at the half-finished crossword and read fifteen down. *A confused poet faces a vast emptiness.* Four letters.

'When?' she finally asked, planting the mug in front of him. It was one of the thick pottery ones she had bought in Lewes. He hated the feel of the fat rim against his mouth. It was like drinking from a chamber pot. Not that he had ever done that. The fact Kath was using those mugs suggested she was less than pleased by his news.

'When?'

'Friday.'

'Friday? *This* Friday?'

'It's a newspaper, Kath. They like to strike while—'

Adam never got to complete the platitude. 'Conor is coming home for the weekend. You know that.'

He knew his son too well to allow him to be used as a weapon. 'Conor is coming home to lock himself in his room between trips out to Brighton getting pissed with his mates. He isn't coming to see me.'

Kath pursed her lips and he thought about telling her she shouldn't. The resulting lines didn't flatter and . . .

He smothered the thought.

He could talk. Neither of them was getting any younger. *What's that coming over the hill?* as the old pop song went. Why, it's fifty. Well, in *his* case it was. Kath could look in the rear-view mirror and still see forty.

She sat in front of him, both hands cradling the mug, head over it as if she were hoping the steam would clear her sinuses.

'Did Rory do it just to piss me off?'

Adam shook his head. 'What you or I think doesn't come into it—'

'Oh, bollocks. He must know I can't even bear to hear the name of that fucking place.'

*Albania.*

'Look, he knows I speak the language. Well, sort of. And I'm associated with . . .' The rest of his sentence deserted him, giving an impression of guilt.

'*Associated* with? Is that what you call it in the office?'

Adam closed his eyes. At work on the newspaper, on the five-a-side pitch and in his seat at Brighton & Hove Albion, he had a reputation for . . . robustness. For the odd hard tackle and a command of fruity language.

11

But faced with this, his defences crumbled and he was continually on the back foot.

With Kath making all the running he felt like Superman must whenever Lex Luther plucked out a chunk of Kryptonite.

Powerless.

It was the guilt that sucked the energy out of him, of course; the nagging feeling that he had done her wrong, as they said in country and western songs.

'Look, Kath, there are two towns locked in a power struggle. It's like *A Fistful of Dollars*: two families facing off against each other ...'

Kath gave a hoot of laughter. 'And you're John Wayne, are you?'

*Clint Eastwood.* But he kept quiet. Pedantry never ended well with Kath.

'In which case, you shouldn't have given up the gym membership when we moved, should you?'

Kath had recently commented on his 'man boobs', which he thought unfair. He was in pretty good shape for his age, especially compared to some of his colleagues. But it was possible that Tuesday night five-a-side wasn't enough to combat his red wine and curry (albeit not together) habit.

'And look, I know you went to Helmand and to Syria, but you're no longer a front-line reporter. No John Simpson, anyway, ploughing the same furrow as an elder statesman. Your cutting-edge days are over. Human interest is your beat—'

A flash of anger made his words bright and brittle.

'Don't tell me what my beat is. I did that exposé on cam girls in Romania, didn't I?'

She sniffed. 'I thought that was just an excuse to look at porn for a week.'

Angry now. 'And the people who make their fortunes from trading poor girls as sex slaves – that's not a cutting-edge story? Or relevant? Or important?'

She had no answer to that. After a while, her voice modulated somewhat and she said: 'And you got death threats after that article. And the book.'

Only on Twitter, he thought. And only if he were to go back to Romania, which he had no intention of doing. Although he wasn't stupid enough to think Albania was a day at the beach.

'I'm not going there to take them down all guns blazing, Kath. Simply to observe and report. And I'll get some material for the novel. It's a good cover. They don't like journos sniffing around, but if they think they might get mentioned in a book . . .'

At least she didn't laugh at that. Adam was working on a semi-fictionalised version of actor Anthony Quayle's time in the Special Operation Executive (SOE) in Albania during the Second World War. His agent hadn't achieved a particularly large advance for the novel – 'Who's even heard of Anthony Quayle these days?' the young editor had asked – so it was coming along very slowly. That and the fact Kath huffed every time she stumbled across one of his books on Albania left on the coffee table or next to their bed, as if she had found a copy of *Men Only* or some such. *Did they still publish such mags in the day of the internet,* he wondered? It was a long time since he had felt the urge to look along a top shelf.

The truth was, the novel was a way out. A fresh start. He felt increasingly alienated from the paper and its so-called core values. And the hordes of millennials that seemed to swell on a weekly basis. He doubted half of them were even on a salary. Barbarians in Supreme hoodies at the gates, ready to sweep the old guard away and take the plum assignments. But he didn't want to go out with a whimper; didn't want to move to editing the puzzle page or some other remote corner of the enterprise.

One last big piece, then he'd be off: head held high, dignity intact. Oh, and maybe a redundancy package after so many years of sterling service.

'So this was Rory's idea?'

Now, this was the tricky part. The tip-off about the two small communities in Albania supplying nearly all the sex traffickers in Europe had come from a Dutch Europol investigator, whom Adam had interviewed for his article. They had stayed in touch and over a drink in London, the Dutchman had told him about Golan and Cerci, the Sodom and Gomorrah of the sex trade. Apparently, the Kurds controlled the general people-smuggling across most borders, but the Albanians were the specialists. They dealt in carnality.

It was Adam who had pitched a story about it at conference. But it might be better to gloss over that . . .

'I think it came from Martin.' Rory was the

magazine's editor. Martin was deputy of the whole paper. 'But the mag is the best home for it, so Rory took it. That bloody Nina wanted it. I've still got the marks from her sharp elbows as she tried to get my own bloody story off me.' Nina was Scottish, abrasive and clearly feeling the same sort of pressures as Adam from the upswell of younger talent. It was a little like fighting for the last seats in a lifeboat. 'I sent her packing, mind.'

He knew from the way she stiffened that he had said the wrong thing. 'You *fought* for this?'

The temperature dropped as if the weather outside had breached the kitchen walls.

'It has nothing to do with her, Kath. I don't even know where she is now. Not in bloody Albania, anyway.'

'I'm still going to kill Rory.' Kath knew Rory of old. Adam and Rory had been something of a double act when they were all at university. Sharing a flat, a high tolerance for alcohol, a love of The Smiths and a lot of women.

'He must have known that it would upset me … Oh, fuck it.'

She got up and strode out with a purposefulness he recognised.

'Don't give him a hard time. He's only doing his job. It'll only be a few …'

There was a rustle of heavy fabric from the hallway as she grabbed her coat. The front door slammed. He heard the throaty growl of her Mini and the spatter of wet gravel against the windows as she wheel-spun down the drive.

15

He sipped his tea, relishing the sudden calm. All things considered, that had gone better than he had expected.

Her name was Roza – Rozafati in full, but she preferred the truncated version. She had just turned nineteen when she had been trafficked from Albania in 2009 with all the usual promises of a soft and affluent life in Western Europe.

She could be a waitress. Perhaps, if she wanted some extra money on the side, a stripper. Or a table dancer in the West End of London. It wasn't exactly the promise of an easy life, but it beat the prospects she had at home.

The reality, though, was much worse than what she left behind when she climbed in a battered Cibro minibus, everything that mattered to her stuffed into a single suitcase.

After being gang-raped several times along the way – a tried-and-tested device to render sex meaningless to the girls – she had ended up in England, in a brothel above a kebab shop in Ealing. After three weeks – three very long weeks with up to a dozen 'clients' a day – she had escaped.

Unusually, not only did Roza speak English, she was articulate and resourceful. She managed to find a refuge and they contacted the newspaper. At last the reporters had someone who could tell their own tale, without translators; a woman who was traumatised but would unflinchingly explain what had happened to her and thousands of others.

The magazine article that Adam wrote grew into a book – *The Shame Road* – using Roza's story to expose the whole cesspit of human trafficking that was going on under everyone's noses. Adam estimated that, in London, everyone was within at least half a mile of a trafficked person.

One night during the book tour, after too much champagne, Adam and Roza had found themselves in the same room and the same bed. He was so drunk he had forgotten that he had invited Kath to join them for the final few dates of the trip.

# TWO

It was a slow and steady climb through the mountains of Northern Albania to the turning that would take Adam to the rendezvous point where he was to pick up a local 'fixer', the newspaper's person on the ground. The road was wide, but covered in potholes, which meant Adam progressed in a series of sinuous curves until oncoming traffic forced him to endure the suspension-threatening jarring of the craters. There were still dirty patches of snow, like frozen cowpats, dotting the sides of the so-called highway, and much more of it capping the mountains. The sky, though, was a clear, crystalline blue, dissected only by the thin white razor-cut of a jet's vapour trail. He wondered if the circling dots he could see beneath the airliner were the fabled eagles of Albania. In reality, they were more likely to be common-or-garden buzzards.

He had been driving for several hours and his arms were growing weary. The further he got from Tirana the more the country looked like the cliché of a place out of time; the way it would have been when the SOE men had landed, only to find themselves pawns in the war between King Zog and the communist partisans.

He passed villages where the rooftops were made from old drop containers from the war, hammered flat and now rusted to a deep, deep brown. There were goats wandering into the road; horse-drawn carts; scrawny, yappy dogs; tiny farms that could barely feed one person, let alone the six he saw working the land; women in shawls and headscarves, age indeterminate. And then he glimpsed a vulgar monstrosity, all pillars and gables and a satellite dish so large it could be used to search for signs of intelligent life in the universe.

Gangsters. Drug lords. Traffickers. *Scum.*

Or was that another cliché and these people actually owned a Starbucks franchise in Tirana?

Maybe. But there were bad men hereabouts.

He wasn't that far from the Yellow House, where terrible atrocities had been perpetrated during the Kosovan war. *Allegedly*, he reminded himself. But trafficking human organs was not his story, and the Yellow House was old news.

He turned the radio on and promptly turned it off again. He wasn't in the mood for Albanian hip-hop. In fact, he'd never be.

For several miles, the road hugged the shore of a lake created by a monstrous concrete dam visible in the far distance, the artificial waters black and uninviting. Shortly after passing the dam itself, the air around it humming with power, a sign indicated he should turn left and begin his ascent. The road up to the rendezvous point was steep and sharply curved, but its surface was mercifully free of potholes. It was etched into the side of a mountain with a sheer drop on one side and laughably flimsy crash barriers in place only at selected corners.

As he continued to climb, the trees thinned before disappearing completely as the bends tightened. He tried not to look down over the cliff edge to his right.

Adam felt content. So far the research for the novel was progressing nicely. As it was largely fictional, he didn't have to worry too much about nailing down the exact topographical – or geographical – details. Quayle had spent most of his time in the south, living in sea caves, but Adam's novel was to be more impressionistic than historically accurate. He had managed to get a stack of self-published wartime diaries by men nearly all long dead, who had come to this cold, inhospitable country to help the partisans. He was planning on weaving their stories into Quayle's. *Inspired by actual events*. Isn't that the phrase to use when you've made a lot of stuff up?

Tirana had gone well. In a dilapidated, fusty bar to the north of King Zog's brutalist Royal Palace, Adam had met with two old men who had known Enver Hoxha, the future ruler of Albania, back when he was leading the partisans against the Nazis. Neither of them remembered Quayle, although one of them had met his predecessor. The other bloke had been born near Golan, one of the villages Adam was heading to. He had provided deep background about its rivalry with neighbouring town Cerci, which dated back hundreds of years. He had given the pair a card with his email address, asking them to contact him if they remembered anything else. But at their age, they probably forgot a little more about the war with each passing day.

Through Viora, the paper's attractive but sullen Tirana fixer, he had also met a 'retired' people-smuggler who'd sworn it was a humanitarian calling. No sex involved. Just desperate, frightened human beings. Willing, no doubt, to pay a fortune to cross from Libya to Greece. He had made Adam's flesh crawl as he'd plied him with bottle after bottle of Birra Tirana. *But, of course, he knew about Cerci and Golan. Who didn't?* the man had said with a wink.

Adam couldn't bring himself to give the man a card. He never wanted to hear from that creep again. But the information he had obtained was copper-bottomed and flexing his journalistic muscles had put a spring in Adam's step. He felt a long way from Pets' Corner.

A battered piece of wood nailed to a tree, full of what looked like buckshot scars, displayed partially erased symbols for food, drinks and washing facilities two kilometres ahead. He slowed a little. Behind him a Fiat he hadn't noticed honked and pulled around, scattering stones and dust over Adam's bonnet.

The inn was a surprisingly grand structure: two wooden storeys, a slate roof and a terrace out front, with metal tables and chairs spread across it. Next to the main building, a new wing was being constructed out of breeze-block. The severe, square, flat-roofed box showed no heed to the style of the original architecture. It would look like a brutalist parasite latched onto the side of the traditional inn.

*Wait outside,* had been his instruction. *We'll find you.*

Adam parked up, collected his map, notebook and the two-day-old *Times* from the passenger seat and got out. Despite the sun, the chill of the air at that altitude bit at him so he fetched his jacket from the rear. There were two other sets of customers outside: a group of three men, each dark and moustachioed, and two women, thirties maybe – one fair, the other dark – who had their own map spread out on the table and appeared to be arguing.

He sat just out of earshot of the others and ordered a coffee from the waiter. As an afterthought, he added a slice of *ravani*. With luck it would be syrupy sweet and sickly to counteract the bitterness of the coffee. He began to work through the newspaper's crossword.

Four down. *Dog – a stray – circling English person who enunciates badly?* Eight letters.

He put his elbows on the marble table top and it tipped. The heavy disc was merely resting on the metal base. He took his weight off the top and it banged back down into place.

The noise made the women look over and he smiled; a quick tight grin that was simply an acknowledgement of his clumsiness. However, one of them – the blonde – took this as permission to come over.

'Excuse me,' she said, in English. 'Can we borrow

your map? Our satnav is playing up. I just want to compare yours to ours.'

'Sure. Where are you going?'

'Golan.'

It was one of his stops, but he didn't say anything. He had no intention of getting embroiled. But why would two Englishwomen want Golan? Unless, he thought queasily, they were reporters, also on the story. He looked the woman up and down. There was a flintiness about her that suggested she might be in the game.

He handed over the folded map. 'How did you know I was English?'

'It must have been the Union Jack on your back,' she said with a smile.

'That obvious?'

'The clothes. The shoes. *The Times* crossword. Yes, pretty obvious. I'll bring it straight back.'

Observant, anyway. Maybe she was a copper.

The coffee and cake arrived and he lost himself in the puzzle for a while. A tap on the shoulder startled him. 'Thank you,' said the woman, returning the map. 'All sorted.'

'You're welcome.'

She hesitated, but he let the silence hang.

'What brings you here?' she asked eventually.

'I'm researching something on Anthony Quayle. The actor. He was here during the war.'

'I don't know him.'

'*The Guns of Navarone. Ice Cold in Alex.* That sort of thing.'

'Oh. Well, my husband used to love those films. Good luck.'

'And you?'

'Hiking.'

He glanced at her feet and she caught his disbelieving look as he clocked her battered trainers.

'The boots are in the car,' she laughed, pointing at a Dacia FWD. 'Right, thanks for the map.'

Adam watched her return to her table. He wasn't quite sure what had occurred, but he was certain both parties hadn't been entirely truthful. *He* definitely hadn't been. The two women sniggered about something. He hoped it wasn't him.

*Mutterer* – Four down, eight letters.

'Mr Bryant?' the waiter asked in a thick accent.

'Yes?'

'Phone call for you. Inside.'

He stood and looked at his phone. It had signal. But then plenty of people didn't trust mobiles. He went to gather up his map and notebook but instead gestured to the women, asking them to keep an eye on his stuff. They nodded. He took the phone with him, though.

Inside was dark and warm, the air slightly gritty from an open fire, and he wished he could meet his fixer in there. The barman pointed to the rear of a long, wood-panelled corridor where, next to the foul-smelling toilets, a receiver dangled by its cord. He walked down the passage and picked it up.

'Hello?'

There was a click and the line went dead.

'Hello? Hello?'

After a few seconds of interrogating dead wires, Adam replaced the receiver and walked out. He found the waiter serving the women a second cup of coffee and vegetable pie.

'Excuse me,' he said in his halting Albanian. 'Nobody there. Did they give a name?'

'No, they didn't say,' the waiter replied in English.

'Man or a woman?'

'Woman, I think.'

Adam walked slowly back towards his table, checking his phone again. It wasn't until it was almost upon him that he noticed the mosquito-buzz of a high-revving motorbike and looked up to see the rider and his pillion passenger, their faces obscured by heavily tinted visors. The passenger was trying to extract something from his unzipped leather jacket. Suddenly, an automatic pistol was in his hand.

It was then that Adam knew he was about to die.

# THREE

It was only much later that Adam was able to piece together what had happened, replaying the few sound and visual clues that were stored in his subconscious. Just as he realised exactly what the rider and his passenger were about, he was hit from the right by what felt like a steam train whose brakes had failed. As he went down, an apparent flying saucer appeared, spinning through the air before him. He heard three or more cracks, which – thanks to his time in Helmand – he recognised as gunfire.

He hit the hard, unyielding terrace with a bone-jarring – and it later transpired, rib-cracking – force that propelled all the breath from him. There was a flash of light and then the world turned to smoke. He must have passed out for a moment because he awoke on his back, a woman's face inches from his own. At first he thought she was going to kiss him, but then he felt the jittery little slaps she was delivering to his cheek.

'You OK?' she asked. It was the dark–haired hiker.

'Yes,' he croaked. 'You can stop hitting me now.'

'OK, but don't move. I heard something pop as you went down.'

'I think that was my pride.'

Adam twisted his head slightly. One of the circular café table tops – the flying saucer – was lying in the road. The blonde was talking to the three other customers, who were standing next to it. One of them held a big automatic pistol in his hand. Adam could smell the fumes from discharged weapons swirling in the air.

His stomach cramped and he thought he might be sick.

'What happened?' he asked the woman. Then, as she touched his torso: 'Ow, FUCK!'

'Ribs bruised or cracked,' she announced.

'Who are you?'

'Call me Freddie.'

'Are you a doctor, Freddie?'

She shook her head. 'Are you a gangster of some kind?'

'What?' he replied. Why would she think that? 'No, of course not.'

'Well, who have you been rubbing up the wrong way?'

'Nobody.'

Now the blonde was standing over him. He had to squint as he looked up at her, the sun flaring behind her head. 'Really?' Blondie said. 'Because someone just called in a hit on you.'

# FOUR

They moved to the inside of the inn and switched on the lights, revealing necklaces of cobwebs hanging from cornices and picture frames that the dimness had helped mask. The three armed Albanians were left outside, to keep watch. In case the bikers returned, Adam supposed.

As Freddie bandaged him up using the first-aid bag from their car, the other one – Sam – told Adam what had happened.

The mystery phone call had tipped them off. Apparently, it was an old way to finger the right person. The 'mark' would be the one who took the call. As the motorbike approached, the pair had snapped into action before the passenger had even fully drawn his weapon. Freddie – the steam train – had launched herself at Adam while Sam had frisbee'd the unfixed table top through the air, pulling a muscle as she did so.

There were two bullet holes in the table, both meant for Adam.

One thing was for sure: whoever or *whatever* these women were, they weren't on a hiking holiday.

The three Albanians were locals and, affronted by the attempted assassination, one of them had loosed off a couple of shots of his own at the bikers. Sensing they were outgunned, the pair on the bike had taken off.

'What now?' Adam asked as he gingerly slipped his T-shirt and sweater back on.

'Rakia!' said the barman, putting a tray of glasses on the bar. They were half full of a golden, syrupy-looking liquid.

Sam and Freddie both smiled at the barman and knocked their drinks back. Adam did the same, keeping his grin fixed as the fruit brandy scorched its way down his throat.

'Who the hell are you?' he asked.

The two woman exchanged glances. 'Hikers.'

'Bollocks.' The journalist in him had finally kicked in. Hikers who knew the choreography of a drive-by shooting? Unlikely, it seemed to him. There was a story here.

'Ex-army hikers,' said Freddie.

'Right.' At least one part of that rang true. 'What now? Is this *Assault on Precinct 13*?'

Blank looks.

'Are we trapped here?'

Sam shook her head. 'I don't think so. My guess is those were a couple of kids. Cheap. Disposable. The men who sent them will be thinking carefully about their next move now they know they have opposition.'

'Those guys?' Adam pointed to the three men now drinking free brandy on the terrace. 'I'm guessing them being here and armed was just blind luck. As was you two being here.'

'Maybe, but they don't know that. The kids won't go back and say they were scared off by a woman with a loaded café table,' said Freddie. 'It'll be an army they faced down by the time they get back to their bosses.'

'They will beat the truth out of them,' said the barman. He had laid a shotgun across the bar. He nodded at it. 'If you need.'

Adam thought the mottled barrel and chipped hammers meant it looked old and neglected enough to blow up in your face, but Sam said, 'Thank you. We'll see how it goes. You know the men who did this?'

'From Golan, I would guess,' growled the barman. Adam half-expected him to hawk and spit from the way he said it. 'Only the people there still doing this shit. Them and Cerci.'

Those were the two villages fighting for control of the trafficking business across Europe.

'What are you really doing here?' asked Sam. 'And don't give me that guff about Anthony Hopkins.'

'Quayle,' he corrected. 'And it's true. He was here in the war.'

'But there's more,' Sam said flatly, 'more you aren't telling us.'

Adam lowered his voice. 'I'm a journalist. I was sent to do a story on ... on those two villages he just mentioned.'

Freddie took the shotgun off the bar, broke it, peered down the barrels and sniffed it. The barman put a handful of shells on the bar and she nodded her thanks before pocketing them. 'They fuckin' hate journalists round here.'

'But I haven't started,' Adam protested. 'Asking questions, I mean. Apart from in Tirana.'

Sam's brow furrowed and Adam could almost hear the cogs meshing as she processed what little information she had. 'Which means somebody tipped them off.'

# FIVE

'Why would anyone tip off the locals?' asked Adam.

Sam shrugged. 'I don't know. You upset anyone in Tirana?'

'Not that I know of.'

'Who were you waiting for at the café?'

'The local stringer-cum-fixer, arranged through the paper. A decent guy by all accounts. I doubt he would bite the hand that feeds him.'

Freddie inserted two shells into the black holes of the gun barrels. 'The Sayonara Syndrome.'

'The what?' Adam asked.

'I don't think so,' said Sam, throwing a steely look in her friend's direction. 'And right now, it doesn't matter. We have to get down that hill.'

'But I have to go to Golan to do the story. I'm on assignment.'

'Both cars?' asked Freddie. It wasn't addressed to Adam. In fact, it was as if he hadn't spoken.

Sam shook her head. The next sentence was for his benefit. 'No, we take the four-wheel drive. Adam can tell the hire company to come and get his. I'm sure Saban here will look after the keys.'

The barman nodded.

'What about Leka?' Freddie asked.

Adam looked at each woman in turn. 'Who's Leka?'

'Leka is a man from Golan we have some interest in,' Sam said.

'I thought you were going there?'

'We were.'

'So we could all go. I have to get the story. My editor will kill me if I don't.'

'I don't think that's a good idea,' said Sam. 'Not now you've been fingered. We'd better stash you somewhere.'

'How am I going to write a story if I'm stashed somewhere?'

'You don't think this is a story?' asked Freddie. 'Fuck me, you've got high standards, mate. You've almost been executed in a drive-by and now we have to get you down that mountain in one piece. Besides, I'll bet you can get chapter and verse about the feuding villages from Saban. It's Albania, not the moon. Barmen are still the source of all knowledge.' Freddie held up ten fingers to emphasise her next point. 'You've got ten minutes.'

But Saban was looking at Freddie. 'Leka who?'

'Leka Zogolli,' said Sam.

Saban made a low snorting sound, like a bull gearing up for a charge. 'How do you say in English? Cunt?'

'Yup, that's close enough,' said Freddie.

'Why are you interested in Leka Zogolli?' Saban asked.

'We … he … he's causing us some trouble,' said Sam. *By trying to kill my boyfriend*, she didn't add. If 'boyfriend' was the correct term for Tom. She never could settle on a suitable description of their relationship. Whatever it was, Sam would rather he wasn't murdered by Albanians.

Saban guffawed and banged the bar top. 'I know how *you* can cause trouble for Leka Zogolli.'

'We're all ears,' said Freddie.

Saban spoke quickly and softly, so softly that Adam couldn't hear all the details. He caught a few stray words. *Paris. Family. Children. Bastard.*

When he had finished, Sam shook his hand like she meant it.

Then she said: 'I need to ask another favour.'

'What?'

'Can you sell us some cement?'

'Why?' Saban asked.

Sam shot a glance at Adam. 'Because we're going down the mountain.'

# SIX

Adam had emailed Kath but received no reply. He thought about sending a message to Rory, but decided to wait. Editors didn't like being told a story had gone tits up, and he wasn't sure how this was going to pan out. It all depended on two mysterious women.

He had been sent to sit at a table out of earshot, with a beer and an order to take shallow breaths to give his ribs a rest. As he did so, he watched the two women talk in hushed tones to the barman. At one point, a grin flashed across Sam's face, softening her features. They were both attractive women, though the kind he would be wary of complimenting for fear they might take it the wrong way and crush his windpipe.

He had met women like that in Helmand: tough, capable, confident. But that was in an army situation. Off duty, they reverted to something softer, more – although he wouldn't say it to their faces – feminine. But this pair ... it was like they were 'on' all the time. Whenever one spoke to Saban, the other kept an eye on the door, and then they switched roles, instinctively, it seemed.

And knowing there was a hit coming? They had to be some kind of Special Forces. But thank God for that.

When Adam reached for his beer he noticed his hand was shaking. He held it out and watched his trembling fingers.

'Just a little shock.' It was Freddie, standing over him. 'Nothing to worry about.'

From the corner of his eye, Adam saw Sam slide a stack of money over to Saban and they shook hands once more. Then she went outside.

'What now?'

'She's bought the cement from next door. And a bit of sand. Now she's buying a gun.'

'Look, I don't understand—'

'No, I know. But based on what Saban told us, we no longer have a need to go up to Golan. We have our story. You'll get yours.'

Adam looked doubtful. 'That's easy for you to say. You don't have to answer to editors who have forked out cash for this trip. What are you two going to do, then?'

'Sam and I need to go to Paris – that's where our leverage over Leka is – which means flying out of Tirana. So we can drop you at the airport. Now, take your beer, go and talk to Saban and ask him about what's going on in those villages. Do not identify him as your source when you write it up. Understand?'

'Yes.'

She grabbed his bicep as he got to his feet. 'Or mention us by name or description. Clear?'

He laughed and winced as his ribs protested. 'I never argue with a woman who owns a shotgun.'

'Especially one who knows where you live.'

'How's that?'

'We know where you work. Which newspaper. The next step is simple.'

'I'll keep it vague,' Adam said.

'Vague is good. We'll be outside.'

When he had finished with Saban – the man really did have all the information he needed to write his piece – Adam went outside. The women had backed their Dacia up to the breeze-block shell and were busy loading hefty sacks of cement and sand into the back of it. With the rear seats down, they had created a walled area in the back.

'What's going in there?' he asked.

'You are,' said Freddie.

'They won't stop an AK round,' said Sam, pointing at the bags, 'but pretty much anything else. Just as long as you keep your head down.'

Adam bristled. 'No way. I'm not cowering in the back while you two play Calamity Jane.'

The women exchanged glances. 'Well, yes you are. Either conscious ...'

'Or unconscious,' completed Sam with a shrug. 'Which might be better for us. Get your gear from your car. Don't forget your passport.'

Adam's phone beeped. It was a message from Kath: *What kind of bother?*

*I'll tell you when I get home.*

If I get home, he thought. I'm trusting my life to two women who, despite their grim expressions, seem to be enjoying this. What if this was all a scam? He only had their word for the attempted hit.

Then he remembered what Saban had told him about the people further up the mountain and their disdain for human lives, which made him feel sick inside.

Another message from Kath: *Are you OK?*

*Yes. Are you? Is Conor OK?*

*I'll tell you when you get home.*

Touché.

After he had fetched his bag and given the keys of his hire car to Saban, he threw his belongings into the Dacia.

'You get in, we'll put a layer between you and the rear door,' said Sam.

He was about to climb in when he hesitated. 'What is the Sayonara Syndrome?'

'It doesn't matter,' said Sam.

'It clearly does,' he replied.

It was Freddie who told him. 'We had a captain in Iraq who used to make sure that every risky patrol was led by the same young lieutenant. To the point where it became a joke. We couldn't understand it. He even made the guy use the Vallon – which is the metal detector for IEDs. I mean, a decent lieutenant will always take his turn. Just to show he won't ask someone to do something he wouldn't do. But it's not his primary role. And every time the lieutenant went out, Dawson always said the same thing: "Sayonara".

Which doesn't just mean goodbye, it has a we-won't-meet-again finality about it. Sure enough, the lieutenant stood on an IED one day and boom. Dead. The following year, the captain married his widow.'

'Nice. So he'd been . . .?'

'Well, according to Freddie here, deliberately putting the lieutenant in harm's way,' said Sam. 'He and the wife had been having an affair long before deployment. But that was war, not journalism. Get in.'

'That's ridiculous.'

'Just a thought,' said Freddie.

'Although not a good one,' added Sam. 'Freddie has a vivid imagination.'

'I do when it comes to sex.'

Adam decided to change the subject. 'Why are you helping me?' he asked.

Freddie shrugged. 'We're PPOs. Bodyguards, to you. It's what we do.'

That begged a whole fresh set of questions. But Adam kept his mouth shut and climbed into the rear of the car as they put an extra two layers of bags in position, so that he was barricaded in on all sides. He felt like a pig in a very dusty pen. As he tried to make himself comfortable he thought about the Sayonara Syndrome and laughed to himself. Not because of the captain's shenanigans – that was monstrous – but the thought that Rory might have sent him to Albania to get to Kath. As if.

The Dacia rocked as the women climbed in the front and he heard them checking their weapons. Sam had gained an automatic pistol from the Albanian customers, who had now departed in a black Mercedes. Were they friend or foe? Who knew? Maybe it would be those guys waiting for them down the hill. He felt the fingers of paranoia squeezing his heart.

'Who were the men with guns?' he asked. 'Cops?'

'Not regular cops,' said Sam. 'Maybe Sigurimi or whatever the equivalent is now.'

Adam knew that the Sigurimi was the Albanian equivalent of the Stasi. And equally feared.

'You trust them?' he asked.

'No,' said Freddie. 'Hard to tell white hats from black hats over here.'

'What about all this extra weight?' Adam asked, trying to get his mind off useless speculation about the loyalties of the men who had sold Sam a pistol. 'Will this thing even move?'

'We'll mainly be going downhill,' said Sam. 'We'll dump the cement when we're in the clear.'

*In the clear.* She made it sound so simple. Like driving through a rainstorm. Except it looked like they were heading for a *shit*storm. Christ, I'm really frightened, he thought.

He heard Freddie snap the barrels shut once more. 'You ever see that film *The Magnificent Seven*? The original?' Of course he had, but he didn't answer. She was speaking to Sam.

'It was hard to get away from it. Paul loved it. That and the bloody *Great Escape*.'

'This reminds me of that movie. Steve McQueen

says to Yul Brynner: "Never ridden shotgun on a hearse before".'

'Doesn't that make me bald?' asked Sam.

'Doesn't that make me dead?' Adam shouted from the back, a slight tremor to the words undercutting his attempt at levity.

They both answered at once: 'Not yet.'

The engine caught first time and grumbled a little as Sam gave it enough gas to compensate for the extra load, and they bumped out of the rough car park and onto the road down the mountain.

# PART TWO

*'Let your hook be always cast. In the pool
where you least expect it, will be fish'*

# SEVEN

*How did I know it was a hit?*

As I eased the Dacia out of the car park, trying to get used to the new distribution of weight, I knew I would be asking myself that question for a long time to come.

'How is she?' Freddie asked, tapping the dash with the barrel of the shotgun.

Skittish? I thought. Was that the right word? Though that suggested a prancing colt; something delicate and dainty. The Dacia was only a few steps up from a tractor. I settled on: 'A very pregnant sow on four wheels.'

We'd been in FWD vehicles before, driving towards men who wanted to harm us. Iraq. Afghanistan. Normally, though, we had a bunch of hard-nosed squaddies with us, not a civilian hiding behind bags of cement. Although, to be fair, we hadn't given him much choice.

We began our descent, with my foot hovering over the brake. The rear end felt twitchy due to the extra baggage. I reckoned the Dacia would prefer to come down arse-first. I had placed the automatic pistol in the centre console. It was a Beretta, with the older fifteen-round magazine. Worn, but OK from what I could tell from a quick once-over. In an ideal world I'd strip down and reassemble an unfamiliar weapon half-a-dozen times, putting a round through it at each rebuild. Just as Pavol, my Slovakian weapons tutor, had taught me. But this was a far from ideal world: I wouldn't know if I had been sold a pup until I pulled the trigger. And that might be too late.

So, how had I known it was a hit? Not some sixth sense; not the hairs on the back of my neck or a gut feeling. I think it was the choreography. That's what PPOs like me do. We visualise – or some sketch out on paper, napkins, fag packets, whatever is at hand – the possible lines of attack and escape; the threats and responses. You need to know how to extract the client – the Principal, in PPO speak – safely if shit goes down. So you sit and try to calculate what might be coming and from which direction. Those instincts tick over, even while you are not in paid employment, idling at a White/Yellow status. It is what makes PPOs such crap dining companions. They never just sit, relax and look at the menu. There is always at least one meerkat moment when they look around, calculating the odds.

So, while I was sitting at the café, I had already assessed we were vulnerable to a drive-by. I also knew the trick of identifying a target by phoning the venue. These days it was usually the intended victim's mobile that rang, but maybe those lads on the bike didn't have Adam's number.

'Here?' Freddie asked, as I slowed for a bend. To my left there was a cliff edge with a fifty-metre drop to some scrubby trees and not much in the way of crash barriers, and to my right, a rock face. It was constricted. But it would be for any opposition as well.

If they tried to block us with a car, someone might go over the edge. And that someone might be them.

'Not yet,' I said. I became aware that my heart was pounding in my chest. I wasn't breathing properly. Too shallow and the heart has to up its game to try to replace lost oxygen. I gulped in some air and then regulated my breathing to deep and slow. 'Soon enough though, don't worry about that.'

'Who the hell are you two again?' Adam queried from the rear.

'You already asked that,' I reminded him. 'And we told you.'

'Well, it wasn't what you might call full disclosure, was it?'

Freddie gave him a fuller answer. She gave a quick outline of two ex-military medics who had ended up on the Circuit, the international brotherhood – and, increasingly, sisterhood – of those in the security industry.

'You haven't really explained who this Leka bloke is you are so concerned with.'

I could, of course, have explained about my 'boyfriend' Tom, who, as a British soldier, was part of the Kosovo Force (KFOR), four international brigades of peacekeeping troops. It also included my late husband Paul, who, alongside Tom, had been involved in a rather one-sided fight with some Albanian would-be rapists. I remembered the words, the anguish in them, as Tom described the scene, the memory still raw as they stood and watched a group of men surround a young goatherd, just thirteen or fourteen years old.

*One of the men – an older one – started to jeer at us. They made all sorts of obscene gestures.*

*Goading us.*

*They knew we couldn't touch them.*

*Some of the younger ones had begun to paw and prod at the girl. She was lashing out at them, which only made them laugh more. It was like a vile game of 'It'.*

*Then another guy – I'd say about thirty, the one with the AK –walked ten, fifteen metres down the hill, so he was closer to us. He unbuttoned his pants and flipped out one of the biggest cocks I've ever seen. I mean, there's always one in a group like that, isn't there? Always one hung like a donkey who takes every opportunity to whip it out. His looked like he should have a licence to take it for a walk.*

*The others cheered. He waved it about at us, pointed at it, then at the girl. Just in case we were particularly slow.*

*So he started working at it while we watched, running his hand up and down the shaft, pulling back the foreskin, until he had this great stonker on. Two of the men had the girl by her wrists at this point, so she couldn't go anywhere. The rest were clapping, this sort of rhythmic, almost flamenco-like dance clapping. As if it were some kind of cabaret ...*

And then one of the Brits opened fire, hitting the guy with the hard-on. At which point they realised that, by interfering, they had broken the KFOR non-intervention mandate.

So they killed them all.

It was the logic of madness, but, as he said, the whole world seemed turned on its head in Kosovo at that time.

Paul, my future husband, had tried to stop the slaughter. And Tom had let one of the potential rapists – a young kid – live, pretending to shoot him in the head, but deliberately missing. Now Leka, that boy, was an all-grown-up warlord intent on getting revenge on the British squad.

They may have let him live, but the Brits had killed the others; his family and friends. Maybe Leka reasoned he had been spared to avenge them.

It was certainly possible he had already managed to kill Paul, who was shot coming off a shift for a British Nuclear Police/MI5 operation.

And Leka knew he could get to Tom through me. I couldn't just let that go.

I couldn't go on thinking Tom might get hurt or I might be followed and kidnapped to use as bait for him, as they had once tried in Zurich.

But I didn't tell that story to Adam. I also didn't tell

him the bigger reason I had for wanting to resolve the situation with Leka, and fast.

The truth was, I was needed over the other side of the world, where my daughter Jess was with her father. Her father who had taken her without my permission; had snatched her from under my nose. They were last seen in Bali. But I knew Jess was no longer there.

When the photographs that my old mentor, the Colonel, had extracted from the internet had showed she was in Bali, I contacted the UK police, who asked the Balinese cops to investigate. However, with there being no current extradition treaty between Indonesia and the UK, all they could do was check 'on a friendly basis'.

A frustratingly vague report had come back: *Our enquiries show that, while the suspect had been in the country, sources indicate he has now left the island of Bali with the girl.*

I had always known that the chances of Jess still being there were slim – Matt, my ex, knew enough to keep moving, especially if he ever caught wind of the fact I was coming for them – but Bali was where I could pick up the trail. And I would.

*If you live that long.*

Not helpful.

I made an effort to stop thinking about Matt and Jess, and Laura, the treacherous au pair who had helped him take my daughter. I really didn't want that anger out there yet, clouding my vision, not given our current situation.

What had Adam asked?

Oh, yes. About Leka. I just said: 'It's complicated. I needed to get something to use against him.'

'For what?'

I said nothing.

'And have you?'

'Yes.' I didn't expand. My leverage came from Saban, the barman, who had been at school with Leka. Though I suspected his association went beyond that. Saban was coy about how he knew so much about Leka's operations in Europe, but it was clear he hated him. My guess was this: Saban had been part of Leka's organisation in France. They had fallen out. Saban had come back home to open his café, but he still despised Leka enough to dish the dirt on him when asked, even by a couple of strangers in town. I suspected Saban had some skeletons of his own in some worm-riddled cupboard, but that wasn't my concern. Neutralising Leka was.

'That's good,' Adam said.

I grunted. Saban had given me decent stuff all right, but leverage was only worthwhile if you lived to use it.

I was looking down at the rusty skeleton of a bus nestled among the spindly spruce on the slope below us – always a reassuring sight when driving mountain passes – when a real, live one came barrelling around the bend in the middle of the road. It honked a horn so loud it might have been signalling Armageddon was on the way, and it almost was. I swerved, but the Dacia decided I hadn't swerved enough. I lost grip and we clipped the cliff face to my right. The side panel gave a squeal of protest as I scored a gouge in the rock, and then, with a final punch of air, the bus was past us and carried on up the mountain road.

'We're not going to get that deposit back at this rate,' said Freddie, as I managed to pull us away from the cliff edge. I felt the snag in my shoulder from a damaged muscle or tendon, but ignored it.

A six-hundred-Euro deposit was the least of my worries.

'Look, I'm sorry I've got you into this. You still think someone told them I was here?' Adam asked.

I shook my head. 'I don't know. The stringer you were waiting for is still the best bet.'

Freddie threw me a glance that suggested she disagreed. She thought the answer was closer to Adam's home. Someone wanted him out of the way.

The Sayonara Syndrome.

Unlike Freddie, I was never certain that was true of Captain Dawson. The marriage to the widow of the man he sent out to be blown up by an IED didn't prove the captain was putting the lieutenant in harm's way. But then, human nature – and lust – was pretty unpredictable at the best of times. I just didn't buy it in this case.

Adam's phone pinged.

I hoped he had the Seventh Cavalry on speed dial but somehow doubted it.

'Voicemail. Hold on.'

I was still negotiating a long series of switchbacks

that had taken us around the sides of the mountain and down towards the valley below. I could see part of the road we had already traversed above us, the bus that had nearly sideswiped the Dacia climbing at still-indecent speed and, just passing it on the way down, a black four-door saloon.

'They might not be waiting for us down below,' I said.

Adam sounded distracted. 'Great. Hold on, I'll just listen to this.'

Freddie knew I wasn't talking to Adam. She followed the direction of my gaze, and probably caught a flash of dark paint before it disappeared from our view. She shifted in her seat, as if ungluing herself from it. 'You could be right.'

I looked in the mirror. Adam was sitting up, holding his phone to his ear, his face furrowed in concentration as he tried to hear the message. 'Adam, get down,' I said.

'It's Kath.'

Phone addiction. It'll kill you. I knew it still hadn't got through to him just what danger he was in. Correction: *we* were in.

Status: glowing red-hot.

'Adam, for fuck's sake. It'll wait. Get your fuckin' head down.'

Freddie swivelled. 'This is what we do, remember? Do as she says.'

He gave a petulant huff and slid down behind the screen of cement. I now had a half-decent view out of the rear window, enough to see that the saloon, as it rounded the bend immediately behind us, was one of the bigger-model Peugeots. I could hear the smooth, low growl of its engine over the bag-of-nails rattle of ours. I pressed the accelerator, knowing I couldn't outrun him. Or her. But this was Albania; *him* was a good guess. I couldn't keep my eyes on the mirror long enough to ID who was in the car, not now that the Dacia was acting like a toboggan on sheet ice, slithering into the bends and rolling so much it felt like we'd be up on two wheels at any moment.

I was right on the edge, in more ways than one.

'Two of them,' said Freddie, who had twisted to take a look. 'Two blokes.'

The Peugeot's horn blared – not as loud as the bus's, but in three impatient bursts. I risked another few millimetres on the pedal, pulling away by a couple of extra yards. My hands were gripping the wheel hard now. I'd have to do some serious steering if I lost it on any of the shallow curves I could see ahead.

'Impatient driver or persons of interest?' I asked.

The shattering of the rear window into ice crystals answered my question.

I heard Adam shout in alarm as he was showered with fragments of glass. I reckoned it was just shock, but asked, 'You OK?'

'They're shooting at us.'

I couldn't quite figure out whether that was a question or not. But the quiver in his voice told me that something about our predicament had finally got through his thick skull.

'Ya reckon?' Freddie offered as she clambered into the back, over the cement sacks and into the well we had created in the rear. I heard a thump, like the sound of a glove on a punch bag. A gritty dust filled the cabin of the car as the bags puffed out their contents through the bullet holes.

'Not AKs, then,' said Freddie, with something akin to relief. Me, I think any old bullet can kill you if the shooter gets lucky, but she meant they weren't penetrating our defensive shield.

I checked my wing mirror and the car weaved into view. The Peugeot's passenger was leaning out of his side window holding something small, which we both knew wouldn't have the penetrating power of an AK, but, if it had an automatic selection, could still spray us with bullets. On our side was the fact that I was a slippery target – not all of which was deliberate – and that aiming one of those Skorpions or Uzis, even while stationary, is no easy option. He could waste a whole magazine before he got a bead on us.

'Brake.'

I didn't need to be asked twice. I stomped. The Dacia fishtailed as we took the bend and slowed dramatically. The Peugeot didn't have much time to react and was almost at our bumper when Freddie shouted: 'Ears.'

I got a finger in my right ear before she discharged the shotgun. In my mirror, I watched the windscreen of the Peugeot turn opaque and the car dance across the road. Its tyres bounced over the stones that marked the road edge and, for a second, I hoped it would flip, but already the driver had punched a jagged hole in the screen and he recovered nicely.

Bastard.

'Incoming!' Freddie yelled, and then I felt as much as heard rounds sparking off the rear door. There was a clunk as the metal was pierced. More dust rose and I heard Adam coughing.

I watched as the sole of a boot stomped at the Peugeot's damaged windscreen repeatedly until it peeled away and spun backwards. It twisted through the air and into the valley, glinting as it cartwheeled down to the trees.

Christ, now they could fire straight through the space where the windscreen had been, which would make for far more accurate fire than leaning out of the door. Freddie clearly thought the same thing, as she said: 'Oops.'

I began to yank the wheel back and forth, setting up an oscillation that was at the very brink of the car's stability.

'Ears!' Freddie fired three quick rounds from the Beretta before it jammed. 'Fuck.'

I couldn't have put it better myself.

The road was opening out as we reached the last section of the hairpin. Ahead of us, it entered a long straight section where the cliff, now more of a low bluff, and the road edge, were hundreds of metres apart. It's not the place I would have chosen for a road-block – too wide – but they had made a good fist of it. They had positioned two big white vans facing each other about three metres apart and then a number of what were probably concrete- or water-filled barrels to take care of any gaps in the blockade that I might try to drive through. There was no way I could force my way past without totalling our vehicle.

'Hold on!' I yanked the Dacia to the right and spun it, and this time it really did lift onto two wheels. As it thumped back down, I put it in reverse and drove us back towards what was left of the diminished cliff face where I had spotted a fissure or crevice – an indentation, anyway. As I approached, I realised it was larger than I had first thought and I pulled on the wheel so that the car, now parked sideways, blocked the entrance. It was the closest I could get to circling the wagons.

'Out! Out!'

I went through the passenger door as Freddie and Adam came out of the back over the cement sacks. Freddie tossed me the pistol.

I pulled the slide back. The chamber was empty. But it had been a full mag and she had only fired three shots.

I could hear Pavol's voice in my head: *Misfeed! You know what to do.* I hoped I remembered correctly. I slammed the palm of my left hand into the base of the butt, then racked the slide back to its full extent in the smoothest movement I could manage with shaking hands.

I felt the round chamber: sticky bullets, bad spring – who knew? I took a breath and shook my head. My ears were whistling from the gunshots.

I gave Freddie and Adam a quick once-over. Adam looked like he had aged three decades, but that might have been because he was covered in grey cement dust. Freddie was similarly coated, but she just looked pissed off that someone had spoiled her top.

Her eyes told a different story, though. She knew we were not in a good place.

*This might be where it ends.*

I stifled that voice and peeked over the bonnet. The Peugeot had stopped some way short of the barricade. The two men had exited from it and were walking towards another group of four – the ones who had set up the roadblock.

The Peugeot guys were unharmed by the looks of it.

*Damn.*

The passenger had the Skorpion pistol held in his right hand; the other had a hefty-looking handgun. The roadblock men were carrying an assortment of shotguns and rifles, one of which looked like an Armalite. Not an AK, perhaps, but trouble all the same.

The two parties met up, shook hands and slapped backs, as if they were long-lost friends meeting for a drink. We barely merited a glance as they jabbered and gesticulated. But then they knew we weren't going anywhere. The indent in the cliff was a dead end. And if we tried to climb ... well, that would count as sport to these guys.

Now, finally, they all turned towards us. They carried on talking and it was clear they were discussing what to do about us. I aimed down the barrel of the pistol, knowing they were too far away for me to able to count on even one of the three bullets finding a target.

Fifty metres was the claimed effective range, but that was in the hands of someone at the top of their game. Truth be told, I was rusty with a handgun at anything other than close range.

'I can't do anything with this thing from here,' said Freddie, echoing my thoughts as she popped her head up next to mine. She meant the shotgun. 'I was hoping it was loaded for bear, but I think I got bunnies. That windscreen didn't cave the way I'd hoped.'

I became aware of our ad hoc Principal breathing down my neck. 'What's happening?'

'Adam,' I instructed. 'Sit behind that tyre with your back to it, crouched down, arms over your head.'

'I can't do that,' he protested. 'Not with you up here.'

'Don't give me that wounded male pride bullshit again. Get over there.'

I yelled the last part as the first of the bullets snapped over my head and hit the cliff. Rock fragments rained down and I crouched behind the front wheel, with the engine block between me and the fusillade. Another batch, from the Armalite by the sound of it, sprayed the bodywork, sparking across the metal and shattering glass. The Dacia rocked and twitched under the impact.

Freddie was right. We wouldn't be getting our six hundred Euros back.

'You OK?' I asked Freddie.

She inclined her head to one side and raised her eyebrows. I translated it as: *Yeah, I'm stuck in a dead end behind a piece of shit car about to be murdered by Albanians with big guns. What's not to like?*

I felt a wobble, a surge of panic, and I closed my eyes for a second. I pushed the tide away. 'I'm glad you're here,' I said. 'Even if you aren't so keen.'

'All things considered—'

She never finished the sentence. The wall behind us was disappearing under a layer of dust as stray rounds pulverised the stone. I felt something sharp and hot sting my cheek. I didn't have to poke my head up to know what was happening. They were walking towards us, line abreast, firing just enough to keep us cowed.

As the unfortunate Dacia disintegrated into iron filings along one side, I reckoned the situation couldn't be much worse.

That's when the AKs opened up.

# EIGHT

I called Colonel d'Arcy from the airside at Tirana International Airport Nënë Tereza, once I was sure we were going to get on the plane.

That's never a given when you've left six dead bodies on a mountain.

Well, *we* didn't actually kill them, but we did act as the magnet that brought them to the spot where the men standing above us with AKs could mow them down, like skittles all in a row. Those guys up there on the bluff must have realised where the roadblock would be and taken advantage of our situation to improvise a little score-settling of their own.

Our saviours didn't say anything to us. The three men from the café were there; the ones I thought might be the Sigurimi. I doubted that now. They waved their smoking barrels from their vantage point, indicating we should get out of there.

They allowed us to take one of the vans – the Dacia now only good for use as a pepper pot – and drive off. We had been caught in the crossfire of a turf war between the black car/white van guys who wanted Adam and a group who didn't care about us, just wanted to take out their rivals. Whatever the truth of the matter, I certainly didn't want to hang around while the victors wondered whether it was wise to let three witnesses leave the scene of the crime. Especially as we didn't know whether this incident was a case of good guys vs bad guys, or, the more likely scenario, bad guys vs more bad guys.

'Colonel?' I asked when someone picked up without identifying themselves. 'It's Sam, Sam Wylde.'

'Sam,' he said in his strange pan-European accent. 'Where are you?'

'Albania.'

'Albania? I'm hearing some strange things coming out of Albania. Anything to do with you, Sam?'

The old bastard was still able to pull rabbits out of the hat. How did he know there had been trouble? 'It's possible. But why would you care? I thought you'd retired.'

'My hearing is still good, though.' He gave his dry-leaves-rustling laugh. 'Can't turn that off.'

Colonel d'Arcy had been at the epicentre of the personal protection racket in Europe for decades. He trained me in the basics, sent me to Slovakia to get firearms training from Pavol and found me my early assignments looking after pop stars and princesses.

He had given me a job when I needed one to fund my search for Jess. It wasn't his fault that the latter went sour. It was his son's. And when that son took a leap/

was pushed off a high building – delete as you think most likely: even the cops couldn't decide – the Colonel jacked it all in. But I knew he still kept those jug-handle ears of his close to the ground.

'Nothing to see here, Colonel. Move along.'

Another chortle. 'I miss you, Sam. Miss all of you; my boys and girls.' It wasn't like the Colonel to be sentimental. All he cared about was whether the wind was going to blow him some hard cash. Maybe retirement had made him soft. That or losing a son, I added to myself with a pang of guilt.

'You can always go back into the game,' I said. 'Pick up where you left off.' Even at one hundred and fifty, or however old the man was. Maybe you had to count the wrinkles on his face, like the rings on a tree, to be certain of his age. It would take quite a while.

'I can't go back, Sam. Sold all my files and contacts to someone forty years younger.'

'What, some pensioner?'

'Don't be cheeky.'

I looked across the cramped waiting area in front of the airport gates. Adam was on his feet, shaking hands with Freddie. We had all cleaned up at the Tirana International Hotel, which wasn't fussy enough to object to three apparent tin miners fresh off shift, still covered in tailings, asking for a day room and directions to the nearest clothes shops. From the room, I had called Hertz to report the Dacia stolen. They weren't happy. I suspected I'd be hearing a lot more from them.

'You sold all your files?' I asked, surprised. Shame, because they might have been useful to me.

'Most of them. I hung on to a few.' This was good. It meant he'd kept those most valuable; the ones he felt someone forty years his junior didn't deserve.

Adam was heading for me. I made various hand signals that tried to convey: *Just wait. I won't be long.* He pointed to the Departures display and the flashing 'boarding' sign next to his flight to London and did his own hand-dance to convey I'd better be quick.

Could I trust this man at the other end of the phone? I ran through my options and came to the conclusion that I had no choice. I took a breath. 'Colonel, I need to know how I can get a police document saying I reported a vehicle stolen, dated yesterday.' As well as bodyguards and information, the Colonel once offered a comprehensive service in fine forgeries.

'Stolen where?'

'A town called Pulana here in Albania.' It was a jumble of buildings we had driven through after the ambush, so small it couldn't afford the one horse that would put it on the map. But I didn't want anyone to trace us to that mountain if I could help it. The story had to be it was stolen and then, unbeknown to us, used as a shield in a gun battle between rival trafficking gangs. It was almost the truth.

'Send me the full details. Same email as ever. I'll see what I can do. No promises.'

'Of course not.' But I could sense a little frisson in

his voice, like an old racehorse being taken out on the gallops one more time, just to stretch its legs.

'And?'

I stepped away out of Adam's earshot and gabbled what I had in mind. There was silence on the line and for a second I thought he had hung up on me. 'Colonel?'

'I can send you a scenario or two for that.'

'OK.' He meant ways of solving my problem. Solutions might be a better word, but the Colonel had always dealt in 'scenarios'. They varied from a single paragraph to a full-blown dossier complete with PowerPoint presentation. I was inclining towards the former. It would be cheaper, for one thing.

'How much money do you have?' Now that's more like it, I thought. It's just business to him, sentimentality be damned.

'I'm good for a few scenarios.'

'No, you'll need more than that. A lot more.'

'What for, exactly?'

'You can't face Leka without suitable provision.'

That sounded expensive. I opened my virtual wallet. 'What do you suggest?'

'Oktane.'

There was a sound in my head like water going down a drain. I think it was actually cash flowing out of my bank account. Oktane did not come cheap.

As soon as I ended the call, Adam came up and gingerly put his arms around me. I could smell the faint aroma of cheap cement on him. It'll never catch on as an aftershave. He squeaked a little as he squeezed me.

'You get those ribs checked as soon as you get home,' I said.

'Yes, Nurse Ratched.'

I could talk. I still had what I hoped was just a pulled muscle in my shoulder from my table-flinging practice and yanking the wheel of the Dacia.

He pecked me on the cheek and released me from his grip. 'I don't know how to thank you. If you hadn't been there . . .'

'But we were.' Who knew, if he hadn't been there, I might not have met Saban and got my leverage. 'Maybe it was all meant to be,' I said.

He looked surprised. 'You believe in that sort of thing? Kismet?'

'No.' But sometimes I am tempted to give it just a little credence. As in: *sometimes life is just fucking weird*. 'And don't worry about the Sayonara stuff. As I said, Freddie has a vivid imagination. I think you might have tipped someone off in Tirana that you were doing more than just researching that actor of yours.'

'Or I was just unlucky. Mistaken identity.'

'There's always that.' I wasn't convinced. If I were Adam Bryant I wouldn't head back to Albania in a hurry. If at all.

As we spoke, he pulled out his passport and a business card fluttered to the floor. He scooped it up and slotted it away. 'Hold on,' I said.

I logged on to the airport Wi-Fi and googled his full name.

'I've got to—'

'Hold your horses.' The page loaded. 'You wrote a book called *The Shame Road*?'

'I did, yes.'

'About sex slaves.'

'Sex trafficking, yes.'

'And that article about sex workers in Romania. It was a finalist in the Features Journalism section of the British Journalism Awards?'

'Yes, but—'

I held up the screen to show him. 'Someone just had to do a search on you. Someone you gave your card to, perhaps. And once they had seen the top two entries in this list, they'd begin to think that maybe you were interested in more than Anthony whatsit.'

'Quayle.'

'Whatever. You see what I mean, though? Isn't there someone's razor that deals with this sort of thing?'

'Occam's razor,' he said. 'The simplest solution is usually the right one.'

'There you go. You were rumbled somewhere along the line and some calls were made to let people know that a nosy journalist with an interest in people-trafficking was coming up the mountain.'

He looked a little disappointed that it could be something so prosaic. 'I guess so. But the people I gave my cards to were harmless old men.'

'No such thing,' I said. 'You should know that.'

'I should. Look, I'd better . . .'

'Yup, off you go. Take it easy, eh? And good luck with your story. And remember: no names.'

'I remember. No names, no pack drill, whatever that means. Or you'll hunt me down and hurt me.'

'Not me. Freddie.'

'Sold.' He mimed zipping his mouth. 'Look, if there's anything I can ever do. To repay you.' He fished in his pocket and passed me the card that had fallen on the floor. I handled it gingerly. I'd had a bad time with business cards of late. Not all are what they seem. 'Although, I can't imagine what that might be.'

'You never know,' I said. I held out my hand and we shook.

'I still don't fully understand what you are up to next.'

I wasn't sure either. But with Oktane in the picture, it wasn't going to be pretty. Or legal.

'Best it stays that way. See you, Adam.'

'Good luck. And thanks again,' he said as he hurried off, raising a hand to Freddie.

She came over as he had his passport checked once more and disappeared through the gate.

'Would you?' Freddie asked.

'What?'

'Fuck him.'

'Adam?'

'No, the guy at the gate who looks like the love child of Joseph Stalin and Rosa Klebb. Of course, Adam. He has a pretty decent-sized cock.'

68

Despite myself, I let her draw me into her sordid little world. 'Freddie, how the hell do you know that?'

'I walked in on him in the shower while you were blabbing to the car-hire people. How was I to know the screen was transparent?'

'I don't know, probably because you scoped it out first.'

'No, I didn't. It was a pure accident.'

'But you didn't avert your eyes.'

'How could I? It came at me like some fuckin' anaconda. I had to pay full attention.'

I never really knew if Freddie was as horny as a promiscuous old goat most of the time, or she just liked winding my prudish – in her eyes – arse up. A mixture of the two, I suspected. 'In your dreams.'

She gave an impish grin. 'And I am very much looking forward to dreaming that one again. Coffee?'

I knew that even by the execrable standards of airport coffee, the little stall's effort was going to be vile sludge. But I said, 'Yes. Why not?'

As we waited for the girl to push the buttons on the machine, I sent Colonel d'Arcy a rough outline of our car 'theft', as it should appear on an official document.

Freddie asked, 'What did the Colonel say when you spoke to him?'

'He's going to lay out some options,' I said.

'OK. Options we could do with.'

I sensed a weariness in her voice. I was still running on adrenaline from the mountain but Freddie's shoulders had dropped, as if her tank was empty. It would happen to Adam, too. The moment he buckled up on that plane he would start feeling cold and hollow.

And then he'd remember what dead men looked like up close.

What a hail of 9mm bullets does to a human being.

Freddie and me, we'd seen a lot of that in our time, patched up plenty of broken bodies. We just added those new ones to the library of images we'd rather forget. Adam didn't have that luxury. He didn't have a library. I didn't envy him for the nightmares he had to come.

'Look, Freddie, you can butt out of all this now if you wish. Jesus, I wouldn't blame you.'

'Butt out?' She took the coffees and we stepped away from the cart. I sipped something black and tar-like. 'Why the hell would I do that?'

'Because I nearly got you killed up some godforsaken mountain.'

'I think we were pretty much at the bottom when it looked like we were going to die.'

I ignored that. 'And the next part is mine. Neutralising Leka and going after Jess.'

'That's fine talk coming from my friend and partner.'

'Friend, yes. Partner in what? Crime, you mean?'

'No, the agency.' Before I could ask *what agency?* she ploughed on. 'Your suspension from the SIA, that's up soon, right?'

I nodded. The protection industry's professional body had canned me for kidnapping and threatening my old boss. Misdemeanours, really. 'Two months and I can re-apply.'

'Right, I was going to mention this anyway at some point. There was a piece in *The Times*—'

'Wait, you've started reading *The Times*?'

'No, I can't actually read, I have a social worker who reads it out to me every day. Don't be such a snob, just because some broadsheet journalist fancies you.'

'Adam? Me?' I felt myself blush for no good reason.

'He hugged you. Not me. Gave you a smacker on the cheek. Not me. I got the limp handshake.'

'Maybe it's because I didn't burst into the bathroom and start measuring his cock. Perhaps he was worried what the next step would be if he were to move any closer.'

'Possibly,' she conceded. 'I might not have been able to resist finding out if my eyes had been deceiving me ...'

'*The Times*?' I prompted, before she got out of hand.

'Yes, *The Times* said that rich Americans are hiring bodyguards for their tours of Europe. In case of further terrorist outrages. It said female close protection is much in demand, a demand that agencies are struggling to fill.'

It wasn't really news, except for the nationality of the clients. We London-based PPOs got a lot from the Middle East, especially in summer, with Asia and Russia coming up on the rails. The USA, not so much. But with plenty of bad press about the situation in Europe, it was probably a comfort blanket for those who could afford it. If a waste of money. Foiling kidnap and robbery attempts we were good at. But there was no way an unarmed PPO was going to help against a rucksack bomb or a van mounting a pavement, unless you got lucky. I think a lot of vacationers would bristle at the restrictions needed to protect a client absolutely. Then again, a PPO team might be the new must-have accessory for any well-heeled American tourist: *Darling, we had the most divine bodyguard ...*

Which might mean there was good money to be had while it lasted. But I kept quiet; Freddie obviously wasn't finished.

'So what if we set up an all-female agency? Nothing but women PPOs. Maybe we name it after a Greek goddess. Like Callipygos.'

'Who's she?'

'I'm not sure, but it means "beautiful arse", so count me in.'

'Really? Is that the image an all-female agency wants to project? The receptionist picks up the phone and goes: "Beautiful Arse. How can I help you?"'

She laughed at that. 'OK. Maybe not. I did some research. Eos, the Morning Star, or Nemea, who breast-fed some monster—'

'Or Wylde and Winter?' I suggested, before she started reciting *The Odyssey*. Winter was Freddie's married name, which she no longer used, having ditched the husband, but I quite liked the combo. 'Or Winter and Wylde if you prefer.'

She moved her head from side to side, like a Bollywood dancer, thinking. 'Well, we could toss for the order, but what about—'

She hadn't finished before the crackly tannoy interrupted us. The accent was thicker than the coffee in my paper cup, but I got the message. 'Would Miss Sam Wylde, Miss Sam Wylde, travelling on the Transavia flight to Paris, please return to passport control.'

# NINE

Back at passport control, I was shunted between various hatchet-faced uniformed officials – some dressed as if auditioning for the SAS – before I ended up in a room smelling of eggs with someone in civilian clothes.

Nice civilian clothes.

Not Savile Row, but made by someone who knew what that once looked like.

The double-breasted jacket fell in the 'English Drape', which meant it gathered into vertical folds across the chest. Good for hiding guns, although I doubt the designer intended it for that purpose.

He sat opposite me at a rectangular desk, the varnish full of scratches and carved initials. There was even a swastika on there. No doubt, a comment by a previous interviewee on the techniques employed by his interrogators. Or maybe it was just an ill-advised doodle. The latter, I hoped.

His hands were well-manicured and moisturised, with no rings of any description. There was a very faint tattoo on one finger, but it was indistinct. He had fine, sharp features, slicked-back hair and green eyes that raked over me as he flicked at my passport with his left hand and turned my phone over with his right.

I tried to keep my breathing easy. Why had they pulled me and not Freddie? Or did they have her in another room right now? What did they actually have on me?

'Miss Wylde,' he said eventually. 'I am Inspector Gazim. I shall be handling your case. Do you know why you are here?'

'Because I have a plane to catch?' I almost bit my lip. The same lip that everyone warned would get me killed one day. Or, in this case, thrown into an Albanian jail.

'I think I'll be the judge of that.' He paused and looked down at the phone. Did he need a warrant to look at its contents? In Albania, I doubted it. But I'd have to tell him the code to unlock it first. Although, a couple of his combat-equipped pals outside could hold me while he held the screen to my face. Facial recognition had its flaws.

'A car registered in your name has been discovered on the Gencian Road.'

'Well, thank goodness it has been recovered. Where is the Gencian Road?'

He didn't answer that one. 'Recovered, yes. All in one piece? No.'

'Had it been in an accident?'

'It was – *is* – full of bullet holes.'

'Bullet holes? Really?' I made my mouth into an 'O' of surprise, like I couldn't possibly imagine guns or gunfights ever entering my life. Luckily, our own weapons were at the bottom of the lake in Tirana's Grand Park. I wouldn't miss that jam-prone piece-of-shit Beretta anyway.

'Yes. Quite a number of them. Of course, we checked with the hire company and you were the renter.' What he wasn't mentioning were the dead bodies. It was possible the AK men had disposed of them, or the families had come and collected their fallen. 'And now we find you leaving the country. What was your business here?'

'Holiday. Walking holiday.'

His eyes flicked down to the passport and up again to me in the way all border officials and police are trained to do. I think the Gestapo first invented the 'papers please scan'. Or maybe it was the Hollywood version of Nazis. Either way, it really caught on. 'Yet, you have been here only a few days. It normally requires at least a week, or even two, to see our beautiful country.'

'Your English is very good.'

He nodded, accepting the truth without explaining it. 'Why the short visit?'

'Well, the car was stolen, which was upsetting, and it rather ruined the holiday.'

'But you didn't report it stolen.'

'I did. To the police station in Pulana.'

He gave me his weary-policeman smile. 'There is no police station in Pulana.'

Fuck. Then something told me he was fishing. I had nothing to lose by spitting out the hook. I bristled a little. 'Well, there was some sort of building full of cops who mostly ignored me.'

He nodded. 'What I meant to say was, there is no permanently manned police station in Pulana. Four days a week. When did you report the vehicle stolen?'

'Yesterday. We'd been for a walk around the town, which didn't take long ...'

He wasn't ready for the details yet, which was a relief. I didn't have any to give him.

'What is it you do back in England, Miss Wylde?'

'I'm a personal ...' Just the merest gulp as I swallowed the next word, which had tried to tag along. I hoped he hadn't noticed. 'Trainer.'

'A what?'

'A personal trainer. I help people get fit, lose weight, become toned.' *Release their inner selves, empower them, put them on the path to wellness*. I'd had enough motivational gym sessions over the years to know the lingo, but I decided to spare him. 'You have them here? Personal trainers?'

'For the lazy elite, yes. Body gurus, we call them. But most people in Albania keep fit by working hard.' He sniffed to emphasise the point. 'Your final destination today?'

'London.'

'Yet, you have only a ticket to Paris.'

'Sorry, we are stopping off in Paris for a few days. Sightseeing.'

'And your companion will confirm everything you have told me?'

Be a bleedin' miracle if she did, I thought, because I've been making all this up on the hoof. I considered claiming Freddie was a fantasist suffering from a form of amnesiac autism that made her an unreliable witness. But I thought better of it. 'Of course she will.'

'Will you excuse me for a moment? I have some calls to make.'

He rose, readjusted the line of his jacket and slipped my passport and phone into his right-hand pocket. He left, closed the door and I heard a bolt snick across.

I turned and surveyed the room. There was no camera I could spot. Maybe they didn't want whatever happened in here on tape. The floor was covered in scuffed, marbled linoleum tiles, but I could see no signs of blood. Only spilled coffee and food. And I guessed some of the latter contained the eggs that now perfumed the air. Maybe I was just being paranoid about the inspector being a rubber-truncheon man. That was the Albania of thirty years ago. Or so I hoped.

The room's only decoration was a poster in English: *Welcome to the Land of the Eagle.* The eagle in question was swooping over jagged peaks that rather queasily reminded me of where we had just seen men slaughtered. The bird had a crudely drawn bubble coming out of its mouth, containing something written in what I assumed was Albanian. Maybe it said: *Better they were slaughtered than you.*

How long until the flight left without me? It had been forty-five minutes to boarding when they had called me in. I reckoned half that time had now elapsed. I knew there was a vast reservoir of panic inside me that I had managed to keep a lid on. All this, this chasing around the toilet bowls of Europe, had one endgame: get to Bali and find Jess, my lovely daughter whose face I couldn't quite visualise any more. Who, in the many months she had been gone, would have blossomed into a beautiful young woman. And I was missing it all, thanks to her fucking father, who took her from me.

I could feel myself welling up – the reservoir had clearly sprung a leak – when I heard the bolt on the outside of the door draw back and Inspector Gazim re-entered, a pained expression on his face. He didn't sit. He simply threw a red folder on the desk in front of me.

I waited. He let our lack of communication stretch out.

'I have spoken to the duty sergeant at the police station at Pulana,' he said eventually.

I raised a quizzical eyebrow. *And?* it said. While my brain said: *Oh, fuck, here we go.*

Gazim sighed. 'He confirmed your account. There is a copy of the report in the folder. I have emailed a version to your car-hire company.'

It took a while for me to process this. Then I said: 'You bastard.'

A brief smile flitted across his face, lightening those

serious features, as if the sun had broken cover from behind cloud for a second. 'Were it all too swift, my colleagues might have suspected I had not investigated properly.' As soon as he had finished the sentence, it became gloomily overcast again and he was cop-like once more.

'How long have you known the Colonel?' I asked.

Nothing came back. He stared at me, impassive, that smile an anomaly to be disowned. Eventually he spoke, as if he were reading off a cue card. 'I hope this unfortunate incident has not coloured your impression of our country.'

Well, if that was how he wanted to play it. 'No, not at all.'

'In which case ...' He extracted a pen from his pocket. 'In the folder is a form saying that you have been treated fairly and courteously by the *Policia e Shtetit* and have no cause for complaint. It is standard procedure.'

Jesus, even the police want reviews now. *CopAdviser.*

I opened the red file, removed, folded and pocketed the official police report on our stolen car and signed the *How did we do?* form. At least it didn't ask for star ratings.

'Why did you bring me in here?'

He glanced up at the corner of the room. The meaning was clear. I had been right. There were no cameras to record him talking to the Englishwoman. Fair enough.

When I was done, he closed the folder and placed my

passport and phone on the desk in front of me. 'Thank you, Miss Wylde. Have a nice flight.'

As I collected my things I couldn't help but notice that, whereas I had arrived in the room with just one phone, I was leaving with two.

# TEN

Looking back, I am ashamed of the plan we came up with in Paris. We took advantage of a decent man. Lost him his job, possibly his career. To be fair, Freddie didn't like it from the get-go.

'There must be easier ways to get Leka's attention,' she had said. There were probably cheaper ones, too. But she couldn't think of anything that gave us such copper-bottomed leverage and so she went along with it.

I suspected she was beginning to doubt my sanity. But she was a loyal enough friend to keep that to herself.

We had been in Paris for seventy-two hours and had slept for about eight of them. The rest of the time was spent sourcing a vehicle, checking our quarry's routines, estimating the strength of the opposition and buying drugs. Lots of drugs.

Eventually, we had worked out a plan. Sorry, *scenario*. It involved Freddie and me stripping down to vests and tight jeans. We were no youngsters, but we looked pretty good, the musculature of our arms still well defined and with something reasonably substantial to push up in a push-up bra.

It wasn't the flaunting of our bodies that made me ashamed, though. It was the fact that Jens van Welz, a member of my profession ID'd from a picture sent to the Colonel in Zurich, was fooled by one of the oldest tricks in a very well-thumbed book. It was like Fool's Mate in chess – a hoary old move that nobody ever fell for. Until they did.

When Jens pulled up outside the grand mansard-roofed house in the suburb of Saint-Germain-en-Laye that morning, he was confronted with two women struggling to lift a chest into the back of a small van. He watched us for a second until Freddie flashed him a we're-just-weak-women smile and he came over, flexing his shoulders like a weightlifter. 'What you got in there?' he asked in French. 'A dead body?'

'Not yet,' said Freddie.

I could slap that girl sometimes.

We both stepped back so he could take a shot at it. He planted his feet wide apart, bent his knees and spread his arms so he could grab both handles at once. The moment he put his back into it and realised the chest was almost empty, that was when we had him off balance. We grabbed a leg each and heaved him inside. Freddie was on top of him in a second, administering a punch to the back of his neck. I held my breath and closed my mouth while I released powder from a talc-dispenser into his face. Cable ties took care of his arms and legs, and within a matter of seconds we were inside the van with an angry, thrashing bodyguard. He stopped when I relieved him of his Glock and put it to his temple.

Honestly, it was so slick, any watching Formula One drivers would have welcomed us into their pit team.

'Who the fuck *are* you?' he asked, but I could tell he already felt like his tongue had been replaced by a fat baguette.

'If I had a penny . . .' replied Freddie.

I waited until his eyelids drooped before I wiped the excess powder away from his nose and mouth.

The Devil's Breath.

Surprisingly easy to get in Paris.

Some weeks before I'd actually been dosed with it myself when I'd stroked the embossing on a business card. So I knew just how effective it could be. And what the hangover was like.

We removed the nasal screens from our nostrils and Freddie opened the chest and began dressing for the part of bodyguard/driver. I removed the car keys, ID and lanyard from Jens' pocket. I slit the plastic casing and inserted Freddie's photograph over Jens'. It needed trimming down, but it would pass a brief once-over.

'How do I look?'

Freddie now had on a dark jacket and trousers with a black silk blouse underneath. Her hair was pulled back in a compact ponytail, her face devoid of any make-up. Unlike me, she never seemed to need it, even on a few hours' sleep. 'Like a bodyguard,' I said.

'If she phones the agency to check, we're fucked.'

'I know.' I offered Freddie the Glock but she shook her head.

'It won't come to that.'

I had to admire her optimism. It was bound to come to that sooner or later.

North of Saint-Germain-en-Laye is the Forêt Domaniale de-Saint-Germain-en-Laye, which, on a weekday morning, has quiet sections of road and a network of tracks to shield ne'er-do-wells from prying eyes. At night, they are a favourite for locals who fancy a bit of car-hopping, *shique-shaque*. One of these dogging areas was our RV spot. By the time Freddie returned to the rendezvous, Jens was stirring. I almost felt sorry for him as his eyes snapped open and his brain tried to make sense of how he had ended up in the back of a van.

'What . . .?'

'What, how, who, where, when?' I said in English. He was Dutch, so his English was bound to be better than my French. 'You can try to figure it out all you want, but the memory of how you got here is gone. Retroactive amnesia. You probably recall setting off for work in your Mercedes for certain. Maybe the drive to Mrs Cosovanu's house. Maybe you even recall seeing two women struggling with a chest . . . but I doubt it. The Devil's Breath. Like Rohypnol or GHB, but faster-acting.'

'What . . . what do you want? The kids?'

I shook my head. 'The kids are at school. Dropped off just like you would.'

'The wife?'

'Probably fucking her tennis coach as we speak.' He looked even more puzzled, if that were possible. 'Or whatever she does on a Wednesday morning.'

'I don't have any money. You kidnapped the wrong guy.'

The door opened and Freddie held up her phone and took a picture of the hapless bodyguard. 'We don't want your money,' she said. 'We just want to show your boss how easy it is to fuck him over.'

'He'll kill me.'

'Leka?' I asked.

'Mr Cosovanu. When he finds out I—'

'Yup. When he finds out you let strangers get to his kids. Strangers who could have raped, murdered and dismembered them, if they'd so wished.'

'Thank your lucky stars we are nice people,' added Freddie. I wasn't sure he would buy that, considering his situation.

'What about me?' he asked.

As if I really did give a flying fuck. 'You can go back and tell them what happened. But you are right, I don't think Mr Cosovanu, as you call him, offers generous severance packages to employees who screw up where his children are involved. Your best bet is this: in that chest is a Swiss Army knife. We are going to put the chest, and you, on the road. It may take you a while, but I reckon you can cut those ties. We will even leave you the keys to the Merc. Now, all you have to do is call your agency and make sure those kids are picked up from school safely. Because you'll be leaving the country and looking for a new job, won't you?'

He called us some choice name in Dutch.

Freddie chimed in with an alternative. 'Or we can put you in the boot of the Merc and you can hope someone hears your screams.'

I don't think he liked Freddie's option. 'Who the fuck *are* you and what do you want?'

'I'm just your average pissed-off mother who wants her daughter back.'

'A pissed-off mother with a Glock,' Freddie said.

'Ah, yes. Sorry, Jens. We'll be keeping the Glock.'

We were bait once more. It was getting to be a habit. Then again, maybe men shouldn't be so damn predictable. We were two women at the café on the outskirts of Calais, minding their own business, enjoying a coffee in the morning sun. Our VW Campervan, powder-blue and white with English plates, was nearby. We didn't ask to be interrupted. They made all the running. The men.

Neither of us paid any apparent attention as a Citroën drove slowly past and then again three minutes later. It parked up behind the VW and two men exited. They were dressed from the Thug section at Zara: leather jackets, jeans, dental-white trainers. Both had bullet heads and mirrored shades, which they took off as they approached. The one who spoke had a thick black moustache.

'Ladies, how are you today?'

Freddie and I exchanged glances. 'Fine,' I said.

'Can we help you?' Freddie sounded defensive.

'May I?' he asked, pulling out a chair and sitting down. His pal stood behind him, arms folded. The sitter pointed a thumb over his shoulder. 'Nice van. Yours?'

I nodded. 'Daisy.' Everyone names their bloody VW Campervans something like that. Daisy, Clementine, Ruby. The twee-er the better.

'Daisy. Cute. The thing is, ladies, we'd like to buy it. We'll give a good price. You could pay for your holiday.'

'Daisy is not for sale,' I said. Which was the truth. It wasn't really ours. We had hired it. And those English plates were fake.

'Well, in which case, we will hire it from you. Just for a few hours. You drive it across on the ferry, we give you, what, five hundred Euros?'

I leaned in, like I was interested. 'With how many people in it? Van like that, it's a GG, isn't it?'

A GG was a Guaranteed Game.

Now he looked offended. 'What do you mean?'

'How many refugees can you get in there?'

'Well, what we do with it while we have hired it is our business. All you have to do is be in the front and minding your own business.' Because two women in a VW Campervan called Daisy are a good bet for getting over the Channel and into the UK unchecked. Meaning the smugglers were pretty sure they could stuff the rear with live bodies to bring across, at up to nine grand per person.

Prices changed all the time. It wasn't only Ryanair and easyJet who had dynamic pricing algorithms, although the people-smugglers' computers were all in their heads. Just as commercially savvy as the real thing, though.

'We want to see Leka,' said Freddie.

It was like she had electrocuted them. Both gave a little spasm of shock. The moustachioed one shot to his feet. 'Who are you?'

Christ, I was getting bored with that question. 'We're not cops. We're not journalists. We just want to see your boss. For a chat.'

'About what?' It was the second man, finding his voice at last.

'That's between him and us,' I said. 'We have business to discuss. We'll be here.'

They stood and stared for a few seconds, unsure of their next move. Mr Moustache gave a jerk of his head and they walked back to the Citroën, muttering to each other. The Colonel had told us about people-smugglers targeting van owners on the Shuttle and ferries, offering to rent or buy their vehicles and stashing desperate men and boys inside – they were nearly all male – for the crossing. God knows why they still thought the UK was the Promised Land. Didn't they read the newspapers? Well, probably not, but it was no secret that there were better final destinations than blighted Blighty.

We ordered another coffee and it had only just arrived when the Citroën returned. There were three of them now, the newcomer a lanky lad with greasy hair to his shoulders and an acne-savaged complexion. He came and sat. 'Just one of you,' said the moustache.

We had expected that. I picked up my phone and pocketed it. Freddie had the Glock. I knew I'd be searched at some point, but she might not be. I'd like to see the pockmarked lad try to pat her down. 'If I haven't called or if I'm not back in thirty minutes ...' I pointed to crater-face. 'Break his neck and call the police. I'll be at the Hotel Neptune.'

I enjoyed the look of confusion on their faces. We *knew* where Leka's office was?

Of course we did.

Our Man in Zurich was bound to know where all the best people-traffickers hung out. But we couldn't just swan in. We needed them to get us to Leka.

We needed more than that to make sure we got out.

'Count on it.'

And they thought we were joking.

The Hotel Neptune was a blocky modern building on Avenue Louis Blériot, and Leka had taken over the entire top floor. The two men from the café took me up in the lift, and I was given a quick pat-down by the mostly silent one. They took my phone, then handed it back so I could turn it on. They ran through various apps to ensure it was as it appeared to be. A phone. And not a bomb. Part of me wished I'd thought of that. It would be cleaner than what was to come. And cheaper.

When the lift stopped and the doors opened, I was led along a corridor carpeted in deep red with a gold

Neptune motif, to a set of double doors where I got a second pat-down from the sombre-looking sentry outside. After he'd finished with a final poke of my breasts he nodded for us to enter.

It is fair to say that Leka wasn't what I had expected. The Colonel had sent me a photograph, but in that he looked like any other Albanian hustler. The man sitting behind a desk you could land a helicopter on was smart and handsome, with none of the pudginess seen on some of his more simian colleagues, and he had a haircut that didn't look like it was done with secateurs. He was wearing a dark pinstriped suit, light-blue shirt and a geometrically patterned tie.

The room was decorated in fake Louis XIV style: lots of gilt, portraits of noblemen with horses and a red carpet a few shades darker than its sibling in the corridor, with a single large Neptune image in the centre. There were padded and quilted carver chairs and, somewhat incongruously, an antique high-backed settle that looked seriously uncomfortable.

Mr Moustache put my phone and passport on the desk. Leka reached into a drawer and placed a silver revolver with a polished wooden grip on the table next to the items. It was a Ruger or a Smith & Wesson, I couldn't be sure. Although revolvers are less fashionable in the world Leka inhabited, they were often more practical. They didn't jam like my Beretta had on the mountain.

When he spoke, Leka had that curious mid-Atlantic twang of people who learned most of their English from watching TV. 'You wanted to see me?' He picked up the passport. 'Miss Wylde ...'

And then, as the penny dropped, he laughed. 'Miss Samantha Wylde. I was expecting you some weeks ago.'

Leka had sent two 'retrievers' to pick me up in Zurich. The idea was they would use me as bait to lure Tom, the man who had spared a young Leka after the attempted rape of the young goatherd, to my rescue. It hadn't worked out well for them.

'I had business to take care of.'

'So now you have delivered yourself here, right to my place of work. Very thoughtful of you.'

I saw the inclination of the head. Knew what it meant. I heard the shuffle of white trainers on the carpet and felt the air behind me displaced. It was meant to be a blow to the kidneys, I reckoned. That's a quick way to get someone on their knees. I side-stepped, spun around, punched the attacker's ear hard and pushed him towards Leka. Then I stepped away and raised my arms in the air to show I was done.

It was the clean-shaven one who had tried for me, and he levered himself up from the desk and spun to face me.

'You know, this isn't my first rodeo,' I said, dropping to a defensive crouch. I knew I could take him.

'Enough,' said Leka. The young man glared at me and curled his upper lip to show me his teeth. I guessed that it meant: You'll pay for that. He padded back so he was out of my line of sight when I turned back to face Leka.

'I prefer to do my talking on my feet, not my knees.'

'Keegan said you were tough. I didn't believe him.' Keegan was the chief retriever who had tried to parcel me up for Leka so he could use me to access Tom. 'I could just shoot you.'

'But you want to get to someone through me. Can't do that if I'm dead.'

'Who said anything about you being dead?'

'You shoot me, you better kill me,' I said. I didn't mind that it was some cliché I had heard. I meant it. 'But I'm here to persuade you not to. And to leave my friend alone. The man who spared your life once. Doesn't that count for anything?'

He thought about that for a moment. 'Wait outside,' he said to his goons.

I expected objections, but none came. They knew I couldn't make it to his gun before he could pick it up. Besides, I wasn't here to put a bullet in him. That was someone else's job.

I waited until the pair had left. 'You killed my husband. Or had him killed. Which is the same thing.'

I gave him the brief summary of how Paul, who had worked for the British Nuclear Police, had been shot down in cold blood on the streets of London.

Executed.

'That had nothing to do with me,' he insisted.

'Yet other members of the same army unit have died. At least one is still a hunted man.' Tom, who was hiding out at a boatyard in Nottinghamshire. 'Maybe the others are, too.'

He shook his head. 'You are barking up the wrong tree. And making a lot of noise while you are at it.'

'So why did you set the retrievers on me in Zurich to bring me in?'

'To straighten this out.'

'I don't believe you.'

He gave a shrug that managed to be insolent. 'That's not my problem.'

'It is if you are lying. And just in case you are, I have insurance. Pick up the phone.' He did so. 'It's unlocked. Hit camera. Play the video.'

As he did so, I watched all sorts of emotions speed across his face, like fast-moving clouds. He was seeing his kids skip into school, filmed by Freddie. The final cloud settled. It was black with rage.

I could tell from the tension in his body he was about to reach for the revolver. A bullet hit the desk before he could even stretch out his hand, sending his gun spinning to the floor. It was only afterwards the room filled with the sound of glass shimmering and shattering.

The pistol was three paces from me. I let it stay there. The door behind me opened. Leka kicked his chair back, so he was no longer visible from outside the room. 'Across the street, shooter. Go!'

I was impressed he had pieced it together so quickly.

'If he'd wanted you dead, you'd be dead,' I said. 'But call them off if you want them to live.'

He didn't ask why, so I told him.

'That's Oktane over there.'

*

It was a good ten minutes before order was restored. We moved to a room on the other side of the hotel, where he stayed well away from the windows. But Leka knew the threat wasn't me. I wouldn't hurt his kids. But I knew a man who would.

Oktane was, I suppose, like the Banksy of the Circuit in some ways. The best hit man – and rumour had it the richest, given his *per diem* – in the business. Mysterious and elusive, nobody was even certain of his nationality. Except, perhaps, the Colonel, who had once been his manager – yes, some of them do have managers who act as a cut-out between them and law enforcement – some years past, before the old man decided there was more money in stopping people getting whacked than actually whacking them. The dead don't pay, after all.

I could have put Freddie out there, except I guessed they would lock her down as collateral. And Oktane had one big advantage. The name. It was enough to tell anyone: I'm serious about this. Deadly serious.

Leka sat in a chair, the gun held limply by his side, while I stood. 'I'm guessing your father-in-law, or indeed your real wife, don't know about the second family in Saint-Germain-en-Laye,' I said. 'Which is one of the reasons you use agency security for the school run. So word doesn't get back.'

'Word has clearly got back somehow.'

It had. To Saban, the café owner. But I didn't say that. Saban was very clear on that point. He had shared his knowledge on the condition of total anonymity.

'So what are you threatening me with, Sam Wylde?

Telling my people that I am a bigamist, or harming my children? Or shooting me?'

'Or all of it,' I said. 'I have a daughter of my own. She is missing. I have to find her. I can't with you looming over us like a bogeyman. I don't want to be distracted watching my back the whole time.'

'This man of yours, he lets women fight his battles?'

'Yes, if the woman in question is me.' I said it with a confidence I didn't quite feel. But a little bombast goes a long way sometimes.

He frowned, still not quite grasping what was on the table here. Or perhaps pretending not to. 'So the deal is?'

'The deal is, it was all a long time ago. People got hurt, people died. Not for the first nor the last time. This blood feud belongs in the past. Let it go.'

'Let it go?' He ran his free hand through his hair. 'You didn't see what they did to my family.'

'There would be some who would say they deserved it.'

'Which someone? It was unprovoked. We were unarmed.'

I shook my head. He wasn't going to wrong-foot me so easily. 'That's not how I heard it.'

'OK, one of us, my Uncle Ramiz, had a shotgun. It is normal. What did the British have? Submachine guns. It was what you call shooting fish in a barrel. Except they weren't fish. They were my family.'

He sounded as if he genuinely believed he had been wronged. I could feel something hideous squirming in my stomach. 'Your family were going to rape the girl.

That's why they got involved. That's why they broke the non-intervention protocol.'

A sneer twisted the lower part of his face. 'Is that what he told you? Did he tell you what your fine British soldiers were doing when we found them? Why they had to kill my friends and family? Why I had to play dead with my cousin on top of me, his blood running onto my face?'

My mouth was dry and the next sentence came out as a croak. 'You're lying.'

His face relaxed. The clouds of hate suddenly cleared. He smiled, as if confident that he was in the right. And that he had me on his hook. 'Am I? Look into your boyfriend's eyes and ask him to tell you the truth for once.'

And what he told me next made me want the earth to open up and swallow me whole, bury me deep and never let me go.

I know I am in trouble when I dream of Bojan. He only comes when I am at my lowest ebb. He was a Serbian gangster, a man who had tricked me into fighting him twice in the basement of an oligarch's house in The Bishops Avenue. I had won both times, although the second was more by luck than skill. I had managed to stab him with his own knife. Although he later disappeared, he had lost so much blood, I was certain he was dead. That didn't worry me. It was self-defence and his wound was self-inflicted, with just a little help from me.

But whenever Bojan comes into my dreams, the situation changes. It is me who gets stabbed. Me who bleeds out. Sometimes the knife slides up and under my ribs; in other versions he slices the blade across my throat; a third scenario has him inflicting my death by a hundred tiny cuts.

He always wins.

I know whenever Bojan and his knife appear, my world is about to turn upside down. And he came to me with that blade every night until I finally made it to Tom.

# ELEVEN

The boatyard smelled of bitumen and two-pack epoxy. It was blacking season. Narrowboats had been craned, trailered and dry-docked out of the water. From one of the sheds came the sound of metal being shot-blasted. It suited Tom. Outdoors, lots of machinery, the chance to collect and deliver the boats across the canal network and be paid for it.

I arrived just as Tom was on his break. He came over and tried to hug me, but I twisted away. Hugging could wait. Hugging might be off the agenda permanently. He looked confused and asked if anything was wrong. I told him we needed to talk.

We found a picnic-style table in the garden of the pub next to the boatyard. He had put on some bulk since I last saw him. He was wind-tanned, and muscles rippled under his T-shirt. His face was streaked with oil and his fingernails would need an excavator to get the dirt out.

He was happy. I was about to ruin that.

Tom had come into my life at a turbulent time. I was still getting over the shock of Paul's death and back into the world of personal protection. Tom, the itinerant narrowboat man, cruising the canals like a waterborne nomad, had provided warmth, humour and sex. And, oddly, a living link to Paul, as they had served in the army together.

In return, I nearly got him killed in a house on The Bishops Avenue. And then I knocked him unconscious so I could take on Bojan alone.

Boyfriend and girlfriend? Not quite. It was more complicated than that. I liked him. Did I love him? I loved the sex we had whenever we were together. But I suspected that wasn't quite the same thing.

When he came back from the bar with the drinks – a pint for him, half for me because I was driving – I had arranged some photos on the table; print-offs from my phone. My heart was racing in anticipation. I had a tremendous desire to pee, but I knew that was just nerves. I used to get that phantom bladder pressure in Iraq, too.

'What's this?' he asked. 'Holiday snaps?' Then he saw my face. 'Sam?'

'These were taken in a small town outside Paris. Her name is Mrs Cosovanu, although it is possible she isn't really married. Elona Cosovanu is her full name.'

He sat and sipped his drink. I pushed the photograph closer. 'Elona. The goatherd you apparently saved in Kosovo.' I might have accidentally put too much emphasis on 'apparently'.

'Good God. Really? In Paris?'

'Near Paris,' I corrected. 'Is it her?'

He shook his head. 'Nah. Can't be.'

100

'Well, have a good look at her before you say that. Is it her?'

He rubbed his mouth, smearing more dirt onto his face. 'Christ, Sam, it was such a long time ago.'

'Try the next picture. It's a close-up. Is it her?'

A sigh. 'I thought you were coming up to see me; to catch up.'

'Is it her?' I wanted an answer.

Irritation flared in his words. 'No. No, I don't think so.'

'No, or you don't think so?'

I saw his eyes flick back towards the boatyard. He wanted to be away from that pub. Away from me and these questions. Back in the sanctuary of hard, physical graft. 'Why are you doing this? What happened while you were away?'

'Is it her, Tom?'

'I don't know. OK?'

'*Could* it be her?'

'It *could* be anyone, Sam.'

I examined his expression, as detached as I could manage. 'You don't look like it could be anyone. You look like you don't want it to be her.'

He almost growled at me, his face reddening. 'For crying out loud—'

'Is it Elona? Is this the girl you saved?'

'Why are you saying it like that?'

'Like what?'

'"Saved", as if it has inverted commas around it.'

'It's a simple question.'

101

'No, it isn't. Not the way you're asking it.'

'Then just answer me.'

'It could be. All right? It *could* be her. Are you going to tell me what this is about?'

'It's about the truth.'

'Where did you get the photos anyway? How did you find her?'

'Never mind that.'

'You're scaring me, Sam. What is this all about?'

'I am just wondering how a man who was part of a group that almost raped a young goatherd called Elona comes to be keeping her and their two children on the outskirts of Paris? They are, to all intents and purposes, married. Except, he couldn't marry her because she had been raped.'

'She wasn't raped. We saved her,' Tom protested.

I kept my voice as level as I could. 'I heard differently. And I heard she was blamed for it. Always the woman's fault, the world over. She should have fought back; better to have died. She was an outcast. Unclean.'

'I don't know what you're talking about.'

'I'm beginning to think you know exactly what I am talking about.'

'I don't,' he insisted. 'But you've seen Leka?'

'Yes. He said it was you who sodomised her.'

'What? Don't be ridiculous. Nobody sodomised her. And how would she identify me anyway?'

'There's pictures of KFOR units all over the internet. Band of Brothers and all that shit. Wouldn't be hard to find you and Paul's squad.'

He banged the table, slopping his drink. 'Let me tell you what happened—'

I cut him short. 'I know your version of events, Tom. Lived with them for a couple of years; never doubted them. But let me tell you what Leka remembers of that day.'

# TWELVE

'And do you believe him?' Nina asked.

'Tom? I want to believe him.'

We were lying on daybeds in the relaxation room of a spa in central London. The air was filled with ylang-ylang and yuzu, and dolphins and other cetaceans made plaintive noises over the loudspeakers.

Through a plate-glass window I could see a circular Romanesque pool, complete with fluted columns and curvaceous stone gods. A series of tall, elegant women in expensively sculpted swimsuits carefully risked a few head-up strokes, swimming in a don't-smudge-my-make-up way. I automatically sorted them into two categories: Work Done and No Work Done. WDs outnumbered NWDs by about two to one. There was more filler out there than in a branch of B&Q. This was the idle rich at ... well, idle. In what seemed increasingly to be my previous life, they might have been my clients.

What I couldn't quite figure out was why Nina had brought me here. An old university friend of Paul's, she worked as a journalist on a national newspaper – the same one as Adam from Albania as it happened, although I thought it best not to bring that little escapade up – and would normally rain vitriol down on the slim-limbed, meticulously depilated women exiling themselves in this private club.

Nina sat up on one elbow, pulling the neck of her robe together. Perhaps she thought natural breasts were against club rules.

'That's not really an answer.'

'Well, it's he says/he says, isn't it?'

'So, do you believe your friend and lover, or some gangster who traffics in human misery?'

I was stumped for an answer. I knew it should be an easy choice. Except, even traffickers in human misery have to switch off some time. It could be that Leka was telling the truth and that Tom – and Paul – had played a part in the cover-up of a rape. Possibly a gang rape. If Leka's version of events was true.

Leka had claimed that it was the British soldiers who assaulted the girl, and when they, the locals, tried to stop them, the Brits opened fire. Leka had survived, not because of anybody's mercy, but by playing dead. The thought of Tom and Paul being mixed up in that sent acid into my throat. I couldn't look that scenario in the eye just yet.

'What are we doing here, Nina?' I asked.

'Didn't you enjoy that massage?'

'Not knowing it cost three hundred quid, no.'

'Ach, I told you, it's on the house.'

'Which makes me feel even more uncomfortable.'

Nina used to specialise in making me feel uncomfortable, pointing out my lack of knowledge about art, politics and literature whenever she could. Being able to field-strip a Sig was, in her book, a poor substitute for being able to say Edvard Munch properly. *How was I to know his surname wasn't pronounced like the eating sound?*

This had improved somewhat since Matt and Laura had enticed Jess away while she was at Nina's house. Guilt – even misplaced guilt – had a way of softening her hard edges. But I had that toxic guilt as well. In spades.

Matt was a fuck-up. I'd met him while I was in the army as a medic and I went to Afghanistan while, unbeknown to me, pregnant with his child.

Our child. Jess.

I left the service and decided to settle down. Then Matt decided he hadn't quite used up his lifetime clubbing/drug allowance and set about touring the party islands of Europe. Somewhere along the way, he realised he couldn't face coming back to domesticity.

Matt returned to my life some time after my second husband Paul was murdered, looking for a way into the same family he had rejected years earlier. If I hadn't batted him away, somewhat forcefully, he might not have taken Jess. I never quite understood why he wanted custody of her. Where did his late burst of paternalism come from? Wherever it was, he probably shouldn't have had a vasectomy until he was certain he never wanted any more children. But he did and, given he would have no future chance at fatherhood, had been prepared to steal Jess. An eventuality I hadn't even considered.

Nina might have fallen for Matt and Laura's ploy to lure Jess away from her care, but the guilt I felt for not second-guessing it was far more acute.

Nina sipped some water. 'You should rehydrate.'

I took some just to keep any lectures at bay. Her skin did look better than mine, that much was certain. Then again, the skin on the stone gods around the pool looked better than mine.

I had an excuse. It's difficult to get your fifty litres a day, or whatever it is, when you're being chased down a mountain by men who want to kill you, or when you are trying to bully an Albanian people-smuggler into getting the fuck out of your life. And gunfights play havoc with any moisturising regime.

Nina put on her serious face. It didn't wrinkle much and I thought: *Botox?* No, not Nina, scourge of artifice.

'Last year, ten thousand journalism jobs disappeared in the UK,' said Nina. 'Did you know that?'

'Have you been fired? Is this your redundancy we're spending on being stroked by Amazonians?'

'No. Let me finish. Last year, there were forty thousand PR jobs created. *Forty thousand*. Most in social media.'

'Your favourite.'

She looked like I had just punched her dog on the nose. 'You can't play favourites with the future.'

It sounded like something Elon Musk or James Dyson might say. 'Where did you get that line from?'

The door opened and a WD put her head in, tried to sneer, failed and retreated. I recalled there was a 'Please keep your conversation to a minimum' sign outside. Fuck them, that's easy when you have nothing worthwhile to say.

I dialled down on the scorn a little. It wasn't the club or the women or even Nina putting me in a bad mood. It was the whole Tom and Leka situation.

'I'm setting up an agency. Managing influencers, mainly. Making sure celebrities come down to the clients' places and post about their visits. This place is going to be the first. If we sign.'

It took a while for me to process this. 'But, you're a journalist. You hate PR as much as you hate social media.'

'What I hate is being in a dying industry. Oh, I'll stay in writing for a while. But look, some of these celebs will need bodyguards, or ELOs, or whatever you call yourselves.'

She knew damn well we were PPOs. She also knew I was right. She hated that world. But I was making her defensive. Her spines would come out soon. I softened my tone.

'Sounds good.'

'Well, not good. But a way forward.' I think her eyes were asking for approval. I didn't know what to say. It didn't sound like a career she would relish. 'Talking of journalism, I read a great piece by Adam Bryant the other day. You know him?'

I kept quiet. I might have known they were acquaintances. Colleagues. Rivals, perhaps.

'It was about two women he met who got him out of a confrontation with some Albanian brigands.'

Gangsters, not brigands, I wanted to say. 'Brigands' suggests some sort of romantic bandit. Those guys had been anything but romantic. 'Really?' I said it with a what's-this-got-to-do-with-me flatness.

'Really,' she continued. 'It's a great read. He even swears it's true.'

'Sounds interesting. When's it running?'

'It's not,' said Nina with an irritated shake of the head. 'Rory spiked it. The editor,' she said, answering my next question. 'Said it read too much like *Boy's Own* fiction. It's one of the reasons I want to leave. If all we write about is a celebrity's fragrant farts, we may as well just get out there and take the celebrity's shilling. Anyway, you were in Albania recently, weren't you? With Little Minx?' She meant Freddie. They didn't see eye to eye on ... well, anything really.

'Didn't meet any brigands,' I said.

'Bollocks. Your Leka is Albanian.'

'He's hardly my Leka.'

'No.' She leaned across the gap between the two daybeds and lowered her voice, even though we were alone. 'You know, it strikes me that there is only one way to solve your dilemma about who is telling the truth. About the rape.'

I knew what she was about to suggest because I had already considered it. 'Ask Elona what she remembers.'

'Yes. If you've already thought of it—'

'I suggested it to Leka. He said he didn't want the past stirred up. That Elona had suffered enough. He said if I ever went near her he would kill me.' In fact, he also said if he ever saw me again he'd kill me. But he promised a truce, at least while I confronted Tom about that day in Kosovo.

'Shame.'

'Being killed? A real bummer. So, I'm not doing that.'

'You know what I mean. She is the one witness that could tell you the truth.'

'Tom reckons not. He says she is either traumatised or has been brainwashed, or both.'

'How convenient for him. Then what are you going to do?'

'I told you, I'm going to Asia to get Jess from Matt.' With Freddie. Although, how I was going to pay for both of us was a moot point. Oktane, as the Colonel had warned, had not been cheap. And I never even saw the guy. We had only communicated via the extra phone I had been given by Inspector Gazim at Tirana airport, which I had destroyed as instructed once our business was concluded.

I needed cash. There was a job being advertised that might have tempted me in the old days. The whole-page ad that had appeared in *Security Gazette* swam into my vision.

We are looking for a PPO to accompany our well-known international celebrity client on a visit to

Hong Kong for personal reasons. The successful applicant will be discreet and well versed in defensive surveillance. The client has received kidnap threats that she – and we – take seriously. The successful applicant will be part of a team offering 24-hour protection for the duration of the trip. Client stipulation is for at least one female to cover all possibilities. Mandarin or Cantonese an advantage. Clean passport essential. Proof of self-defence skills expected. Must be willing to submit to random drug testing. Salary negotiable.

'International celebrity' was always worrying. If it were true, it meant they drew unwarranted attention wherever they went. The Beckhams were a prime example. Very hard to keep them under the radar completely. If it weren't really true, then it was a client with ideas above their station. And I couldn't promise Mandarin or Cantonese.

No, it was a bust. Especially as HK wasn't where I wanted to be. Close, but no cicadas.

Nina burst my speculation bubble. 'How have you left it with Tom?'

'He's hurt that I don't believe him. I'm ... ambivalent. Also, he thinks I'm mad running after Jess.'

'Why?'

'He thinks she'll find her way home eventually. Matt might be an arse, but he'll keep her safe. He thinks I'll just stir up trouble.'

'Well, you're good at that,' said Nina.

111

'Thanks, sister.'

'So, it's all over between you two?'

I puffed out my cheeks, a move I doubted many women in that spa could manage. I remembered my first meeting with Tom on the canal near King's Cross, when he had cut his arm trying to repair his narrowboat. He had seemed so confident, yet so vulnerable. And how we very awkwardly fell into his bed. Or was that his bunk? But Leka had cast a shadow over all of that. My feelings at this point were probably what they call bittersweet. With the former probably ahead by a length. 'I think it is.'

Most spas in London hotels are built in the basement. It's one of the reasons I don't feel comfortable in them. I prefer clear views of the outside world and obvious exit strategies. Whenever a client has a day in the spa, I feel jittery. Especially if I have to join in and wear those gowns and mule slippers they all seem to favour. Have you ever tried running in those things? I have. I'd rather do it in Blahniks.

So, even though I wasn't working, I was glad to emerge into the fresh air – of sorts – near Trafalgar Square and get a phone signal. After I had said goodbye to Nina, wishing her all the best turning from gamekeeper into poacher – although I didn't use that phrase – I walked around the corner to a wine bar called Terroirs, ordered a large glass of Viognier to counter the effects of all that subterranean rehydration, and checked my messages. Several were from

Freddie, who was comparing fares out to Singapore and on to Bali.

*Economy or Business?*

Well, my heart said one, my wallet another. I texted back, *Premium Economy*?

There was a request to get in touch from my Personal Finance Planner at the bank. I really didn't want my PFP to know what I was planning to do with the rest of my money. There were missed calls from Tom, which made my insides do somersaults I couldn't actually interpret. The final one was a voicemail from a number I didn't recognise. It also took me a moment to place the woman's voice when I played it back.

'Hiya, Miss Wylde. Long time no speak. Look, I might need your help. Just for a few days. It pays well. I'm putting my head above the – what's it called? – parapet. Can you call me on this number? Be great to hear from you. Oh, it's Noor, by the way.'

Noor. Short for Nourisha. AKA the Angel of Harlow. I hadn't heard from her since . . . since the days when stretch limos seemed cool. I'd always liked her. Despite everything. I took a sip of wine and pressed the call-back button. I might as well tell her straight away that Sam Wylde was out of the bodyguarding game for the foreseeable future.

# THIRTEEN

She wasn't an angel and she wasn't actually from Harlow. But *Angel of Bishop's Stortford* didn't scan as well in the press. Noor was signed by a record company when she was fourteen – this was pre-streaming, when CDs still ruled and there was money in the industry's coffers – released her first album at sixteen and her second just before her seventeenth birthday. The quality was astonishing given the speed with which they were recorded. Most of that was down to Noor's voice. The young girl could transmute at will, aurally at least, into Billie Holiday, Aretha Franklin or Nina Simone. Add to that an ear for pop hooks and Noor was quite the package, appealing across a wide demographic.

She also looked great: tall, sharp-boned and funky. Her dad was an engineer from Grenada, her mother a teacher from Switzerland. She had been one of the first teen pop stars to resurrect the Afro and flaunt her many piercings, which she preferred to tattoos on the grounds that they were more easily reversed.

I was pulled in during the time when the tabloids

went sour on her. You know, after about ten minutes. She had turned eighteen and was hanging out in clubs and bars. There were a few stumbling-from-the-Groucho-at-two-in-the-morning shots and a couple of her bleary-eyed and hungover having breakfast with her disapproving manager.

And then the Angel of Harlow got a boyfriend and wouldn't play ball. *Who was he? How did they meet? Have they had sex yet?* All of which was met with a resounding: *fuck off.* One of the rags was offering fifty grand for an ID and an interview with Noor's Nookie, as they'd called him.

So I had been roped in as a media blocker; someone to stand between the paps and Noor. I might not have had the bulk, but I was young enough – still in my twenties, with a young child and a prospective husband called Paul – to get into the same clubs as Noor and her pals without attracting too much attention. Sometimes a 'lump', as we call the big, beefy refrigerators some stars prefer as minders, is like a curiosity magnet. I was also new to the game and, I am ashamed to say now, I displayed a vestigial misogyny from my army days. As I said, I was young.

So there I was, sitting in the back of a stretch limo, three teenage girls opposite me, and no Mr Nookie, mysterious or not, in sight. In the centre of the trio was Noor, playing on her new iPhone 3G and cooing every time she found a fresh function. Like she would ever really have to use a spirit level.

To Noor's right was Kassie, her bestie from school.

Kassie was – and this is an example of me being very unsisterly, but here we go – the archetypal fat friend, so beloved of Hollywood. She was squeezed into some strapless, stretchy-yet-clingy material that she was always tugging out of one crevice or another, or pulling up over her considerable cleavage. Her cheeks were already red from the champagne she had necked out of the bottle she was holding, and her eyes had what I'd suspected was a Colombian-sourced sheen to them.

On Noor's left was Romana, aka Romy. She was like a darker-skinned proto-Kardashian – again, this was before that particular plague escaped from the lab – with cheekbones so prominent they cast shadows down her face, a permanent pout and a striking aquiline nose, perfect for when she wanted to look down it at you. I'd quite liked her. She'd always acted as if something about the whole set-up smelled fishy. She was also wearing a similar little black dress to me, except hers never seemed to bunch or wrinkle whereas mine felt like it was only a single evolutionary step above a pound-store bin liner. Which was unfair as it was from Whistles, which must be several evolutionary steps up.

We were heading for a club in Mayfair, driving there from the Sanderson, Noor's second-favourite hotel after the Portobello. It was fifteen minutes if traffic was light, down Regent Street, along Conduit, right at Berkeley Square. But we weren't going directly to the club, which was on Albemarle Street. It had been set up with the deliberate intention to mimic/rival Mahiki and, although the newbie hadn't bagged any royal princes yet, they had enough visiting celebs to make it worthwhile for some of the paparazzi to divide their time between the two clubs.

We wanted to avoid them.

To that end, there was another way into the new club from Stafford Street, through the premises of a personal trainer who catered to the time-poor, monied rich, including the odd pop star. Of course, the limo sort of gave the game away and I'd argued against using it. But Kassie had decided she never ever wanted to ride in anything but a pap-magnet again. And Noor had indulged her, over my objections.

Soon after we'd set off, I had issued some instructions.

'Right, the idea is that we get dropped opposite the entrance to Joe Roberts' place. It's down the steps. There will be someone waiting to take you through to the entrance to the club. It opens directly into the VIP room.' I had already scoped the place out while Noor was having a nap after a morning of radio and press interviews. Kassie and Romy also needed a kip, having run themselves ragged executing a harrowing Bond Street shopping sprint. 'So, when we stop, don't stick around to admire the view. There isn't one. Straight in. I'll be right behind you, just in case.'

'Yes, Miss Wylde,' said Kassie, giggling.

'Are you coming in with us?' asked Romy, making a valiant effort to keep the horror from her voice. 'To the VIP area?'

'I'll be around,' I said. I didn't add that what happened to Kassie and Romy was not my concern, unless

117

it impinged on my client. They could have sex in the toilets with a donkey for all I cared.

Always protect the Principal.

'If I say leave, Noor, don't ask questions. Just come with me. You two follow if you want to. The club has its own security and they're pretty good. We've got a safe area set out, and we'll have Vic parked up for a fast exit.' Vic was the limo driver, an old-school chauffeur-cum-heavy who had done the job since the days of Led Zeppelin.

The stories he could tell.

In fact, he did, some of them at least, in a memoir called *Rock'n'Roll Getaway Driver*, a few years back. Sadly, the lawyers had gutted it, so the most salacious stories ended up on the cutting-room floor. Or in a safe somewhere.

'Wasn't like this when we used to go to Marlon's in Harrow,' said Kassie, playing with the various controls on her armrest. For a second, Inner City's 'Good Life' boomed out at a volume that threatened to blow the speakers. She apologised and turned it down.

'Well, Noor wasn't worth millions to a record company when you were going to Marlon's,' I said. It was the record company paying my bill. Actually, that wasn't quite true. The record company had hired me, but eventually Noor would find herself footing the bill for me, the limo, Vic, the champagne, the club bar bill, maybe even the snowstorm up Kassie's nostrils. One day, Noor would wonder where her generous advance had gone.

You can usually see enough out of a heavily tinted limo window to make out people gawping, trying to figure out who's inside. This was before camera phones became ubiquitous, but still there were a few futile shots towards the glass as we slowed at the lights at the top of Regent Street.

Just as we were lining up for the right turn, a blast of cold night air hit me. The roof panel had been slid back and, before I could stop her, Kassie was through it, arms waving in the air.

She began to whoop at the top of her voice and wave the champagne bottle. Then she began to sing. Or, more accurately, wail. 'Goodlifegoodlifegoodlife. GOOD LIFE!'

There was a thud on the window next to me. A snail-trail of froth was smeared down the glass. Someone had thrown a can. I wasn't certain I blamed them.

'Kassie, get in,' I said.

'Goodlifegoodlifegoodlife. GOOD LIFE!'

'Kassie, now.'

I heard some lads jeering or cheering at her, I couldn't be sure which. But we were crawling up to the right turn and exposed to the world. A thought reinforced when the next half-drunk can of beer plopped like a slam-dunk into the car and spewed all over the leather seat next to me.

I lost a little of my PPO cool at that point, duck-walked across to her side of the cabin and pulled Kassie down. 'Close the roof!' I yelled at Noor.

As I grabbed hold of Kassie's waist and pulled,

that pesky elasticated material decided to ping down, unleashing her breasts in a blancmange of white flesh. As I yanked her away from the sunroof, she staggered as one of her heels bent under her and she lurched on top of me. I managed to shuffle a few steps back to reach my seat before collapsing with her full weight on me. It was like being attacked by an albino boxing kangaroo.

'Get off me, you lezza!' she'd cried as we had slithered on the wet leather. 'I'll do you like a fucking kipper.'

Exactly what that entailed I didn't know, so I gave her a little slap. 'Behave.'

'You hit me!'

'Not yet.'

I managed to push her away and across to her own seat, where she set about corralling her escaped prisoners back into captivity. Noor and Romy couldn't speak for laughing at whatever the former was holding up for them to view. Noor, I realised, had found the camera function on her phone. I'd made a mental note to get that off her and delete the evidence before the night was out.

We'd ridden the rest of the way to the club in silence, the odd outburst of giggles apart.

# FOURTEEN

I had lasted another ten days as a celebrity bodyguard.
It was like herding drunken cats: exhausting, frustrat-
ing and far from rewarding.

I had been trained in small-arms combat, defensive
driving and Krav Maga. What Noor and her chums
needed was a babysitter with attitude. The attitude
being: it's all good fun. I wasn't prepared to settle for
that. My job was to protect my Principal. It didn't
always chime with the Principal's besties having a
good time.

I had asked the agency for something more chal-
lenging and they got me three months protecting a
woman who feared her estranged husband was out
to kill her. Better. But I made sure I had left Noor on
reasonable terms.

Back then, I didn't believe in burning bridges. These
days, I take out both riverbanks too.

I waited until I was home and could FaceTime her.
The call connected and she appeared on the screen,
looking much as she had as a teenager. Face a little

121

fuller, maybe, but skin still flawless, eyes bright and a smile on those lips.

'Miss Wylde. How are you? Been a while.'

'I'm OK. Surprised to hear from you. I thought you were a hermit in Wales.'

'I am. Although I own most of Pembrokeshire now.' She gave a husky laugh, aware of how ridiculous that sounded. 'Look, Sam – is it OK to call you Sam?' She didn't wait for an answer. 'I know I was a spoiled little twat the last time we worked together. Too much too soon, as they say. But ... will you just hear me out?'

'Go on.'

'I need your help. I have to go to this wedding and, well, I need some security.'

'After all this time?' I asked.

'Hey, some people remember me. I turn down those *Remember the Noughties* tours on a weekly basis,' she laughed. 'And I'm still big in Basildon.'

I guess some pop fans do stay focused on the idols of their youth. 'So you have stalkers? Is that it?'

'Well, I did. I do sometimes. Thing is, the last few months I have been getting threats. Twitter, Instagram, texts. All untraceable. Accounts opened and shut down.'

'Threats such as ...'

'Rape, mostly.'

'Nice.'

'Yeah, but it's *where* they want to rape me that bothers me.'

'Up the arse?' I guessed.

'Worse. Bishop's Stortford.'

'Your home town?'

'Right. They say if I ever show my face there again there'll be trouble. I think it's someone I knew back in the day, I mean before all the music shit. And a bunch of my friends from home have been invited to this wedding. It might be one of them, know what I mean? So, I need someone to watch my back. And my backside, just in case you're right.' She was making light of it, but I could tell she was worried. Who wouldn't be? The papers were full of internet threats, dismissed as the work of a crank, which turned out to be all too real. However, my sympathy didn't extend to actually going to Bishop's Stortford.

'Look, I'm sorry, I'm not in that game at the moment.' I gave her a brief run-down about needing to find Jess.

'That's well fucked up,' she said, by way of empathising.

'Yeah. Look, I might be able to suggest some people. Good people,' I offered.

'Nah. I wanted someone I knew was the business.' She thought for a minute. 'I could blackmail you. I still have a photo of you sucking Kassie's tits in the limo. Well, that's what it looks like, anyway. What then?'

'Then I'd be the one coming round to stick something big up your arse.'

A chuckle. 'Yeah. I reckon you would an' all.'

Foolishly, I'd neglected to retrieve those snapshots taken in the back of the limo, not realising at the time just how toxic snatched photographs can be. 'And

I think that's illegal. Blackmailing with old photos.'

'Kiddin'. If you won't do it, I s'pose I can always ask my old record company to lend me someone. They love me again.'

'How come?'

'That last record? The one that they all said was too stark, too Eighties synth pop? Look at the streaming charts. About half of those songs have a sample of me in there somewhere. I make a fortune without stepping foot in a studio. Kanye, Post Malone, Rich Brian ... they all love me.'

I knew exactly one of those names. 'Congratulations.'

'You still sound like a schoolteacher, Sam. So, you can't help out an old pupil, huh?'

'Not really. I'm sorry, Noor. Like I said, I've got problems of my own. But if you do need recommendations, let me know. You might want to think about having two bodies, if you can afford it.' She tutted to let me know she could. 'Who's getting married?'

'Kassie.'

'Kassie?' I instantly regretted the amount of shock I let creep into my voice at the thought of the big girl's nuptials.

'Had to happen sooner or later. Except she's not Kassie, not like you knew her. She's not even called that any more. She's Kate. She's about half the size she was when you met her and she doesn't sound like the girl who used to let boys finger her for a fag behind the science block.'

That's going to be a great wedding speech, I thought.

'Hubbie-to-be is dead posh. Minted.'

'So why is she still getting married in Bishop's Stortford?' I asked.

'She isn't. Like I said, some people from Bish and Harlow are invited. But he's loaded, he ain't doing the nuptials in this country.'

'So where is it?' I asked.

'Didn't I tell you? It's in fuckin' Bali.'

# FIFTEEN

'So, your pet pop star pays for us to go to Bali?' This was the third time Freddie had asked this, as if it were too much to believe: a stroke of luck at last.

We were drinking tea at the café in Parliament Hill Fields. We had run up the hill ten times, to the viewing point across London – the cityscape mostly shrouded in an early autumnal mist – and then had done a circuit of the Heath. I had stretched at the end of all that, but, although my shoulder was better, I could still feel a tightness in my hamstrings. I decided I'd get a massage – a real massage, not the airy-fairy wellness shit that Nina was peddling – and keep stretching over the next few days. I didn't want to turn up in Bali limping from a pulled muscle or damaged tendon.

'Look, three or four days' work, max,' I said to her. 'While one of us is looking after the former Princess of Pop, the other can be out asking around known locations.' Of which we had but a handful: a clear picture of my daughter at a hotel pool and a couple in hard-to-make-out bars.

'No time for sightseeing, then,' said Freddie. 'I've always wanted to go to Bali.'

'My great-grandfather visited Bali in the Thirties. My mother had letters and postcards he had sent to her mother.' She also had ones from the Japanese prison where he eventually died. But I didn't mention that. 'From what I can gather, these days it's full of lairy young Australian lads. I'll toss you one of those.'

'Oh, you can leave the tossing to me.'

I ignored that. She was only chumming bait to get a response.

I watched a parade of strollers and attached parents pass by, rustling through the fall of russet, bronze and copper leaves that had coated the pathway. The crowd was mostly heading for the organic, sourdough, knit-your-own-quiche farmers' market that was held every Saturday morning. The parents had a variety of artisan dogs in tow: cockapoos, labradoodles, jackhuahuas, that sort of thing. It was like a canine version of *The Island of Doctor Moreau* out there. Not that I had ever read any H. G. Wells, but Paul had been a hardcore classic sci-fi fan. He was always trying to get me to read some doorstop called *Dune*. I saw the film. That was enough. I can never hear the word 'Sting' without shuddering.

'Plus,' I said, getting back on topic, 'we have our passage paid – Premium Economy, not Business, but better than a poke in the eye. And decent wages to fund the whole trip. We'll be in Bali, for God's sake, last known sighting of Jess.' Mentioning her name caused a spasm of pain in my chest, like for a second my heart forgot its real job was to keep me alive. It passed, though. Because, although I had no idea where she was now, I had to focus on the fact that I was finally going after her. As I had promised her in my head almost every hour, I was coming to see her. Hold her. Kiss her. With the added bonus of having the chance to punch Matt into the next century.

'Noor's been to Bali, she says, and isn't bothered about hanging around. Last time she got bitten by a monkey, which didn't endear her to the place. So it won't detain us long. And it's a wedding. Everyone will be in a good mood.'

Freddie wasn't buying that one. 'You must go to different weddings from me. Where I come from, there is usually a fight. My sister got arrested at her own daughter's nuptials. I hate weddings. I particularly hated my own. And there wasn't even a fight at that. Mind you, there were only six of us there in total, so it would have taken some doing.'

'I'm pretty sure that you're *really* going to hate this one,' I said. 'But there's hotel security for the bride and groom. Our only concern is to look after Noor and make sure whoever is threatening her doesn't spoil the Big Day. Or anything else.'

'You have any clue who it might be making the threats?'

'She's sending everything over. All the texts and what have you.'

'She's shown them to the police?'

'Yes. They've filed it under "harmless crank". You know how much manpower they have to deal with such things. They wait until there is clear physical danger.'

'By which time it's often too late.'

'Yeah. Often. But most of the time, Noor is tucked away in Wales with her gentlemanly farmer husband, two kids and a couple of bull mastiffs. She feels safe there. But out among her old friends . . .'

'Not so much,' Freddie completed. 'Shall we get a pint at the Bull and Last?' she asked.

'Nah. Body's a temple.'

Freddie made a clucking noise. Disbelief, I think it was. 'Like Angkor Wat is a temple – old, ruined and beyond repair.'

'You're thinking of your fanny,' I said automatically. That old army habit of crude banter sometimes comes back without being formally summoned.

She leaned over and kissed me on the cheek. 'I love you, Buster.'

The rules of crude banter demanded no unseemly show of emotion, at least not while sober. 'I think you're meant to call me a fuckin' cow,' I said.

'Oh, all right,' she said, a smirk playing about her lips. She stood. 'I love you, you fuckin' cow.'

I got the call two days later.

We were due to fly to Hong Kong that evening and then on to Bali. It was the Royal Free who called. Freddie told them I was her next of kin, which

129

made things easier, in that they would tell me what had happened.

It was a moped robbery.

Most people were baffled by the rise in moped crime in London. I reckoned it could be explained in one word: *Gomorrah*.

That Italian TV series was, like *Narcos*, a huge hit among kids during the Year of the Mopeds. Both contained lots of drugs and lashings of violence. It was only *Gomorrah*, though, that was set in a recognisably European world of tower blocks and tenements. And it showed how highly mobile groups of kids, on two wheels, could kill, maim, rob and intimidate with impunity.

OK, so maybe life wasn't imitating art, it was just a coincidence that young, brazen and reckless Londoners had adopted similar tactics – without, thankfully, the machine guns – to the Mafia in Naples. And the trick they pulled on Freddie was a refinement all their own.

It had happened on the Heath when she was running. The two mopeds had entered via the gate near the tennis courts, then ducked right, scattering joggers and dog walkers as they went. One of the passengers was holding a long piece of dull metal, which turned out to be a scaffold pole, pointing skywards as if the rider and passenger were about to enter a jousting contest.

Freddie had entered further down the road, by the cafés on Swain's Lane, and was running towards the ponds. She had headphones in. Her taste in music is surprisingly unabrasive, given her personality and background. Where you might expect thrash metal, you got soft rock. She was listening to Belle and Sebastian when she became aware of a noise over the top of 'The Boy With The Arab Strap'.

She turned and saw them bearing down on her. The two pillion riders were now holding the pole between them to form a solid bar, bridging the two mopeds at about knee height.

Had she more warning, I know Freddie could have jumped out of the way, or even leapt over it, but as she clocked them, the drivers twisted the throttles and accelerated.

She was hit on her left shin, which fractured, spun over the bar and landed on the path, breaking her wrist. As she tried to get up, the two passengers dismounted and set on her with wooden rounders bats, cracking a rib. She lashed out with her feet, doing some damage, but not enough. Nobody is certain when her Achilles tendon snapped, but snap it did.

They snatched the pouch she had at her hip, which contained cash, cards and her phone, and roared off, leaving Freddie battered, bruised and mightily pissed off at herself.

I pieced all this together at her bedside in the private room that I – as her next of kin – had her moved to. Her face had turned a mottled yellow, her top lip was swollen to Kylie Jenner proportions, her ribs were bandaged and her wrist was in plaster. They also had to re-attach her Achilles, asap.

'I'm sorry,' she said, with some difficulty. 'I . . . fuck, I could have taken them.'

'Four of them? Come on. You're lucky to be alive. It's only a matter of time before they kill someone with that shit. Don't waste your time being angry.' This was rich coming from me. Inside, I was seething, and I was ready to unleash my full Charles 'Death Wish' Bronson mode and set about taking out every scummy moped rider I could find.

'You'll need to get someone else. For Bali.'

I squeezed her good hand. 'There is nobody else like you.' I wasn't kidding. There wasn't another person close to me with her skills, her balls, whom I could trust to put herself on the line for me. Or to forgive me when I fucked up.

'Really, Sam,' she lisped. 'You need back-up.'

'No, I'll manage. I'll recruit locally if I have to. You just get better.'

She tried to raise her voice, but winced. 'Sam, listen to me. As your friend. I've been lying here thinking. You can't go by yourself. What we did in France was crazy. I see that now. And you're . . .'

'Crazy?'

'Not thinking straight.'

'She's not your daughter.'

There was pain in her eyes as she processed that.

'I'm sorry,' I said. 'That was mean. Mouth working before brain. You don't deserve it after all I've put you through.'

'I want you to stay till I'm better.'

132

'And you know I can't.'

She sighed. Freddie knew it was fruitless. I was going no matter what protests she made. And she wasn't in any physical condition to stop me.

Maybe I was crazy. But crazy can be good.

Rationalism is over-rated. It can act as a brake, feeding into a kind of paralysis. Do nothing or do something potentially stupid? I was going for the latter.

Freddie tried to smile. 'I guess those Aussies will have to get by without my killer bod.'

It was my turn to kiss Freddie, squeeze her hand and tell her I loved her. 'And I'll let the Oz boys know what they're missing.'

She squeezed my hand back. I could see tears of frustration in her eyes. 'Buster, I really am sorry. You be careful, eh? I'll come as soon as I can. Promise.'

I suspected her flying days wouldn't be resumed for a while. Doctors don't like patients with damaged eye sockets subjected to pressure changes. 'I know you will. Don't worry. Like I said, put yourself back together. I'll be fine.'

But I wasn't so sure. The wedding didn't worry me. That was contained, straightforward if – *if* – Noor did what I told her. But afterwards, I was going in search of a man who dabbled in the drug trade, a man who knew bad people, who had my – our – daughter. A man who didn't want to be found. And let's face it: Freddie was right. I was a woman down.

*

133

That night I lay on my bed, bathed and scrubbed, scrolling through photographs on my phone. I stopped at one of Jess when she was about eight or nine, standing in front of a stable door. It was the year when she had decided dance wasn't for her. Out had gone the leotards, the tutus, the tap shoes. In had come the adorable jodhpurs she was wearing in the picture, long-sleeved striped tops, fleeces, a riding crop and a hat that made her head look huge. She has a gap-toothed smile on her face – her new adult teeth were slowly filling the spaces left by the front baby teeth.

In the image filling the screen, the pony she rode that day – Patch, a stout Dartmoor pony – was poking his head over the stable door, looking as if he was deciding whether to investigate Jess's pocket for Polos. Jess had taken a good number of lessons and had done some pony days at stables in and around North London – Crews Hill, Trent Park – as well as a couple of trips to the country for less expensive and less urban hacks with me and our new friend Nina, who was a better rider than either of us.

I had encouraged her as, when I was a little older than Jess – early teens, perhaps – I was half-decent on a horse. However, my older unused muscles reminded me with each ride that it was a long time ago.

This hack was in Devon, in the South Hams through tiny lanes, down a steep hill and onto Mothecombe Beach, where I had ridden with Matt. This was because it wasn't far from where Matt and I had spent part of our honeymoon, in a pretty village called Newton

Ferrers. The marriage might have soured – and by this point Paul was firmly on the scene – but it hadn't dimmed the beauty of the place in my eyes. I was looking forward to recreating a canter I'd done back then across the unspoiled long sandy beach, the air full of sand and seawater.

The ride to the beach was smooth and uneventful, bar the odd car taking a blind bend in front of us at speed. There were eight of us in all, mostly regular riders, chatting across the heads and swishing tails of the horses as we walked along. Directly ahead of me, Jess was too concerned with her seat and keeping her back straight to chat. All I got was a quick reassuring smile.

I was happy with the silence, sitting high above the hedgerows, sniffing the mix of horseshit and leather tack, rocking my hips against the saddle on a handsome Cleveland Bay called Star, due, I guessed, to the white splodge on his head. He was a nice horse. I drifted off and tried to imagine how he would cope in London if I took him home.

I snapped out of a daft fantasy as we moved as a group into an easy trot up a straight incline, and instead watched Jess, my heart swelling with pride at how she kept Patch firmly under control and managed a perfect rise. We slowed into a walk around a corner as the beach came into view. It looked serene in the late afternoon winter sun, the rivulets of water left by the retreating sea glistening invitingly, a vast expanse of sea and sky.

I realised my attention had drifted from my daughter

when Star had 'bunched' up under me, his muscles firmly contracted and bouncing on his toes. It became clear to me that the horses were not going to walk, trot and build to a steady canter. They were going off now. And fast.

I had barely formed that thought when the lead five horses released the brakes and, no matter how decent a rider I thought I was, there was no way I could stop Star from taking off too.

I managed to shout to Jess to hold on as the sand flew up all around us and the group went from a standstill to a gallop. We must have gone for less than a minute when I heard a distant cry. I knew immediately it was Jess. I used all my strength, stubbornness and panic to slow and turn Star.

Jess was lying in a foetal position around fifty metres behind me. Patch had wandered down to the water's edge and was looking confused. I slipped my boots out of the stirrups to get off the horse. The lead rider barked: 'Stay on your horse. We can't get you back on if you get off.'

Fuck that.

I slid off ungracefully and sprinted to Jess's side just as she rolled over and sat up. I fell to my knees and did a quick check for misshapen limbs or other signs of trauma, but she looked to be in one piece. The soft sand must have broken the fall. I pulled her close to me. 'Oh, Jess, I am so sorry.'

She gave a chest-heaving sob. 'Why did you leave me?'

I had only ridden on for a matter of seconds, but

perhaps it felt like an eternity to her, a mother galloping away with no concern for her plight. I looked down into Jess's eyes as I cradled her. There was shock and doubt in there. 'Why didn't you come and get me, Mummy?' she asked.

I closed down the photos, unable to face any more memories, painful or otherwise. I opened the WhatsApp Family Chat on my phone. There it was, as one-sided as ever.

Periodically, I wrote her a note and sent it out into the servers. I checked every few days, hoping for a tick to show it had been received, another that it had been read. They never came. Still, I composed yet another pointless missive.

*Dear Jess,*

*Some days I almost manage to forget you are out there. Never completely. There's always a nagging at the back of my mind, as if I have left the gas on. And then I realise what it is. You aren't at home. I can't come and see you, cuddle you, kiss you, nag you. And it hurts. Please don't forget that I am here, desperate to see you. I have not forgotten or abandoned you. I had things to do, important things. I know, what is more important than you? Nothing, my lovely daughter. Nothing. But I have to be strong now. I have to forget I left the gas on. Just for a few days while I work. Then I'll be back on the case. Because I am coming to find you,*

*Jess. I'm going to bring you home. Love you, love you, love you.*

And then I pressed send, just as a tear dropped onto the phone and pooled on the screen.

# SIXTEEN

Four million people live on Bali. There are three million registered vehicles. That's what the guidebook I read on the flight from Hong Kong told me. It didn't warn me that they would be on the road all at once when I arrived.

We had flown via Hong Kong because every other guest was going via Singapore or Kuala Lumpur. This way, I knew Noor could sit up in Business and me in Premium Economy without worrying too much. I passed the time reading through some of her emails and texts, and scrolling through the wedding itinerary as well as the guest list. I made a note to ask Noor which of the latter she had ever met.

What were the chances that the promises to 'fuck you up if you ever show your black face at home' or 'do you like a kipper' or 'kick your half-nigger arse' were a real threat? In my experience, about a one-in-twenty chance. But – and it was a big but – there was always the possibility that it was the work of a genuine nutter. So there just might be an obsessive character, with a real or imagined slight, who posed a risk.

It didn't mean they'd 'fuck up' Noor literally. It might be an attempt at embarrassment or a confrontation. Of course, there was also the possibility they didn't get an invite. Or couldn't come. Nipping over to Bali isn't cheap.

I went through the taunts again. No actual mention of rape. The most graphic threat of physical violence was: 'You'd better have a bowl at your arse to catch your teeth'. Either Noor had read between the lines about the sexual intimidation or she'd exaggerated to get me on board. Still, they were pretty severe – the insults were either racist or misogynist, sometimes both. Certainly enough to be getting on with.

The drive from Ngurah Rai airport to the hotel was meant to take a shade over an hour, but that looked optimistic, as we had arrived in time for a furious downpour. Rather than risk a local cab, I had arranged for a hotel car to meet us, but even the Mercedes' wipers found it hard to cope with the deluge.

So far, I'd seen clogged roads, a cat's cradle of power lines, lost tourists and an endless strip of concrete shops festooned with colourful signs for local services and homestays. The run was broken only by the odd thatched or gilded roof, shrines, arrogant I'm-not-moving cattle and overloaded bikes that gave no quarter.

Mangy dogs sloped along the roadside, nosing at piles of garbage and the offerings on shrines. Every few yards there was a cluster of snack bars and restaurants – *warungs* – that ranged from a simple bamboo shed with a hatch to serve standing customers, to more substantial breeze-block and concrete structures with seats and tables.

Gradually, this squalid semi-urban huddle fell away, and I got my first glimpse of the famed emerald rice paddies and the sculpted hillside terraces, which looked as if a giant, celestial Albrecht Dürer had carved them. The flags dotting the steeped slopes, designed to keep the birds away, hung sodden and limp. As the rain clattered on the roof of the car, I made sure our doors were locked and closed my eyes.

I was confident I could wind down my status to a mere Yellow.

By the time I opened my eyes again, we had turned off the main road and were driving down an asphalt track between the paddies, which were now steaming in sunshine. Ahead was the hotel, an enormous concrete disc protruding from the hillside, like a crashed spaceship. It was startlingly modern and completely out of keeping with the jungle surroundings.

We were decanted into a rather more conventional bamboo and thatched *bale,* or pavilion, where we were swarmed over by slender young women, all dressed in colourful batik blouses and skirts. Cold towels, frangipani and sweet drinks were proffered. The women darted around with such hummingbird energy and elegance, I felt like a parboiled heifer in comparison.

Eventually, we got to our villa: two bedrooms, a living room, two bathrooms, an outdoor shower and a secluded pool in a walled garden. Nyoman, our 'villa concierge', a keen young man in a white shirt and trousers as black as his hair, invited us to embrace the island's *niskala* energy with a dove release, perhaps try a psychic reading, attend a sacred jewellery-making class or have an afternoon nap suspended in a silk cocoon. I just wanted my bed, but I knew that would have to wait.

After I'd managed to send Nyoman away with a fistful of rupiahs, I told Noor to rest up and make sure to lock her door and sliding windows from the inside. Then I went in search of Erik.

Erik was head of security. We had already exchanged emails. He had heard of Noor, he claimed, loved her music and would do everything he could to help. He was Austrian – blond, tanned and trim – and dressed in a lightweight grey suit, complete with a shirt and tie, which was perversely counterintuitive given the climate and the loose clothing the rest of the staff wore, but he carried it off with cool aplomb.

We sat at the bar, which came with a view down the side of the gorge carved by a rushing river, heard, but not seen, behind its ridiculously lush cloak of vegetation. I risked a gin and tonic, while he sipped a beer. He was in his forties, ex-military and, although he hadn't done a tour of duty in the Middle East, he was impressed that I had. I explained I was a colleague down and would need what, back home, we would call a 'corridor man'.

In this case, I guess I required at least one 'villa man'; someone to control the traffic to and from our rooms.

And twenty-four hours a day if required. We would, of course, pay the going hourly rate, which turned out to be very reasonable compared with what a corridor man could command in London.

Erik assured me that they had hosted presidents from twenty different countries, rock stars, film actors and reality-TV flotsam – not his word – and his people were well trained. And would I like to join him for dinner? Whether he meant me, or me and Noor, or maybe just Noor, I wasn't sure. But I explained I was here on business and that we'd eat in the room. Busy day tomorrow. And the Big Day after that.

He accepted the brush-off with good grace, gave me his card with all of his contact details and told me to ask for anything my heart desired. Everything my heart desired at that moment was back in the villa under a ceiling fan and a silk canopy and came with big, fluffy pillows.

Despite being exhausted, I couldn't sleep that night. Dinner had been served poolside, with floating candles and lotus flowers on the water, and I wondered if the servants thought Noor and I were an item, because they made a point of saying we wouldn't be disturbed for thirty minutes after they had served the main course of grilled prawns and minced fish. Perhaps they thought we'd go skinny-dipping in the pool.

Instead, we went through the wedding guest list. It turned out there were only half a dozen old faces from home. Kassie – sorry, Kate – was paying for hotels, food and booze, but it was up to guests to pay their own way for flights. Noor reckoned that had been a deal-breaker for many who hadn't made a decent whack as a pop star, like Noor, or nabbed themselves someone in the City, like Kate.

As I listened to the air-con push out fingers of frosted air, a deep feeling of unease plagued me. Bali is meant to be an island of spirits, with evil swarming the streets after dark, looking for those who haven't been to the temple, burned incense and said their five supplications. I, of course, didn't believe that, but I did have a feeling that there was a malevolence in my room. It was a presence rather than anything solid, but as I lay under the sheets it leaned over me and whispered in my ear that I should be out looking for Jess, whipping up my feelings of guilt and helplessness.

In the end, I went back to the pool, wishing I had bought cigarettes. I made do with a Bintang and a Snickers from the minibar that probably cost me – or, strictly speaking, Noor – as much as my last pair of shoes.

The warm, soupy air was filled with the croaking rhythms of tree frogs and the stars were playing peek-a-boo behind clouds. But all I could think was that Jess was – or had been – somewhere on this island. I was probably closer to her at that moment than I had been for over a year. And it hurt; a real physical pain low down in my stomach. I just wanted to get out there and ask questions, knock heads together, but I knew I had to bide my time.

Two days. That was all. Three at the most.

The wedding was due to take place in two days' time. Noor was flying back to her sanctuary in Wales the morning after the nuptials. I'd take her to the airport, she'd be met in London by a driver. The flight was via Doha, just to mix the routes up. She'd be fine.

That's when I would take a trip south of Kuta and make myself a fucking nuisance.

'Can't sleep either?' It was Noor, padding out in a robe. 'You got any mossie repellent on?'

I admitted I hadn't and she went back and returned with her own beer and a pump-spray, with which we both doused ourselves. It was citronella, which I am not convinced works, but I hate DEET so much I'd rather put up with the bites, given the chances of malaria or dengue fever were small. Once I had covered all my exposed places, I returned to the fridge for a second Bintang.

When I returned, Noor was scanning a print-out of several sheets of paper. We sat in silence for a while as she read, while the tree-frog chorus seemed to build in intensity. Some of the nearby guard dogs barked as if telling the amphibians to keep the noise down, then fell silent, defeated.

'Do I want to go and buy some batik, a wooden ukulele, some carvings, bamboo furniture, a stone statue, make a windchime, or see a temple ceremony tomorrow?' she asked eventually. 'Kate has put together activities.' She sniffed. 'Oh look, an Uluwatu hand-made lace demonstration.'

'I don't know, do you?'

She shrugged. 'I can also visit a local school, a gamelan orchestra or learn how rice is grown.'

'Shall we decide tomorrow?'

'Yeah,' she said with a weary grin. 'Maybe just lunch somewhere. I don't think I need a new ukulele. And I fuckin' hate windchimes. And monkeys. It was around here I got bitten last time, near the Temple of the Dead. Anyway, I'll call Kate, see what she's doing for fun tomorrow.'

'How come Kassie became Kate and got herself a hedgie?' I asked.

Noor laughed. 'It cost me a fuck of a lot of money. She was with some guy who spent every penny on the machines at his local bookies. I knew him from school as it happens. A right dick. So, I organised an intervention. Like she was in a cult. And while I was at it, I got her a trainer, a stylist, all the shit they threw at me when I was first signed to the label. Nobody is more surprised than me that it worked. But good on her.'

I was about to ask more, but I saw the projectile glinting in the weak starlight as it arched over from between two of the palm trees that leaned over our compound. It was instinct that took over. I jumped at Noor, wrapping my arms around her upper body to cushion any blow on the tiles. As we landed, the bottle shattered on the poolside, sending glass shards skimming across the surface of the water before sinking.

I had cracked my elbow, but the adrenaline had kicked in, so I hardly noticed. I waited, in case the bottle had contained an explosive or noxious liquid. Once it was clear it hadn't, I pushed myself to my feet, then yanked Noor to hers.

'Get inside,' I said. 'In your room. Lock everything. Stay away from the window.'

I went outside and found Nyoman running up and down with a torch. 'You see anything?'

'No, *Ibu*,' he said. 'You are unhurt?'

'We're OK. There's some glass in the pool that'll need to be cleared tomorrow. But, yes, we are all right. You didn't see anything? Anyone?'

'No. But I not asleep.'

Was that him protesting too much? 'Of course not.'

'I get some more people, *Ibu*. For rest of night.'

'Yes, thank you. I think a circuit of the perimeter every few minutes, eh?'

'Yes, *Ibu*.'

'What does *Ibu* mean?' I asked, remembering my daughter's 'white slut' tattoo that she was told said something else altogether.

'It mean lady. Or miss.'

'OK. And thank you.'

I went back in and checked Noor's room was secure. She was a little shaken. She'd taken a vodka miniature from the minibar and was sucking on the narrow neck. 'What the hell was that for?'

'Just to keep us on our toes.' I didn't say it, but I thought it could have been worse. It could have been a Molotov cocktail.

She finished the vodka and tossed the bottle into

the bin. 'I'm not sure a fuckin' wedding is worth all this shit.'

'You want to leave, just say the word. It's up to you.'

She thought for a moment. 'No. Can't run away just because someone lobbed a bottle. And Kassie'd kill me. Kate, Kate, Kate,' she prompted herself.

'That guy she was living with before you did a Pygmalion on her ...'

'A what?'

'*My Fair Lady*. A makeover. The bloke with the betting habit. He's not here, is he?'

'Alex? Nah. Jesus, he hasn't left William Hill for years. He wouldn't come to Bali, even if he'd been invited. Which he hasn't. You think ...?'

'No, just looking for a motive. He might blame you for giving Kassie ideas above what he thought was her station. But if he's not here ...' I yawned, the adrenaline gone now, leaving me flat and cold inside. 'OK, try to get some sleep. I doubt whoever did it will be back, and we've got some extra bodies outside.'

I didn't go back to bed immediately. I cleaned up around the pool, then I went back to the print-outs of threats and insults as well as the guest list.

And, just as my eyes began to feel like someone had thrown sand in them, a possible solution to the whole stalking thing popped into my head. Problem was, I didn't have a shred of proof.

Like that's ever stopped me.

# SEVENTEEN

The actual ceremony was to be held down on the banks of the roaring Ayung River, at a waterside spa of a different hotel from the one we were staying at. I took Noor along with me for my pre-inspection and parked her with its head of security, a New Zealander called Keith – an ex-rugby player judging by his nose and one of his ears – and Mae, the hotel's wedding planner, while I went down the steep stone steps that switchbacked through the foliage.

About halfway down, the temperature plunged and I could feel cool moisture in the air. I took a deep breath. A few steps away from the bottom, I glimpsed the creamy, frothy water for the first time, rushing between Flintstone-sized boulders. On the opposite bank was what looked like untouched jungle – note to self: search Google Earth for any tracks that might bring paps, or stalkers, to opposite bank – but on my side, there was a series of wooden platforms built over the riverbank. Looking back the way I had come, I could see that a series of ledges had been cleared and *bales* erected to serve as massage stations.

I sat on one of the hammocks strung between the trees close to the water's edge and listened to the insistent stridulation of cicadas and the gurgle of the waters.

I had already checked the staff as far as was possible. Mae was providing outside hair and make-up specialists who were unlikely to have even heard of Noor. The catering was all in-house, cooked and served by staff. Keith had told me that the local villagers would trek down on W-Day and act as a choir for the ceremony. Wedding photography was to be by drone – something I'd have to check before I allowed it to fly over Noor – there would also be a release of doves and a blessing by a local priest. Priest also not a problem, drone operator an American who was unlikely to be able to find Bishop's Stortford on a map.

Back up at the main hotel, there would be a gifting lounge and a huge marquee with 'image mapping' walls – this was where the dancing would take place, with a backdrop of settings from the Sahara to the Grand Canyon, thanks to digital projection. All that was done in-house, too.

I slid off the hammock and walked around to the rear of the area. There was, as Mae had told me, an elevator there, hidden by a screen of shrubbery, meaning those with mobility difficulties could still access the river. They didn't like to advertise its mechanical existence, as it rather dented the natural and spiritual claims of the Ayung spa.

It all sounded great. I just wondered whether Noor would still enjoy it once I told her my suspicions.

When I reached the top of the steps, my shirt clinging to me from the exertion, Kate was sitting with Keith and Noor on the curved deck overlooking the gorge. She was wearing shorts, a halter-top and an engagement ring that was bright enough to cause after-images on my retina.

Her jaw dropped when she saw me.

She shot a glare at Noor that was pure Kassie, which said: *What the fuck is she doing here?*

But the freshly minted Kate persona quickly reasserted itself and she stood up and beamed at me. 'Miss Wylde. What a surprise. Noor said she had security, but she didn't say it was an old friend.'

I thought *old friend* was pushing it, but I suffered through the inevitable hug. 'Hello, Kas—Kate. Congratulations. On the wedding.'

She beamed. 'I know. I still can't quite believe it.'

Mae left to make some calls to the caterers and Keith also made his excuses, promising to send drinks over, so we sat. Kate had cajoled Noor into a temple visit and supper at her hotel – she and Cameron, her husband-to-be, were spending the night before the ceremony apart.

'You'll be welcome too,' said Kate to me. 'Just some of the girls getting together.'

'I'll be there,' I said, 'but I won't join in the fun. Work, not play.'

'Of course.'

151

I gave her a thin smile. 'I just have one question.'

'Yes?'

'Who did you get to toss the bottle over the wall? Cameron? Some local kid? Or did you do it yourself?'

'What?' It was Noor. 'Sam—'

'One line in the threats did it – the promise to do Noor like a kipper. I wondered where I had heard it before. Only once. When a young girl fell on me in the back of a stretch limo. You can take Kassie out of Harlow . . .'

'Hey, you stupid bitch,' said Kate, her lips twisting so that, fleetingly, she looked just like the old Kassie. 'I ought to rip your head off.' She stood up, fists balled as if she fancied having a go. She was welcome to try. 'Noor, you gonna let her talk such bollocks?'

'One phrase?' asked Noor. 'Is that all you have?'

'She's fuckin' mad,' suggested Kate.

'Motive,' I said calmly. 'She has motive. Why would she want to put you off coming? Because every time she looks at you, she sees what she isn't. She isn't Kate. She's a construct. She knows that because you paid for her, you made her. And she's worried that tomorrow you are going to tell anyone who will listen.'

'What a pile of old wank,' said Kate.

'I can't see any other explanation,' I said.

'What about that you're talking shit? Is that an explanation?'

I addressed my answer to Noor. 'Someone threw that bottle over the wall. A bottle that could have hit you.' Or me, I failed to add. 'What sort of friend is that?'

'Chrissake. Can't you get this through your thick skull?' Kate yelled. 'I didn't throw any fuckin' bottle.' Then, in case I had missed the point: 'I don't know nothin' about any bottle, understand?'

'But you did write the emails and texts.'

She spat her answer. 'That's not the same as chuckin' glass at people, is it?'

The silence was immediate and, apart from the roar of the waters below, complete. Eventually Noor managed to find her voice. 'Kate?'

'It was only . . .' But she didn't seem to know what it was, and her face slowly turned a deep crimson. 'Sorry. I gotta go.'

The drinks arrived at that moment: lurid orange and filled with fruit. Kate paused and took a huge gulp. When she spoke, her words were clipped and precise.

'I am afraid I shall have to disinvite you for this evening, Miss Wylde. Noor, we'll talk about this later.' She pointed at me. 'Meanwhile, I suggest throwing this one back into the pond she crawled out of.' With that, she left. *Flounced*, if one can flounce in shorts that skimpy.

I almost laughed at her parting shot. Now it was all *my* fault?

'So you were right?' asked Noor.

'Looks like it. She just wanted to put you off. It's probably why she's getting married in Bali. To make sure most of her old friends wouldn't be able to afford it. But you could.'

Noor sipped at her cocktail. 'She didn't actually say it was her.'

That was true. Even the apology was ambiguous. 'She didn't say it wasn't,' I offered back.

'That's just crazy, innit? Why would she do that to me, of all people?'

'I think she's embarrassed by how she got here. Wouldn't be the first person to reinvent themselves and want to torch all evidence of the past.'

It was my turn to try the drink. It was rum-based and delicious. I reluctantly pushed it away. I needed a clear head.

'And the bottle-throwing?'

I gave a shrug. I suspected she was telling the truth on that.

'Jesus,' said Noor. 'What a fuckin' mess. She could've just asked me to stay away.'

'I don't think that's her style. Let's just say I'm right. What are you going to do?'

Noor turned up her nose, as if at a bad smell. 'Do? Nothing. I'm going to the wedding. She might be an ungrateful old slapper inside, but she's still my friend.'

I accepted that with a nod. 'And I'm still your bodyguard.'

A bodyguard with one nagging question: If Kate didn't lob that bottle, then who did?

# EIGHTEEN

Seeing Noor off at the airport, I felt a great weight lift off my knotted shoulders. The wedding had gone without a hitch. The village choir was brilliant, there was a rather beautiful dance – the *Barong Brutuk* – and the Ayung ravine was thick with the scent of frangipani and jasmine. The bride and groom, who was both startlingly handsome and far nicer than I expected from a hedge fund manager, were anointed with water from the sacred lake by an old woman who was some kind of mystic and, we were told, lived in the shadow of the island's still-troublesome volcano. It was only just over a year since it had sort-of erupted, temporarily devastating the island's tourism economy.

At the meal, Noor decided to skip giving a speech and we all subsequently wished that the horse-faced best man had done the same. Nothing untoward happened, and I mainly kept to the shadows. Kate never admitted to being the culprit – *why would she?* – but, by revealing her motives, her fears, I had ensured Noor stayed away from the whole subject of her reinvention, even in conversation.

Job done.

That was what I told myself, anyway. Now for the real reason for my visit: Jess.

I went back to the hotel and sorted out my things ready for the off. I needed to go down to the south of the island, below Kuta. I took a shower, wrapped myself in the hotel's robe and lay on the bed under the fan. My hand strayed to between my legs and I had myself a quick squeeze. I contemplated masturbating. It was, I knew, a response to being alone at last. A hangover from my army days. It was so unusual to have a genuinely solitary experience that, any time you did, you felt the urge to – as Freddie would say – rub one out.

But something stopped me. The feeling I was being ... *watched*? No, not watched. *Played*, perhaps. There was something off kilter and I couldn't quite pin it down. The bottle and now this sense of unease. The villa didn't have the right karma. Maybe I should have done some ceremony with doves.

I retraced my steps since entering the villa, scanning as if I were casing a client's room.

I found what I was looking for in the bathroom.

I went back to the bed and lay down, hands behind my head, watching the blades of the fan chop the air while I considered my next move. Then I rolled onto my side and called Erik, the security guy, asking if he would kindly come to the villa.

*

Erik arrived wearing a dark-blue linen suit that was creased in all the right places. How did he do that? I had plenty of linen dresses and jackets, but they have a time limit on them. If I was going to be in public for more than an hour they were a no-no. After that time, I looked like I had dressed in a cement mixer.

I had changed out of my robe into a T-shirt and jeans. I asked him to sit at the desk.

'You're leaving then?'

'Can't afford to stay here,' I said.

'I can get you a friends and family rate,' he offered.

Yeah, that would take it down to just *hundreds* of pounds a night. It was too rich for my blood. And my bank balance, even with Noor's final fee promised within days.

'Thanks. But I need to be somewhere else.' I put the first of the photographs down on the table. There was Jess in a hotel pool, elbows on a wooden deck that formed the pool's edge, a grin on her face and an umbrella'd drink in her hand. I tried to ignore the usual gut spasm that the picture – all the pictures – gave me. 'Recognise this place?'

'Four Seasons, Jimbaran Bay,' he said without hesitation.

I nodded. I had known this. In a couple of the other pictures, you could see the company logo. 'What about this bar?'

He leaned in and studied the image. I liked that he took his time. 'Bit dark. What's this about?'

I hesitated. Stay tight-lipped or 'fess up? Well, in

this case there was no harm in spilling the beans about a client, the client being me. 'That girl there is my daughter. She has been missing for over a year. Taken without consent by my ex-husband. You can just about see his one of his syphilitic limbs right there.'

Erik looked shocked. 'Really? He has syphilis?'

'Of the soul,' I said, reminding myself that sarcastic vitriol wasn't Erik's first language. 'What about this one? Or this?'

Again, Erik took his time. 'The problem is these bars all look the same. Illuminated bottles, lots of bamboo, a few ancient Balinese artefacts made in China. This one looks like a beach bar rather than a Kuta one. That one, too. You should show these to Tandoko at the Four Seasons.'

'Tandoko? Japanese?'

'He's Chinese-Indonesian. He's from Jakarta. His parents were required to change their name to something less Chinese during the Suharto regime. Call him Jiànyì, he likes that.'

I gathered up the photos.

'Sorry I couldn't help.'

'Well, there is one thing you might be able to do.'

'Anything.'

The next part was throwing rocks in a pond and seeing where the ripples went. I watched his face intently before I spoke. 'Tell me who searched my room while I was dropping my client at the airport.'

*

My next hotel was more in keeping with my pay grade. Twelve rooms, set back from the beach just above Jimbaran Bay, close to the main road – a little noisy thanks to the endless motorbikes – but with air conditioning and friendly owners. The room was simple and clean and as I sat down on the bed, I thought how pleased I was to be away from breathing rich people's air.

I had spent a good chunk of my life hanging around – literally on some jobs – with them. I knew their foibles. But it was when they were on holiday that they really got up my nose. If there were a dedicated fragrance made for millionaires and oligarchs, it would be called Entitlement. The world owes them a perfect vacation every time. Nothing must go wrong. It wouldn't surprise me to learn that the Amans and the Mandarins and the other top hotels publicly execute a member of staff every morning just to keep the rest on their toes for the pampered guests. It was the attitude that gave the world the much-needed bath butlers and pillow concierges that most high-end hotels have. It's a living, I suppose.

I checked the lock on the door. It wouldn't keep anyone out for long. Not that it mattered. I had very little worth stealing. I don't travel with jewellery. I keep my passport and credit cards either on me or in my safe.

So why had someone bothered to go through my stuff at the last place?

I could tell from the way the narrow lipstick line I had put on the catches of my Globe-Trotter suitcase had been smudged.

Apart from that slip-up, it had been a pretty good turn-over, and it took me a while to find something *off* to confirm it. These days, the intruders take snapshots on their phone to ensure they can put everything back just so. But whoever had done the searching had moved my toothbrush to the wrong side of the sink. Maybe they knocked it off as they went for the bathroom cabinet and put it on the wrong side of the tap. Easy mistake, but I always keep my toothbrush away from the lavatory. Someone had once told me how many germs hit the bristles every time you flush. Such facts bring out the Howard Hughes in me. This time, I had found it making eyes at the toilet bowl.

I had pointed all this out to Erik, who had protested it hadn't been him. Or any of his staff. But he didn't like the alternative much either – someone had come into the hotel and broken into a guest's room.

We were both baffled as to motive. My most precious items were the photographs of Jess, and they hadn't been taken. Even if they had been, I had back-ups stored on my phone and with both Freddie and Nina. So why? And who? I had a feeling that, one way or another, I'd find out. Because I was clearly on some-one's radar.

I showered again and changed into cream cotton trousers and a sleeveless blouse. I pinned my hair back, took more care than usual with my make-up and put on heels. I wanted to look like I belonged in the Four Seasons Jimbaran Bay before I called a cab.

*

I took tea with Jiànyì next to the very pool where Jess had frolicked many months before. It was infinity-sided on the section facing the sea, blending seamlessly into the blue ocean. Staff hovered with iced water, cool towels and offers of snacks from the terrace café. I could see why Jess, judging from her expression in the pictures, had enjoyed herself.

'Well, that certainly is the pool here,' Jiànyì said when I showed him the photograph on my phone. He was a young man in his thirties, not security, but part of guest services, who had nodded energetically when I had mentioned Erik's name. 'But these other bars . . .' He gave a sheepish grin. 'I don't drink, you see. I don't have the genes for alcohol. So, I am the wrong person to ask. But perhaps Carol from the spa.'

If I were Carol, I would have sued for national stereotyping by both Jiànyì and God. She was from Brisbane, broad of shoulder and accent, with blonde hair going on white, scrunched back into a perky ponytail. She was wearing a vest top and shorts, and every inch of exposed skin looked like she had been sprayed with a Pantone colour match for sun-kissed. I liked her, if only because she looked at the photos and said: 'That one's Ricky T's. That one is now Kamala. They change their name a lot.'

'And the girl?'

'I remember her. I gave her a treatment once. Nails, I think, and a facial. She came in with a slightly older woman.'

'Laura?'

161

'I don't know. But I know she told me she was something to do with Dieter's place.'

'Dieter?'

'He's German or Swiss, I'm not sure.' She held up the phone to show me the place she had identified as Ricky T's. 'Drinks here sometimes, not often. Scrawny little twerp. Anyway, he's got a place of his own about two miles from here. It's not either of these in the photos. Bedawang, it's called. Or the Blue Turtle.'

'Did you ever meet Matt? Jess's father?'

'I don't think so.'

'She didn't talk about him?'

She shrugged her impressive shoulders. 'Jeez, I don't know. We get a lot of families, lots of kids.'

'You've been a great help,' I said to her and Jiànyì. 'Thank you.'

'I'll call you a cab,' he said, and walked off towards the café.

As he left, Carol leaned in and lowered her voice. Up close, she smelled like an exotic forest glade. 'I hope you find your daughter. The Turtle doesn't open till six. But be careful, hon. I tell you, the word is that this Dieter is trouble.'

I stood, heady with the feeling I was making progress at last. 'Don't worry,' I said slowly, attaching a smile to it. 'So am I.'

# NINETEEN

A darkness waits for me. I can see it there, out of the corner of my eye. Some claim that's where guardian angels lurk. All I have is a tar-black stain of depression, waiting to knot my stomach and drag me into its sticky embrace.

When and from where this dark devil came, I can't be sure. It might have been there after Iraq and Afghanistan. It was certainly there when Paul died, and it had grown bolder in the days after Jess was taken by Matt and Laura.

I keep it where it belongs by activity. I know that's why I went to Albania. After the debacle in France and the Basque Country where I lost a client, I could feel my dark storm gathering. I should have come to Bali immediately. But by going to Albania, I had managed to put something between me and the events where a woman had lost her life on my watch. That was an act of revenge. She had once been something in the IRA, and her past had caught up with her in a particularly horrible way. But then, she had done terrible things in her time.

While I waited for the Blue Turtle to open, I organised myself a driver on retainer, a keen young man called Kadek. I told him that I didn't want to buy anything: no presents, no batik, no lace, no sodding ukuleles. I told him I would factor the shopping commission into his tip, a tip that would only materialise if he followed those rules. Then I sat on the veranda, drinking green tea, trying to keep the darkness and self-doubt away.

The feeling of worthlessness I knew so well had just started to creep up from my abdomen when my phone pinged. WhatsApp.

*New phone*, said the message. It was Freddie.

You OK? I replied.

*Yup. Never better. No, wait, that's a fucking lie.*

At home?

*Yes, sitting watching something called* MasterCunt. *It's a cookery show.*

How's the leg?

*Itchy. And sore. And I have a boot on the ankle for the Achilles. I have crutches now. Wrist is better, though.*

Wish you were here.

*Me too, partner. How is it going? Kassie divorced yet?*

Honeymoon on Lombok and Gili Islands. We'll see. All went OK at wedding. I have my suspicions about her. I'll tell you when I see you. What's next for you?

*Physiotherapy.*

Sounds exciting.

*I might have to ring some of my old playmates. Horny as hell.*

Even in an Achilles boot?

*Especially in an Achilles boot. Getting anywhere?*

I have a lead. Some slimeball called Dieter who owns a bar. I suspect he was a business partner of Matt's.

*Be careful. We know what kind of business partner Matt liked.*

Of course.

*Let me know how it goes. Any time, day or night, this shop's always open.*

I will x.

I looked at the screen for half a minute, wondering if there would be a comeback. None came. Communicating halfway around the world is impressive, but it always left me with a gnawing, empty feeling, like something was fraudulent or unsatisfying.

The black cloud again.

I texted Kadek to come and pick me up. I'd go for a walk before the Blue Turtle. Fresh air and daylight would help keep the darkness at bay.

# TWENTY

At five past six, I was walking along the beach, past the gaudy fishing boats pulled up to the treeline for the night, and the glowing grills of the fish shacks. The sun was falling and the breeze from the sea was cutting through the residual heat. Several kids were flying kites on the wind, slowly reeling them out in a series of swoops, higher and higher into the sky. A few of the massage women were still in place and looked at me with hope, holding up bottles of coconut oil and offering me a discounted happy-hour price. A handsome young man sitting at one of the stations suggested, using sign language, I might like to indulge in another kind of happy hour. I gave another polite decline. I had heard that many women came to Bali for more than batik, and that the beach boys were willing to provide that kind of service.

I took my Birkenstocks off and let the warm sand squeeze through my toes. From beneath thatched roofs, boys and girls beckoned for me to come and try their food, and waved bottles of Bintang at me. Music

166

seeped across the beach, not yet thumping as it would later in the evening. Bob Marley was popular and one bar was painted in full Rasta colours. Screens in some places showed Australian sports and hand-drawn signs proclaimed Fosters and Tooheys for sale.

'Gintonic,' one young lady shouted at me, and giggled as she performed a few fancy finger moves from a *legong* dance for my benefit. I smiled and shook my head. Some other time. 'Sarong?' she shouted after me.

Busy yellow-headed weaver birds flitted among the coconut palms and tamarind trees, singing and servicing their intricate nests. Behind them, the sky seemed enormous.

In that moment, it was easy to fall into the cliché about Bali being a paradise. But the volcano was apparently grumbling again and beneath all the ritual and symbolism, I knew the island had a tortured history, including mass suicides when the Dutch invaded – their own version of the Cambodian Killing Fields of the 1970s – and, more recently, lava flows and *jihadi* bombs. They also have a propensity to execute drug mules by firing squad. And I was here to begin my search for my missing daughter, kidnapped by my feckless ex.

You have to take the term paradise with a pinch of salt.

I didn't have to search for the Blue Turtle. A giant *umbul-umbul* flag featuring the titular animal was visible over the woven rooftops of the beachfront properties. I put the Birkenstocks back on and walked down a crude track between two buildings, to emerge on a row of bars and restaurants. The music here was louder, less laid-back, some of it full-throated Balinese punk, and each bar had at least one young woman sitting on a stool near the entrance, acting as a come-on.

I dodged one of the ubiquitous offerings laid out along the street – this one coconut leaves, red flowers and what looked like a digestive biscuit – and walked up the two steps and smiled at the Blue Turtle's stool pigeon, who gave a nod and a greeting of *om swastiastu*. She was porcelain-faced, almond-eyed, poised and quite beautiful, even with the slight imperfection around her nose, which looked as if it had been broken at some stage in her job at the club. Occupational hazard, I guessed.

There were already a dozen customers at the bamboo tables, ploughing into pitchers of beer. Mostly Western, except for an overweight local in a floral shirt, who was sipping Japanese whisky at the bar, with the bottle left in front of him. His eyes raked over me as I approached the woman behind the counter and asked for a lime-soda.

'You lonely?' the guy asked.

'Do I look lonely?'

He gave a gap-toothed grin. 'Lots of women come to Bali lonely. Lots of men, too.'

I paid for my drink and asked the barkeep: 'Is Dieter in?'

'Later,' said the girl, off-handedly.

The man to my right huffed, shook his head enough

to get his jowls wobbling and went back to his whisky. Obviously, he wasn't interested in women who were interested in Dieter.

I moved along the bar and sat on a rattan stool, sipping my drink slowly, trying to zone out the gap-year stories being shared nearby.

I had to be careful not to gulp, as I tend to when confronted with a non-alcoholic option. I had once experimented with a stomach matrix, which allows you to drink without – in theory – getting drunk. It worked, but I concluded that the pain of expelling a used matrix just wasn't worth the effort. Best to either not drink, or go for the old pour-in-a-plant-pot trick.

The guy I guessed was Dieter arrived about thirty minutes later. It wasn't such a shot in the dark. After all, he swaggered in like he owned the place. Which he apparently did. He was whippet-thin, with a mass of black curly hair. Dieter had on cut-off denim jeans and one of those vests with armholes so big, you wonder why they bother. A thick gold chain dangled a Hindu swastika symbol against the wiry hair of his chest. He leaned over one of the tables and whispered into a lad's ear and they shared a joke. As he slapped the boy on the shoulder, Dieter's gaze passed over me but didn't linger. Instead, he went to the fat guy, and they exchanged a hurried conversation. Dieter handed the man something – an envelope, I thought, but I didn't want to stare long enough to draw attention to myself – and the man slugged back his whisky, slid his lardy arse off the poor stool and left.

Dieter moved behind the bar, mixed himself a drink, then pointed at mine and widened his eyes in the international Esperanto for 'Another?' I nodded.

'Dieter, right?' I asked as he put the glass before me.

'Yes,' he said without a beat. I guessed lots of people were told: *Go and see Dieter. He'll sort you out.* Sort you out for what, though? He wiped and then held out his hand. 'Welcome to the Blue Turtle.'

'I believe you know my daughter,' I said as I took his hand. With that, he escaped my grip like a frightened eel. I saw the shutters come down behind his baby-blue eyes.

'We get a lot of girls in here,' he said shiftily. His body language couldn't have been more slippery if he'd bathed in a vat of WD40.

'Jess. With her father, Matt.'

A look of relief flickered across his face and he relaxed just a little. I wasn't the kind of mother he feared most, clearly. Well, he might have to reconsider that before I was done.

'Right.'

I showed him a picture on my phone. 'This Jess.'

'Yeah.' His skinny body went all squirmy. I suppressed the urge to slap his slippery face. 'They passed through here a while back.'

I scrolled through my photos. 'And this woman? Laura?'

'Yeah, but she split before he did.' He put his elbows on the counter top. 'Look, I don't know what you want—'

'He has my daughter. Without my permission.'

His eyebrows went up. 'Wow.'

'Yes. Very wow. I'm looking for her. Him, not so much.'

'Listen, lady—'

'Sam.'

'Sam.' I didn't like the way my name sounded in his mouth, but I smiled anyway. 'Your daughter should not be with him. He's not a nice guy. He skimmed money off the top of my place when he worked here.' Now his voice dropped to a whisper. 'He dealt drugs. In Bali, I mean, you have to have a death wish. Literally. That guy in here just now? The fat one?'

'Yeah.'

'Cop. I have to pay him every week just to stay off my back. If I don't, next thing I know I'm in Kerobokan sucking some jailer's dick so I can get tofu with my rice ball. No, thanks. So, we argued about the drugs, Matt and me, and he fucked off.' He straightened up and took a slurp of his drink, as if he had said too much. 'Nice kid by the way, Jess. I liked her. You just can't choose your parents.'

No, but you can choose your partners, I thought. And look at how that turned out for me. 'Thanks.'

'Him, I meant. Not you.'

'Was she OK?' I asked.

'Jess? She was fine. I mean, he kept her away from all that. But, you know, if he'd been caught doing what he does, then she would have been in trouble too.'

Now the Big One. 'Where did they go?'

171

'Like he'd tell me. He owed me millions of rupiahs when he skipped. They just upped and went. Off the island, for sure. If you find out, you let me know, eh? I'll give you a finder's fee.'

'Sorry. This one's personal. Any clues?'

'Under some rock, somewhere. Sorry, I can't help. I hope you find her. Drinks are on the house.'

With that, he turned and walked away to check stock.

Game over. Well, for now, I thought.

I put a pile of rupiahs on the bar – I didn't want his comps – and left, texting Kadek as I did so. I had just pressed send when I heard the shuffle of feet on the lane behind me. '*Ibu.*'

I turned, ready to drop the phone and defend myself if need be. It was the girl from the bar, the one on the stool near the entrance.

'*Ibu*, I heard you in there. I knew Jess. My name is Aja. Did she mention me?'

I shook my head. 'I haven't heard from her.'

'We hung out together.' She looked nervously over her shoulder. 'Dieter thinks I am on comfort break. You have to be careful.' She pointed to her misshapen nose. 'He did this when he thought I went with other man. He mad. Crazy.'

'I'm sorry.'

'Not your fault. His.' She hissed this last word, the sibilance as sharp as a stiletto.

'And Jess? How was she?'

'Mostly happy. Sad when the woman left. But lovely girl.' Another backward glance, as nervous as a chicken

172

with a fox on the prowl. I felt a stab of sympathy for her. I was pretty certain that her hopes and dreams never included being a come-on girl – at the very least – at a bar. 'I have to go. Meet me here. Later. Eleven. Go to very back.'

She pressed something in my hand.

'I know where they went. Matt and Jess.'

My words tumbled over each other and collided in the rush to get out of my mouth. But it was no good, she was speed-walking back towards the Blue Turtle as fast as her long legs in a tight skirt could manage.

I unfolded the slip of paper she had given me. One word: *Bacang*. No address or phone. Was it another bar? Or a street? Or a temple? Go to the very back, she'd said, which suggested a building or business. Kadek would doubtless tell me.

I looked at my watch and did a quick calculation. Four and a bit hours to go. They were going to be the longest four hours of my life. And those words would rattle around my skull for every second.

*I know where they went.*

# TWENTY-ONE

*You don't want to go there.*

I awoke with a start, Kadek's words coming back to me as the fog of sleep lifted. It took half a second to piece together where I was: in my room, under the creaking air conditioning. I had arrived back from the Blue Turtle, showered and lain down to close my eyes. Now it was gone ten.

I cleaned my teeth and recalled showing Kadek the word on the piece of paper.

*Bacang.*

The young man had recoiled from it.

Bad place, he had said. A *bacang* was a glutinous rice dumpling filled with meat, he'd explained. Street food. This *Bacang*, though, was actually located behind a series of stalls selling the buns, noodles and meatballs. It was not a place a nice *Ibu* like Miss Wylde should go, he'd insisted. And I'd insisted back that I had to be there at eleven.

We'd arranged that he would wait for me outside

after he had dropped me off, and I made sure to have him on speed dial. If he got a call from me, he should come in and get me.

But what was *Bacang*, exactly? I had asked. But he either didn't know for sure or wouldn't tell me.

I dressed in a pair of black cotton trousers, flat shoes and a dark-grey T-shirt. I looked in my case and my Ready To Go bag, but there was little I could use for self-protection.

I might not need it. Aja was no threat. But what if it was a set-up by Dieter? What if he had sent her as bait? Although, what would Dieter gain from messing with me? No, I was being paranoid. I was also, I realised, ravenously hungry. I had neglected to eat.

While I waited for Kadek, I went down and ordered a bowl of nasi goreng from the *warung* next to my hotel. It arrived in an enormous cone, with the egg on top just erupting, sending a stream of yellow lava flowing down the rice slopes. It came with a bowl of pickled vegetables on the side.

I wolfed most of it down in a few minutes and felt my confidence and excitement return as my stomach filled, and the sugar from the *temulawak* ginger soda hit my blood stream.

Aja knew where Matt and Jess had gone. OK, knowing him, they might have moved on, but it was the first giant step to overtaking them.

The race was on.

I glanced over my shoulder. A cluster of young men, mostly in mirrored sunglasses, were crouched under the *dadap* trees, sheathed in smoke from their spiced cigarettes. One of them raised a hand.

*Driver?* it asked.

The men were all drivers of Kijangs, the all-purpose four-door workhorses of Bali tourism, which were parked outside most hotels. I smiled, shook my head and went back to the last few morsels of my meal.

The honk of Kadek's horn made me jump. I took a final mouthful of soda, debated going back up to clean my teeth again, decided against it and got into the front next to Kadek. He had changed into yet another crisp white shirt and his black hair was oiled and combed.

'Fifteen, maybe twenty minute to place you want,' he said. It was as if he couldn't bring himself to say the name.

'Let's go.'

'Sure?'

'Let's go,' I said forcefully.

'OK, *Ibu*.'

We set off, navigating between overloaded mopeds carrying extended families with a skill that would shame one of those army motorcycle display teams my father loved, and a series of semi-skeletal dogs with various death wishes. I caught a glimpse of myself in the mirror. A red-faced Westerner with a glistening forehead and damp, lank hair. I helped myself to one of Kadek's wet wipes and dragged it over my skin, grimacing as I examined the greasy patch on the tissue.

Paradise certainly came with a lot of pollution.

'What do you do on your days off?' I asked Kadek once we were properly under way.

'Me?' he asked.

'Well, not the car. I don't care what the car does.'

He shrugged. 'I hang out with friends. Play video games. I go to a mixed martial arts gym.' He looked a little sheepish. 'Sometimes. Go to cinema.'

'Favourite films?'

'*Guardians of the Galaxy. The Fast and the Furious.*' A giggle. 'I like *Baby Driver.* You see it? I wish I could drive like that. But Bali too crowded.' As if to make the point, he swerved to avoid a clutch of chickens that were actually crossing the road to get to the other side.

A simple soul, then. And maybe not the best source of information on the subject I was about to broach.

We passed a parade of carvings, gathered at the roadside like a ragtag version of the Terracotta Army.

This was the Foreign Legion equivalent.

There were gods, dragons, birds and, oddly, a full-sized Batman, complete with cape. Within half a mile, they had gone, replaced by shacks selling gaudy bangles, beads and necklaces.

'What is in the baskets?' I asked.

'Which baskets?'

'At the side of the road. There, look. And there's a pile on that motorcycle.' I pointed to a precarious stack of wicker baskets on the back of a moped.

He didn't have to look. 'Cockerels. For the cock fights. They are next to road to get used to people.

177

Noise. For when they fight. I don't like,' he added hastily. 'Too much gambling. Too much gangsters.'

I wasn't sure I believed him. He would know most Westerners are squeamish about such things. But it gave me an opening. 'Tell me about drugs on Bali, Kadek,' I said.

His voice quivered with shock. 'You want drugs? *Ibu,* that's not—'

I stopped him before his opinion of me crashed and burned altogether. 'No, I don't want drugs. A man I know may have sold them. At least, I think he might have. Isn't there the death penalty here for drugs?'

'Mainly for smugglers,' he said warily. 'Mules, you know?'

'I know.'

'Especially if police not getting a cut.'

'The police are in on it?'

Kadek gave a little bark of a laugh. 'Always. Except maybe where army in control. Army specialises in cannabis. Police, they control ecstasy and ketamine. The people at *Bacang,* they sell *yaa baa* and *putauw.* Very bad. Don't eat or drink anything inside please, *Ibu.*'

I knew what *yaa baa* was, a catch-all term for various strains of methamphetamine, most of it made in Myanmar or the Thai jungles and shipped across Asia. It was consumed like Red Bull is in Europe – something to give taxi and tuk-tuk drivers, bar workers, farmers and students a lift. But, unlike Red Bull, it was highly addictive and unpredictable. 'What's *putauw*?'

Kadek laughed again, but this time it was an empty,

mirthless sound. 'Something that was once heroin. Street grade.' He looked across at me and repeated: 'Very bad. Why you want to go?'

'I was told to meet someone there.'

He grunted at that and we rode on in silence into an area that was dense with bars, clubs, restaurants and a night market. There were people twirling flaming batons on one corner – which looked like a public-safety menace to me, what with all the bamboo around – a few hollow-cheeked, mostly dreadlocked buskers who looked more like scarecrows than musicians and clumps of drunken Western travellers swaying along what passed for a pavement.

Eventually, we pulled into what appeared to be a parking lot, one end of which was colonised by a dozen food stalls, the air dense with their smoke. I was glad I had eaten. Even in the car, the food smelled delicious. Before I got out, I said: 'You'll be here?'

'Just over there, *Ibu*. You be careful.'

'I will.'

The stalls were arranged in a shallow semi-circle, with a single break in the middle. I stood still for a moment, eyes stinging from the smoke, and watched several furtive figures slip through the gap, as if it were a portal to another world.

As I walked across to enter whatever lay behind the car park, I noticed a familiar face – or, at least, a familiar arse – at one of the stalls, scoffing a giant bowl of *gado-gado*.

The cop from the Blue Turtle.

I strode across the pockmarked asphalt as if I belonged there, and straight through between the two lines of stalls, ignoring a half-hearted soft sell from one of the vendors.

I hesitated to let my eyes adjust.

Above me was a stretched tarpaulin, which cut out some of the light from the food stalls' gas and battery lamps. Ahead was a bamboo fence with a single wide door in its centre. It swung open and a tall Westerner, shirt undone to his navel, came by, studiously avoiding eye contact, his cheeks burning with shame or excitement, it was difficult to tell. The door clacked back into place.

Once my night vision had improved a little, I stepped through the opening. The smell that hit me was the olfactory equivalent of sweet, sour and nauseous.

Incense, of course, food, sewers and the musk of too many bodies in close proximity.

A path, squelchy underfoot, led between shanty shacks made of wood and corrugated iron, every one draped with a crown of electrical cables. Each doorway had a different-coloured lantern hanging from it. Women, mostly, sat around on chairs and stools, smoking, uninterested in me. Or anything. The majority were mere carcasses, the meat on them burned away by whatever life they lived and chemicals they took.

I continued to walk down, following the row of torches that marked the route between the shacks. I passed a hut full of hollow-eyed young boys, another of what I would later discover were called *benchongs*;

transvestites or transgenders or whatever the current nomenclature was. One of them smiled at me from under a bright red wig and raised a beer bottle. My return smile might have been somewhat strained. I could see why Kadek didn't like this place.

It began to rain, warm but heavy-ish. Some of the prostitutes shifted back under shelter. There came a sound like the shake of a million tiny tambourines, and from under the huts came an army of cockroaches, which took to the air and flew at me.

I began to bat them away and heard a few barks of laughter. As they hit my skin, I felt the burn of regurgitated *nasi goreng*.

'*Ibu, Ibu*, this way.'

I peered through the shifting screen of insect bodies and saw, some metres ahead, the silhouette of Aja. I stepped forward, but as soon as I moved she spun around and trotted off.

As I followed, the cockroaches thinned. Then, someone turned off the rain tap. As one, the cloud of clacking insects fell to the ground, as if their flying batteries had run out, and they scuttled off back under the shanties.

After the last of the flaming torches, the shacks gave way to a small wooded area, the trees spiralled with fairy lights to mark the new path. Unseen birds chirped from above, with the constant, inevitable rhythm of tree frogs underneath.

It was like going from a Grimms' fairy tale to an Enid Blyton world.

Following the strings of electric lights took me through the woods to a clearing, where an ancient, twisted banyan tree held pride of place. Next to it was a shrine, illuminated by candles and the glowing fireflies of incense sticks, with a statue of Ganesh, the elephant god, sitting on top. A young woman was on her knees before it, pressing rice offerings into a bowl. At the far end of the space, behind the tree, were the lights of another 'village', but these houses looked more substantial, less international refugee camp.

Aja was standing directly in front of me, hands on hips.

'Hi,' I said, my insides knotting at the thought of what she was about to tell me.

'Hello, Sam Wylde.'

It took a second for me to realise that her lips hadn't moved and that this was not an act of ventriloquism, but another person.

She stepped aside. There was a man sitting at a table in the shadow of the banyan tree. There was the flare of a match as he lit a cigarette, and in the brief light I saw a face I recognised and my stomach unravelled itself, ready to vomit up its contents.

I knew him.

Thought he was dead. Hoped he was dead.

In that moment, all the optimism in me drained away, like petrol poured on sand.

It was Bojan.

182

# TWENTY-TWO

I had fought for my life with this man. He was a body-guard of sorts, although closer to a mercenary. He had been instrumental in a plot to convince me I was working for MI5 when, in fact, I had been duped by an organisation trying to ruin the business of one of my clients. The last time I had seen him, he was lying in a pool of blood, a knife sticking out of his torso.

So there was only one way to greet him.

'What the fuck are you doing here?' I asked between clenched teeth. 'And you ...' I pointed to Aja, but she sidled off like one of the roaches before I could fully form my insult. Any compassion I had for her drained away in an instant.

She had set me up.

'Relax, it's not her fault. Just doing as she is told, like the pretty *kupu kupu malam* she is. It means "night butterfly". So much prettier than *whore*, don't you think? Sit down, Sam Wylde, we have to talk. Cigarette?' His voice was raspier than I recalled, like a cat coughing up a fur ball. Maybe it was all the fags.

'No, thanks,' I said, remembering Kadek's warning about eating and drinking. It wasn't difficult to adulterate a smoke. Not somewhere they apparently sold shit-grade heroin.

I walked over, pulled out a chair and sat. The girl at the shrine stood, bowed and walked off to the second village.

'It's more upmarket in there,' growled Bojan as I watched her go. 'Dick less likely to fall off. Back where you walked through, you get a blowjob for three dollars, sex for five. Back here, oh, twenty, thirty, maybe even a hundred for something special.' His eyes narrowed. 'I remember your tits. We could probably get even more for you.' Then he slapped his forehead with the palm of his hand. 'Doh. I forgot. You've had a kid, haven't you? How could I forget? Probably a bit ... what's the word?' He frowned. '*Slack*.' He pointed to my crotch. 'They are very fussy about that when paying top dollar. They want tight pussy.'

I almost laughed. This was playground stuff. He was sparring. Although, I did always hate those women who said they elected for a caesarean so they could keep their husbands happy. I was always there to tell them it didn't turn into the Dartford Tunnel. Besides, they could always get a husband with a decent-sized dick.

'That's why we're here? To discuss tightening my fanny?'

'Come to think of it, I reckon some of the girls have had that done. I could probably get you a rate.'

I bit my tongue, stifling half a dozen smart-arse answers.

184

I could see him properly now. Still bullet-headed and hairless, but he was thinner than when I had fought him for my life, his pale skin stretched taut over tendons and bones.

Bojan was the Serbian thug who haunted my dreams. The one who had tried to humiliate me once and kill me a second time. The knife meant for me had gone into him instead. 'I thought you were dead, Bojan.'

'Me and you both.' He held up his thumb and forefinger a few millimetres apart. 'Came this close.'

'The butler wasn't so lucky.'

A shrug of his broad shoulders. I made a mental note not to underestimate him. After all, as an apparently mortally wounded man, he had killed the Russian oligarch's butler watching over him and made his escape.

Thinner and croakier didn't mean he was any less dangerous.

'So it goes,' he rasped. 'So it goes.'

'Is this a coincidence? That you should be here in Bali?'

'What do you think?'

'I smell a rat.'

He laughed at that, smoke streaming from his nostrils as he did so. 'Is that me you are talking about?'

'Oh, I can do better than "rat" for you, Bojan.'

'Still got that big mouth, eh? Let's see what you have to say about this.' He extracted something from the pocket of his jeans and put it on the table between us. I stared at it for a while before it began to dawn on me what the object was.

And then my insides turned to ice.

'Cat got your tongue?'

'How?'

'Pick it up. Check it's real. I had to break the code, so it'll come straight on. I mean, she blocked the number when it was taken, but all the contents are still there.'

I lifted it off the table, flipped open the case and pressed the button. The screen lit up. I recognised the picture that appeared, of course.

It was me.

First day in Iraq, in my army medic gear with Freddie standing next to me. Young and eager, not yet beaten down or bloodied. A whole series of worlds ago.

I couldn't quite compute what he was doing with it. 'How did you get this? Did you buy it?'

'Ha. Buy it? No. I took it. The moped thieves? My lads.'

Another young lady appeared to make an offering. 'The fuckin' Balinese,' said Bojan, irritably. 'They make an offering on everything—'

I was in no mood for a change of subject. Particularly not from a man like Bojan. 'You mugged Freddie?'

'Well, technically, I had her mugged. But yes. How is she?'

'Banged up.'

'Good, job done. Although my beef isn't with her.'

'How did you track her down? *Us* down.' It was difficult to keep my voice level. The hysteria was bubbling up like lava from that nearby volcano.

He puffed on his cigarette for a few moments, debating whether to tell me. 'I wasn't really looking that hard for you,' he said at last. 'I had to get better. Back in the game. But I knew the time would come when we would meet again. Given the circles we move in. And it did. It was Oktane. You hired Oktane. Word got out. That I couldn't ignore. You were virtually on my doorstep. And by then, I was pretty much back to fighting fit. And so it wasn't so very hard to find you at all.'

'But we never even met him. Oktane.'

He flicked his cigarette away into the undergrowth and lit a second. 'Here's the thing. And I bet you don't know this. You heard of the comic strip *The Phantom*?'

I shook my head. I get shaky beyond Batman.

'OK, big when I was growing up. Superman, Spider-Man, very hard to get in my hometown. But *The Phantom* was everywhere. So, he's a guy who lives in the jungle. The Ghost Who Walks. Like Tarzan, but with a mask and a gun. And the Phantom has been going for like, dozens of years, decades. How come he never ages? There's the trick. There is more than one Phantom. When one gets too old for the masked crime-fighter shit, he trains up a new guy to take over. So, the current one is like the twentieth Phantom.'

*Help, I'm trapped in Forbidden Planet with a comic nerd*. 'I don't see—'

'Oktane is a bit like that. There are several Oktanes.' He laughed. 'It's a franchise.'

'Jesus.' I still remembered when Jess was small, feeling more than a little cheated when I went to a party and there was a different Mr Marvel children's entertainer than the one I had hired. Turned out there was an army of Mr Marvels, all over the country like a rash. It was the party equivalent of a fast-food business, serving kids the same puppet shows, magic and slapstick routine. Only, the server changed. And now, apparently hit men were in on the act. Maybe they were on zero-hour contracts, too.

But the Oktane model was probably closer to the Chechen one. If you can prove you are ruthless and brutal enough, anyone, anywhere in the world, can buy the rights to designate themselves a branch of the Chechen Mafia. Just never, ever do it unofficially, because those guys tend to send cease-and-desist torturers rather than a solicitor's letter.

'And you know one of the Oktanes?' I asked.

'I do. Funny, eh? Small world. He told me about this job that was out for tender and I recognised you from the job description. Two women doing something ballsy but stupid? That's you and your pal Freddie, Sam Wylde. Ballsy but stupid.'

'Hey, that's one therapy session saved, thanks. I still don't understand—'

'You know how much crap is on one of those things once you unlock it?' he asked, pointing at Freddie's phone. 'And how did I unlock it? Piece of piss, as you say. Most people who have been in the army use some variation of their old service number as their password. I bet you do.'

I kept my face idling in neutral. I did. Because it is one number drummed into you so hard, you'll never forget it no matter how senile you become.

'Freddie certainly did,' he continued. 'So, I got all your texts, emails, exchanges. Before she set up her new phone and automatically blocked us, we downloaded all existing WhatsApp chats. I knew about the wedding—'

A weak little light went on in my head. 'Did you throw a bottle over the wall at me the other day? In a hotel in Ubud?'

He smirked. 'Not personally. It was just to keep you on your toes,' he conceded. 'I have copies of the photos of your daughter from here in Bali, the ones you have been hawking around. I know as much about what happened to Jess as you. Maybe more.'

I came half out of my seat, reached over and grabbed his T-shirt, but his hand locked around my wrist. I remembered just how fucking strong he was as he squeezed. 'Don't be even more dumb. You think I didn't arrange insurance?'

I followed his gaze. Standing under one of the trees with the fairy lights was the fat cop, with a uniformed policeman next to him.

An armed uniformed policeman.

I knew that because he had drawn his weapon. I let go of Bojan and he released my wrist. I sat back in the rickety chair.

Any trace of affability disappeared from his voice when he spoke. 'I once said that if you didn't do as you were told, I'd take your daughter. I still intend to. You cost me my spleen, half my stomach and a kidney. I'm going to rip your heart out, woman. She'd be worth a lot to me, somewhere like this. F-O-T-B.'

I didn't want to ask what that meant. My imagination filled it in anyway.

'I brought you here because this is the kind of place she'll end up. Not here, exactly. But there are thousands of versions of *Bacang* around the world. At first, she'll just have a few select clients. Then, once the novelty has worn off, she'll end up back there, in the good place. But once her cunt and ass are worn out, she'll be shunted there, into that shithole you just walked through. By the time she's eighteen, she'll be a husk of a junkie.'

I realised I wasn't breathing and my vision was swimming. Sparring, I reminded myself. Just words.

'And you, you'll be in that very special hell reserved for people who know their children are suffering and they can do fuck all about it. And for those who want to kill the people who have done them harm, but can't. The Suffer Club, you might call it.'

I put my fingers round his throat and squeezed, digging them in until I found the artery, pressing, pressing ...

I blinked.

I hadn't moved. He was still talking.

'But right now, like you, I don't know where she is. That doesn't mean I don't intend to find her. Just like you do. And if you make it to her first, then, the best person has won. But if *I* get to her first ...' Bojan coughed, interrupting his flow. 'Well, ladies and gentlemen, place your bets.' And he laughed.

That was a mistake.

It wasn't much of a punch, but it connected and he reeled back in his chair. I heard a shout from the cops, but Bojan put his hand up. 'OK … it's OK. She gets that one for free.'

I wanted to shake my hand. My knuckles were stinging. He had a red mark on his cheek. I would imagine he wanted to touch that. Neither of us moved. 'You fuckin' monster.'

'That's right.' He leaned in over the table and hissed. 'I'm the fuckin' monster who is going to find your precious Jess and feed her to the wolves. And you, Sam Wylde, made me.'

# TWENTY-THREE

My husband Paul used to tell a story about his colleague, William, who left the services and intended to become a Close Protection Officer. Instead, his father, who reviewed for *Gramophone* magazine, got him a gig as a minder for a renowned classical violinist, who also happened to be blind.

Not only was he a famous player, the violinist was also famously mean. There was no manager to take 15 or 20 per cent, just a booking agency taking 5, and no entourage but William.

The violinist was so tight that, even though he could command thousands of pounds a night, when travelling abroad he made William book twin rooms as an economy, especially in America, where two queen-sized beds in a motel room is quite common.

Sometime in the 1990s, they were touring the Southern states and they settled into a routine: concert, hotel, next city, rehearsal with the local musicians. Repeat.

Every night at the hotel was the same regimen too:

a drink, dinner with a half-bottle of wine, then bed. William would get ready for bed first, tuck up and then start reading a military history book, while his companion navigated the bathroom.

Eventually, the violinist would slide between the sheets and say, 'I want to go to sleep. Is the light out?' And dutifully, William would put the light out, even though he couldn't figure out what difference it made to the violinist, him being blind. Maybe he could see some shades of grey, he thought.

'Is it out?' the maestro would ask.

'Yes,' William would reply.

But one night, William was in the midst of D-Day or Dunkirk and didn't want to stop. So, when the question came: *Is the light out?* William said yes and carried on reading.

'You're sure?'

William flicked the switch off and – silently – back on. 'Yes, there.'

The violinist said, 'OK. Goodnight.' At which point, he threw his covers back to reveal a stonking hard-on, which he proceeded to stroke as vigorously as he could, while not making a single sound that might disturb what he thought was a slumbering William.

Except William wasn't slumbering that night. In fact, he would have trouble sleeping for the rest of his life.

Horrified, he turned off the light as quietly as he could and bought earplugs and an eyeshade the next day.

And he always turned off the light when asked.

And the moral of the story is? You never know when some fucker is watching you.

Bojan had certainly been watching me. Just not in the same room like poor old William.

How long had he been sniffing around? Since Oktane, he'd said. Weeks, then.

And how much would he really have got off Freddie's phone? A lot, probably.

She was a lot more tech savvy than me. She used Facebook, Instagram and various dating services. She, unlike me, had swiped right. Or was it left?

So, I thought as I walked back through the forest and past the ramshackle houses of despair, I had to stop relying on my phone. And my laptop. I had to get off the grid, yet still find a way to communicate with Freddie. We had to assume Bojan and his people were all over us. The bottle over the wall was just a demo of their omnipotence.

*We know where you are.*

But – and it was a but the size of Kim Kardashian's rear – if he was to be believed, he didn't know where Jess and Matt were. Hence the first-past-the-post-wins shit. But what if he was simply relying on me leading him to her?

This man was eaten up inside by a desire for revenge. Just like Leka, or perhaps Elona, a woman out to make the British soldiers who had allegedly raped her suffer? Jesus, it was a big club, the people who had been hurt and wanted some sort of recompense.

*The Suffer Club.*

Wasn't that what Bojan called it? And he was a fully-paid-up member, thanks to me.

I knew what I had to do to get through this. My own guts felt cold and fluid, like iced water had been pumped in.

The flares of pain firing off in my brain were like an electrical storm. For a microsecond, it swamped every other activity in my head, subliminal glimpses of what he threatened would happen to Jess forcing their way to the front of my consciousness. But they weren't going to help me. Just the opposite.

I had to smother the emotions to stop the turmoil. Jess was just the Principal now. Not my daughter. I had to approach this as just another case.

Be cold, be detached. Or you'll fall apart.

*Find the girl.* That's the job.

My old sergeant used to say: *Don't worry about outcomes you can't influence. Worry about those you can.*

So I can influence this; I can get to Jess first. And after that? Well, chances are Bojan would still come after me.

So be it. I'd tackle that problem then.

Any kind of calm was going to be hard to find until he was no longer a threat, that much was certain. I think once you are in the Suffer Club, it's hard to leave. Like Hotel fucking California.

I had some inkling of what I had to do next. As I made it out of that purgatory and to the food stalls,

I had a half-formed plan that hovered behind gauzy curtains in my brain.

I looked across at Kadek's Toyota.

The door was wide open, and there was no sign of the young driver.

# TWENTY-FOUR

Older Balinese believe in *Leyaks*, practitioners of black magic who can take the form of a monkey, a pig, wind or light. In the most extreme manifestations, they take on the form of humans by day – apart from their prominent fangs – but by night the head breaks off and flies, entrails straggling behind.

I had a feeling that Kadek might be one himself when, on my third glance around the car park, I spotted him at one of the food stalls. I could have sworn he hadn't been there seconds ago.

He raised a hand to me and I walked over, trying to keep the anger from my voice.

'What are you doing?'

He pointed to a much-diminished pile of rice and meatballs on a banana leaf. 'I'm eating, *Ibu*. I was hungry.'

'I meant leaving the car door open like that.'

The boy looked puzzled. 'I can see it. I have the keys. And nobody would touch it.'

'I wouldn't bank on that,' I snapped. 'What was it you said about this place being full of bad men?'

He looked alarmed, not about the bad men, but from the expression on my face and my tone of voice. I was shaking. Maybe that made my voice quiver.

'What happened in there? Are you OK, *Ibu*?'

I ran a hand through my hair. It felt matted with sweat, dust and fear. 'No, not really. I need a drink.' Pathetic, I know. But just the one, I told myself.

I looked hopefully at the stallholder, but Kadek put me straight. 'This man is *pendatang*. Muslim. No alcohol. Just a moment.' He slid the remainder of his meal into his mouth and threw down some rupiahs. He washed his fingers in the proffered bowl and shook hands with the vendor, before instructing me to follow him.

We passed the Toyota and he kicked the door shut with his sandalled foot, raising an eyebrow that asked: *Happy now?*

'Lots of Muslims in Bali these days. They come from Java, Sulawesi, all over, because we have more tourists. Too many come,' he said glumly. 'More mosques than temples one day, maybe.'

We did the usual moped roulette as we crossed the street. The air was bitter with their exhausts, mixing with the ever-present scent of cloves from cigarettes. Kadek ducked under a thatched awning and we found ourselves in a substantial *warung* selling bamboo skewers threaded with meat, with a small bar to one side. He said something briefly to the woman manning the station and she poured a single shot of clear liquid into a glass. Then she popped the top off a beer and handed it to Kadek.

I got the unknown fluid. I examined it suspiciously. 'What is it?'

'Arak,' he said. 'It calms the nerve.'

'*Nerves*. There are lots of them to calm.' I took a gulp. It didn't so much calm as cauterise them.

I gave a cough and tried to speak, but I sounded like I'd had a laryngectomy. Eventually I managed: 'Beer.' I gulped half of the second Bintang down in one. 'Jesus.'

'Feel better, *Ibu*?'

'I'm not sure I can feel anything. Thank you.'

We clinked bottles and moved away to sit at one of the three tables.

'How old are you, Kadek?' I asked.

'Twenty-three.'

'Where are you from?'

'Here. Bali,' he said proudly, as if that were unusual.

'I meant which part.'

'A village on the edge of the slopes of Gunung Batur.' I knew that was the island's perfidious volcano.

'Was it evacuated last year? When it blew?'

'Yes. Although not much damage.'

'And your parents? What do they do?'

'Farm. But not rice. Rice not grow well near the volcano. Fruits, vegetables, coconuts . . .'

'They own their own farm?'

He sipped his beer and shook his head. 'They are *sudras*. Lower caste. They still believe in such things.

King owns land; they must pay tribute – fifty coconuts every six months. Not fair.'

I didn't realise a feudal system still existed. My reading had suggested the royal family were mere figureheads, with real power wielded from Jakarta. But, maybe like extant royal families the world over, they were canny enough to hold on to land even as their influence faded. 'And you didn't want to farm?'

He flashed me a wry smile as if it were a stupid question. 'I farm tourists,' he said. 'No offence.'

'None taken. But I think this crop has failed.'

He pursed his lips and tilted his head to the side, as if he couldn't quite compute this. 'What do you mean, *Ibu*?'

'I think I'll have to let you go. There might be trouble. I can't take the risk.'

'Trouble? Who with?'

'Bad men.'

'Bad men don't frighten me.'

I admired his bravado, especially for a kid who barely came up to my shoulders. 'Maybe not. But as I said, I can't take the chance you'll get hurt. I suspect your parents depend on you farming tourists.'

A nod. 'They live near Ulun Danu Batur temple. Very expensive.' He took a slug of beer. 'Which bad men?'

'Well, there was a cop at the food stalls back there. He was one of them.'

He mimed a big belly with his free hand. 'Big cop?'

'Yes. Flowery shirt.'

He gave a little snort. 'Wayan Agung. He mainly

rolls tourists on mopeds for speeding fines or not wearing helmet. Plus some protection.'

'You know him?'

'I know who he is.' He flicked his hand as if shooing a fly. 'He can't hurt me.'

'Why not?'

'My mother's *om*. Uncle. He is local Chief of Police.'

'Wow. That's some connection.' And it explained why he wasn't too worried about leaving the door of his car open. He had protection.

Kadek shook a clenched fist. 'He touch me, then Durga bite his ass.'

'Your uncle?'

He giggled. 'She goddess. An evil, evil goddess.'

Another good ally to have, no doubt. With the fat cop taken care of, I wasn't worried about Dieter. He was better suited to life with the roaches under the brothel huts than anything else. But Bojan? He was cut from a different cloth. One with blood all over it. Some of it, as I recalled, mine.

I wasn't sure Bojan would care too much about family connections in the local police force. He'd taken on bigger and badder than that. 'Look, I'll give you the money I owe you and we'll call it quits.'

'No quits,' he said forcefully. 'You are seeing bad side of Bali. Those girls over there.' He pointed back towards *Bacang*. 'Most from Java. Brought by Thais. Bali people good in heart. Outsiders make trouble. I take care of you.'

Well, I was an outsider. And I was going to make

trouble. So he knew what he was getting into. 'OK, Kadek. Thank you. I need to know if I can get a burner phone at this time of night. A non-traceable one. Text, phone, that's all. Not a smartphone.'

'Easy, yes.' He pointed down the street, still gaudy with neon signs blurred by the exhaust fumes.

'And a laptop.'

'Same, same.'

The vague plan I had was beginning to take a more solid form. When I had walked back through the brothel, it had all been scrambled noise, like bad jazz. Now, gradually, I could pick out a tune. My head had cleared. The shakes had gone. I took a breath.

'And there's something else I want to buy,' I said.

'What is it?' he asked.

'Your car.'

# TWENTY-FIVE

It was well past midnight by the time we got back to my digs, but I decided to pack up and move hotels anyway. The clerk wasn't happy that I was leaving without giving a forwarding address. I assured him it was nothing to do with the hotel, that I'd give it a glowing report on Trip Advisor, and then I handed him a fistful of rupiahs to stay shtum about whether I had ever stayed there.

Kadek also added something in the local language, which, judging by the guy's face, might have been more effective than mere money.

After a detour to check out a site that might be useful later on, Kadek drove me to a place he thought would be perfect for me to stay: a collection of six villas, recently completed, not far from Sanur, but away from the tourist strip. It had an eerie feel and, despite having been built from teak reclaimed from a petrified forest, the villa reeked of paint and plastic.

But there were no other guests in the compound, only one way in and out, a competent night watchman, and Kadek agreed to take one of the other rooms in my villa, just in case we had to move quickly. And as it was a 'soft opening' – a kind of trial run before they got to charging full price – it was only costing an arm, rather than the full set of limbs.

Kadek went to bed after checking the locks on the doors and windows and I used the landline to call Freddie. It would be expensive but, as I was calling her home phone, it was unlikely to be compromised. I doubted Bojan was up to bugging BT.

She let out a long sigh when I gave her a run-down of what had happened. 'You are fuckin' kiddin' me. Bojan?'

'Yes.'

'Not his twin brother?'

'I don't think so.'

'Because that cunt is meant to be dead.'

'If there was any justice.'

We both thought about that for a second, before Freddie asked, 'What now?'

'I don't think he knows where Jess is. Of course, he might and could just be torturing me. But my gut instinct is that he doesn't know.'

'I guess you have to assume that. What can I do? Shall I come out? You know I will. Still have an RTG bag packed. '

I expected that. Always Ready To Go for me, that was Freddie. I felt a wave of affection towards her. And then I remembered what I was about to say. 'Don't take this the wrong way . . .'

'I have already,' she said. 'But go on.'

'You'll slow me down. All bandaged and booted up. And I'm not sure they'll even let you fly.'

'Slow you down?' She spat the phrase.

'Think about it. Why did they take you out like that? They could have just mugged you. But no, they took a scaffold pole to your legs, ensuring you'd be out of action. Bojan didn't want you here – he wanted to skew the odds in his favour.'

'Fuck a duck.' I sensed her softening. I wasn't spinning her a line, it was the truth. Without Freddie, I was much less effective. And Bojan realised that.

'But that's an argument for me coming out.'

'Not as you are.'

I let that sink in.

'So, here is what I want you to do.' I heard a noise on the line. 'Is someone there?'

'Yes. He'll be gone soon.'

'Who is it?'

'My physiotherapist.'

'Do you mean your real physio or ... no, don't answer that. Is he on the level?'

'He was. He's on his feet now.'

'Freddie!'

'I think he's legit. I'll put his fingers in the toaster and find out.' She let out a long, heartfelt sigh. 'What can I do, Buster?'

'Go over everything we know. Everything I just told you. Look at the photos of Jess again for clues we might have missed. Trawl the internet for more pictures. Go on the dark web. I don't know ... get one of those white boards they always have in cop shows. I'm bound to have missed something.' That bit wasn't necessarily true. But I was praying it was.

'Desk job?'

'Come on, Fred.'

'I know. I just hate you having all the fun.'

I looked around the soulless room with its cinema-sized TV and a monstrous carving staring me down. 'Yeah. Wall-to-wall fun.'

'Sorry. You got it. Whatever you need.'

'Thank you. I've got a new number. You have a pen?' She had and I gave it to her. 'But call me or text me on a different number from your old one, eh? We have to assume everything we used prior to this moment is compromised. Everything.'

'I have an old BlackBerry that still works. I'll get a new SIM in it.'

'Great. I'll also text you my new Gmail address.'

'What are you going to do now?'

'I want to jump on a plane, fly out of here and scoop up Jess. But I have no idea where to go. I guess the two of them are still in Southeast Asia somewhere. It's a fuckin' big place.'

'You can narrow it down. Matt will always be in Party Town.'

'There are a lot of party towns out this way,' I said, thinking of the hordes of kids following an identical route through the region, like they were pre-programmed by some internal GPS – Get Pissed and Sightsee – device. 'A lot.'

'I suppose.'

I cleared my throat. It was time to tell Freddie about the detour I made Kadek take. 'I do have one idea, though.'

'What is it?'

I outlined my plan, if you could call it that. This time the silence on the other end was longer. When she spoke, her voice was smaller, nervous for me.

'Are you fuckin' mad?'

'Freddie—'

'No, really, you've lost your shit. We're the good guys, remember?' She sounded angry and more than a little frightened. I felt that combo too, but perhaps not in the same ratio as Freddie.

'There's no good and bad.'

'Sam, really? You'd do that to a fellow human being?'

Hell, yes. To get my daughter back safe? To put Bojan back in the box where he belongs?

I'd do *that*. And much more.

# TWENTY-SIX

The next day went slowly. I kept myself busy setting up communications with Freddie and, in a secluded part of the villa compound, tinkering with Kadek's car.

I hadn't bought it. I had just agreed to pay for any damage, which he seemed happy with. I would, of course, compensate him for the inconvenience, too. Luckily, there was still a DIY ethos to car repairs on the island, and his boot contained a full socket set and spanners. I supplied the gaffer tape I needed from my RTG kit.

I also armed myself with the knife he had bought for me; a version of the local *kris*, with a wicked, curved blade. This was not one of those ceremonial daggers, imbued with mystical powers, dense with symbolic engravings.

It was a fighting weapon, pure and simple.

I sent Kadek back to *Bacang* to score some drugs, figuring he would get a better deal than me. And he was less likely to end up in Kerobokan prison, which had an unhealthy percentage of Westerners doing time for drug offences. As little as one gram of crystal meth could get you an extended stay there. And you'd better hope you had relatives who could pay to keep you safe.

Kadek reported back that there was no sign of Bojan, but the word was he had hired himself a posse of *anak merdeka*: street toughs. Kadek explained that these were originally harmless anarchists who had become disaffected outsiders after a crackdown on their subculture by Jakarta. Now, they acted as enforcers and couriers for the gangs that ran places such as *Bacang*.

By mid-afternoon, we were as ready as we'd ever be and I was sweaty and dirty. I sent Kadek off to put some false plates on his car, just in case there was anyone with a smartphone – highly likely in Bali – who might take snaps of us. I needed to protect him, even if his uncle was Lord Krishna.

I drank a litre of water, showered and tried to sleep. But sleep came fitfully and I jerked awake every five minutes, dragged up by yet another spectral image of Jess, sometimes happy and larking, sometimes ...

I opened the minibar and slammed it shut again. That really wouldn't help.

I got dressed – black-on-black – and sat waiting for Kadek, wondering how time was managing to drag its heels quite so much. As the shadows lengthened, I opened the doors, turned off the air conditioning and listened to the scratch orchestra of insects, birds and amphibians outside.

My new phone rang. Only Freddie and Kadek had the number, but even so I was apprehensive as I put it to my ear. It was Kadek. 'OK, the site is all sorted.'

This was the location where, according to Freddie, I would be losing my shit.

*Someone* would be in all likelihood.

But it wouldn't be me.

'Sure?'

'Absolutely. And the target is in place,' he said, before adding, 'Over.'

I ignored that dramatic flourish. 'You've checked? Were you seen?'

'I did a walk-by,' he said. 'Plus I have someone in place to pick up the pieces.'

'Well done.' This kid was earning his money, even if he did seem to think he was in a heist movie. 'I need a couple of other things: a baby's feeding bottle or drinking cup, some nylon rope, three battery-powered lamps and some cigarettes.'

'What kind of cigarettes? Gudang Garam?'

'Don't care.' I wouldn't be smoking them. Well, not much. Just in case I added: 'Something mild that won't rip my throat out. Not clove.' I thought the popping and crackling *kretek* cigarettes smelled like a spice rack on fire.

'OK. I'll be there in thirty minutes, *Ibu*. I'll bring food.'

'I'm not hun—'

But he'd gone.

*

The food was a good idea. Not only would I need all the energy I could get, it helped pass the time until dusk thickened and the sky turned to a star-studded black.

'This is delicious,' I said. 'What is it?'

'*Lawar babi*,' he said, scooping up the mixture with bread.

'And that is ...?'

'Vegetables, local herbs, some coconut, minced meat and ...' He stuffed a parcel into his mouth, crunching down on the vegetables.

I waited. 'And?'

'Blood,' he said eventually.

'Blood?'

'Yes. Pork or chicken. The recipe changes from village to village, but all have blood. This one chicken blood.' He gave a mischievous grin. 'What, you don't like now?'

'No, I still like.' I put the thought of drained poultry out of my head, cleared the plate and drank a tumbler of green tea.

'Make you strong. The blood.'

'Thank you.'

'You know in Bali, we sacrifice animals a lot. When my sister opened restaurant in Denpasar, priests conducted a ceremony. They killed a dog and buried it out front. Then a pig was roasted, worshipped and buried. A hundred chickens were killed and buried in the building too.'

'Sounds expensive.'

He made a little screeching sound. 'Ayyyy. It was. But it kept the demons away. My sister, she makes another sacrifice every fifteen days, to Durga, the goddess. The demons stay away.'

I stood up. I wasn't sure whether he believed all this or if he was just relaying local superstitions as if I were a regular tourist.

But I wasn't.

That night, I would be the demon that people had to worry about. And no dead chicken was going to stop me.

We were a few hundred metres from the Blue Turtle when Kadek's phone rang. He barked something into it and turned to me in the rear seat. 'Still in place.'

'Ready when you are.'

'Five. One. Six. Seven. Two.'

'Is that a Balinese countdown?' I asked as I hunkered down.

'No. *The Fast and the Furious* movies in order of best.' He turned again and shot me a big grin. 'I love Vin Diesel.'

With that, he slapped on a baseball cap, pulled it low over his eyes and slid on a pair of Ray-Ban Aviators. After a quick check in the mirror, he pressed the accelerator and we began our run-up to the strip of bars just behind the beach.

It was tight. We brushed the outside tables and chairs of restaurants with our wing mirrors and startled pedestrians jumped out of the way. Kadek beeped at a group of backpackers, a couple of whom gave him the finger as they stepped aside. The Toyota's engine whined as he gave it more gas.

Not quite *The Fast and the Furious* – or at least, not the first part of the title – but it would have to do.

Now people were turning and leaping out of our path, most with *what-the-fuck* expressions across their startled faces. With some, I glimpsed the fear in their eyes and I realised what they were thinking.

*Terror attack.*

Vans and cars had become motorised weapons in Nice, Barcelona, London, New York ... and now Jimbaran Bay. Well, it was too late to reassure them that, rather than *jihadis*, this vehicle contained one very pissed-off mother.

I snatched the *kris* from the rear seat pocket and sliced through most of the gaffer tape that was holding the rear door on. I had undone the hinge bolts earlier in the day and removed the lock.

'Now!' yelled Kadek.

I braced myself, raised my knees to my chest and straightened my legs with all the explosive force I could muster after a meal of chicken blood. The door hung for a second on a fibrous thread and then split away, rolling behind us. I didn't turn to look, but I knew Kadek had arranged its retrieval.

I could see a cavalcade of horrified faces flashing by the aperture left in the side of the Toyota.

'We're here.'

The car juddered and swerved as it hit part of

the bar next door to the Blue Turtle, but Kadek regained control.

Now we were *really* close to the customers. I could have snatched their drinks had I wanted to. But it wasn't drinks I was after.

I crouched in the open doorway as we reached the Blue Turtle, and there she was, eyes wide, mouth open, still on her stool.

Aja.

I reached out, grabbed her and pulled her feather-light body in on top of me. As Kadek burst onto the beach, tyres slipping as they hunted for grip, I felt Aja's teeth sink into my arm.

It hurt. I hit her twice and, as soon as she went limp, jammed the syringe full of sedative into her arse.

By then, Kadek had managed to find some traction for the wheels and fishtailed us between some of the painted boats, taking paint from both car and hulls as we pushed on into the night.

I pulled Aja onto the seat next to me. She tried to fight, but already her limbs were like rubber, her head too heavy for her neck, her eyes rolling.

They say you can get anything on the black market. I had sent Kadek to score high-quality Demerol, an opioid, and Promethazine, an antihistamine. I had mixed them together to produce a fast-working intra-muscular neuroleptic.

It was risky – to Aja, not me – but I was pretty sure I had the dose right.

Although, I hadn't expected her to go out quite so

quickly. Still, I had a nasal atomiser of naloxone in case it all went tits up, as well as an injectable solution of the anti-opioid.

But all she had to do was keep breathing and we'd be OK.

Well, if she played ball.

With a sudden swerve, Kadek got us off the tarmac road and we bounced onto an old bullock track, throwing Aja around like a rag doll.

I looked back towards the fading lights of the bars and restaurants. Nobody seemed to be following.

The wind whipped past the space left by the missing door, the frogs and crickets so loud they seemed to be in the back seat with us. I checked my arm where Aja had bitten me. The skin wasn't broken. I batted away a couple of opportunist mosquitos and tried to relax a little, to regulate my own breathing.

Stage one of Operation *Wadah* was complete.

I had sent Kadek away. I didn't want him being a witness to this. It would be my fault alone what did and did not happen to Aja.

Kadek was at the end of the phone for when I needed him. But if this went wrong, I wouldn't make the call.

I'd be on my own.

Aja began to stir. I lit another cigarette and waited while the whining mosquitoes circled the edge of the smoke I was exhaling.

I was sat on a low stone wall, its surface slippery with

moss, in a small, seemingly neglected temple that had seen better days.

Aja and I were alone.

Although not completely.

There were shadows, barely illuminated by the lamps, skittering over the larger structures across the centre courtyard.

Monkeys.

Those rapacious, thieving, biting, spitting monkeys that people think are cute. Cute like a mixture of the Krays and Dracula. They were making noises that suggested they weren't happy I had invaded their turf.

Fuck 'em. I had the *kris* next to me, sitting alongside the naloxone. Any of them tried anything, I'd stab them in the eye.

The night air carried the scent of jasmine and frangipani with undertones of old incense and ashes. Somewhere in the night an insomniac rooster crowed. There had been bats, but now, bellies full and night upon them, they had departed. The battery-powered lamps had attracted a halo of small insects that had survived the feeding frenzy, into which lumbered the occasional handkerchief-sized moth.

The temple was still used, so Kadek told me, but rarely, as the village it once served had been abandoned. Something to do with devils. Or maybe they all just went bankrupt. But, occasionally, someone rich who had been born in the village decided they would like to be cremated there. Often, several ex-villagers would have to die and be cremated together to make the cost of the ceremony bearable. It might take two or three years before enough people had died and funds were made available. When that finally happened, a many-tiered *wadah*, a cremation tower, would be built over the dead.

It was the ashes of one of those I could smell.

In the old days, the pyres were built out of wood. Now, gas cylinders fed the flames to the bier on which the body lay in its white shroud.

It was on such a platform that I had used my gaffer tape and rope to tie a spread-eagled Aja, on top of what was effectively a giant grill.

I was sitting next to the tap that would turn on the gas supply. I was smoking because, as soon as Aja was fully conscious, she would realise it would only take one flick of the cigarette to ignite the flames once I'd switched the valve to open.

How far would you go to save a loved one?

*This far.*

# TWENTY-SEVEN

I pushed the mouthpiece of the baby's drinking cup between Aja's lips and tipped. 'It's just water,' I promised. Although, why she should believe anything I said was a moot point.

She swallowed, gulping the contents down. I knew the drugs would have made a sandpit of her mouth. Her head would be thumping, too. As she drank, her eyes widened and narrowed, trying to put me into focus.

I wondered what she was seeing. The devil, I hoped.

I stepped away and she spoke, but it was long and incoherent. 'English,' I said.

She tried English, but it wasn't much clearer. I sat back down on the wall and waited a few minutes.

'Whatthefuckyoudoin'?'

I got that.

I took a breath. Mainly to stifle the voice in my head telling me I had crossed the line with this poor girl. *Crossed*? I'd leapt over it like I was Jessica Ennis-Hill.

'You know, your pal Bojan, the guy you suckered me into going to see, he said an interesting thing. He said we were members of the same club. The Suffer Club. Membership reassuringly painful. Well, I guess you've just been nominated to join.'

'WheeramI? Lemmego ... let me go, you mad bitch.'

'You, my dear Aja, are tied to a funeral pyre. Underneath you are about fifty gas nozzles. Controlled from here – oh, you can't see. Anyway, trust me, I have a handle that opens the valve. I can't believe how much you people spend on funerals. Are you Balinese?'

'No,' she said. 'Malay.'

'Malay? You're a long way from home. You probably don't believe in this shit, do you? Ah well, we aren't going to run it according to strict Hindu principles anyway. No priest. No offering. No widow to throw herself on the pyre.' Although, I was pretty certain the last tradition had died out, on Bali at least.

'What do you want?' The words were clearer now her anger was driving out the fear. For now.

'What do I *want*?' I took a drag on the cigarette. It was hot and coarse on the back of my throat. Kadek had a strange concept of mild. No wonder they came in packets of just twelve; twenty and you'd have a voice like Clint Eastwood. 'I want Jess.'

'Jess? She not here.' Panicky once more, she began to twist and turn.

'I know that. And keep still. You'll only hurt yourself.'

She gave a bark that might have been a laugh. 'You worry about me hurting when you put me on here? And say you going to burn me alive? You fuckin' mad, lady.'

Point well made. 'Well, I might not. Burn you alive, I mean. Depends how our little chat goes.'

She mumbled to herself in her own language and then began to sob.

'Where's Jess?' I asked, unmoved.

She sniffed. 'I told you. Not here. Not Bali.'

'So where did Matt take her?'

'I don't know! Why not ask Dieter?'

Apart from the fact he's a crooked bastard who wouldn't know the truth if you rolled it up and rammed it down his lying throat? 'Because I don't think he knows. If he did, he would have gone after his cash. I don't think Bojan knows either. Otherwise, he wouldn't be keeping up this charade. But I know Jess.'

*Knew*, a voice inside me admonished. You have no idea what she is like as a person now. I ignored it.

'She would want a friend. A woman. I bet she liked you. Bet she thought you were her friend. My guess is you know more than you're letting on.'

'No.'

'But you did get to know her.' It wasn't a question.

'We went out on boat. Had a good time. But then Dieter ...' She began to cry again, mewing like a deranged cat this time. I stifled the stab of pity I felt for her.

'Dieter, what?'

'He was mad at Matt. He tried, you know ...' The next part came out in a rush. 'He tried to fuck your girl.'

Breathe. Stay calm. It's Dieter who should be up

220

there then. But my reasoning remained sound: Jess was more likely to have confided in Aja than Dieter about where she and Matt might be heading.

'And then?'

'Matt beat him up. Beat him up bad.'

'Matt did?' I asked. 'Matt beat up Dieter?'

'Yes. Matt was mad. Dieter was drunk, stoned. Matt beat him up and then he knew Dieter would kill him so he left. With some of Dieter's money. But not as much as Dieter says. Dieter liar.' That wasn't a hold-the-front-page statement.

'Where to? Where did Matt go?'

'I DON'T KNOW! Let me go . . . I don't know.'

So, Matt had taken Jess to protect her from Dieter. And had actually worked the little street rodent over. Well, good for him, the fucker. One tick in the positive column. There were so many crosses in the negative, though. So many.

I lit another cigarette while I worked on getting my heart rate under control. Damn thing was fluttering in my chest. Probably not as much as Aja's, mind.

'And you have no idea where they went?'

'I tell you over and over. No idea. Let me go. I tell you everything.'

'I don't believe you.'

'I did tell you. All.' More mewing. 'I know nothing more. Please. I won't go to police about this . . .'

'Oh, I'm sure you will. One more chance.'

'I don't know any more. And if I did, Dieter would kill me if I told you.'

That was an odd logic. But panic isn't the best mechanism for clarity of thought. 'I'll kill you if you don't.'

'Please. This is crazy. You crazy.'

'Yes, I think I probably am.'

I turned the valve, heard the gas hiss through the nozzles.

'Singapore! Singapore!' she yelled. 'It's Singapore they went.'

I flicked the cigarette and watched the blue flames dance over the platform as Aja screamed her lungs out.

# TWENTY-EIGHT

'Singapore?'

'That's what she said.'

Freddie's image moved in that jerky FaceTime fash-
ion when the link isn't all that great. The first part of
her sentence was white noise. '. . . dangerous for a man
in his line of work?'

I got the gist. 'Yeah. Not like Bali, then?'

'True enough. What are you doing now?'

'Packing. I'm flying to Singapore first thing.'

'Where do you start?' Freddie asked.

It was a good question. One I really didn't want to
answer, because I didn't have one. 'There'll be a few
people I can tap, someone on the Circuit out there.'
Unless they were in opposition or were rivals, PPOs
mostly supported each other when they could. After all,
you never knew when you might need to call upon the
goodwill of this band of brothers and sisters. 'Maybe
get a heads-up from one of them.'

'I dunno . . .' Freddie grimaced into the camera.

'Got any better ideas?'

'Not yet. How's the girl?'

'Lightly singed. And shaken. Even I didn't expect that.'

'She must have crapped herself.'

'I think *I* nearly did,' I admitted.

'Where is she now?'

'Protective custody. Kadek's uncle is keeping her under lock and key till I leave.'

'Handy contact, that boy.'

'Just business to the uncle. I think I just bought him a year's supply of batik shirts.'

Kadek, in prepping the cremation site, had exchanged the gas cylinder for one filled with compressed air so I could threaten Aja with harmless jets. How was I to know I should have flushed the system first to avoid residual gas remaining in the pipes?

It had only flared briefly as my cigarette ignited it, but it had given both of us a scare.

Though, it had the advantage of convincing Aja I really was a psychopath. And that might just be the truth.

Maybe you had to be one to go up against one.

I had, though, left a stash of money with Kadek for Aja. Enough for her to quit the bars and go home for a while. But I kept that back from Freddie too. I didn't want her to think I'd gone soft.

'What about at your end?' I asked.

'Nothing much. I have one idea about getting a tag on Jess. Something we overlooked.'

'What?' I asked.

Her voice turned metallic and distorted.

'What did you say?'

'Woking.'

I shook my head. Overlooked? I'd clean forgotten it. 'What about Woking?' It never featured on my list of places where she might be. Although, when I first met Matt he was a big Paul Weller fan. Wasn't he from Woking? How ironic would it be if I was running around the Far East and Jess was back home in the commuter belt?

'It might be nothing. Long shot. See the straws there? That's me clutchin' at them. Leave it with me. I'll let you know. Get some sleep, eh? You look like shit.'

'Who looks great on FaceTime?'

She ducked that one. 'And watch your back.'

'I have a police guard,' I admitted. 'One at the gate, one on my veranda.' I didn't mention how much over-time those guys were on, courtesy of Noor's generous pay packet. That money wouldn't stretch too far at this rate.

'Don't you wonder what he's up to? Bojan? He's ...'

The screen froze. Her voice turned Dalek again and began to fragment. 'I'm losing you. We'll speak when I'm in Singapore. OK?'

'Oh ... *cchk*.'

I broke the connection and lay back on the bed, watching the ceiling fan spin and listening to the con-stant churn of insects in the background. Some silence would be nice for a change.

I felt stale, spent. I needed to run with a cold wind

in my face; to swim in icy water; to see my breath cloud in the air atop Parliament Hill Fields. The heat and humidity of this island was sucking the energy out of me.

*Don't you wonder what he's up to?*

Damn right I do. But I had a feeling I'd find out soon enough.

I met a bear once. Why I started thinking about it on the way to Bali's airport, I'll never know. But the image came back to me. It was a summer I spent working for a branch of the Kuwaiti royal family. The princess asked me if I would accompany her on a trip to Woodstock. I agreed, as Oxfordshire wasn't that far to drive and it would make a change from hanging around hotel rooms or the shopping emporia of London. But, being a Kuwaiti princess, she meant Woodstock, New York.

Despite being in her late teens, she was a big fan of Jimi Hendrix, and had seen the movie a dozen times. Still, Jess once told me her generation thought Phil Collins was cool, so it shouldn't have surprised me.

She was a little disappointed with Woodstock itself – I think she might even have preferred Oxfordshire's version – especially when I told her the festival didn't actually take place there. But she also wanted to see some nature, so bought us both hiking boots so we could take a trail up the aptly named Overlook Mountain.

One thing you should never do is tackle a steep, relentless four-kilometre climb in new boots.

When we reached a small flat section, which

contained the spooky husk of a once-glamorous hotel, we ignored the signs about timber rattlesnakes, sat on the remains of a wall, took off our boots and compared blisters.

We knew we didn't have far to go to see the view the mountain is named after, but just as I was contemplating getting back into the boots, I heard a rustling to our right. I turned, and saw a black bear had emerged onto the path, blocking our ascent.

'Don't scream or make any sudden moves,' I said, grabbing her wrist. 'But there is a black bear behind us.'

She stayed remarkably calm. 'What do we do?'

I knew there were two types of bear in this part of US: the brown and the black. 'With one of them, you make as much noise as possible and wave your arms,' I said quietly. 'The other, you climb a tree or play dead.'

'Which one do you do for a black bear?' the princess asked.

'I don't remember,' I replied honestly.

All I could recall was that a black bear can run at 35mph. A rough calculation suggested this was about 27mph more than I could manage, even with a bear on my tail.

The bear glanced at us now and then, but mainly sniffed at the base of a couple of trees, as if trying to decide between them.

We sat there for almost twenty minutes, waiting for this tree-junkie of a bear to get bored. Eventually, it looked up into the branches of its favourite trunk and, with an ease I still can't quite comprehend and a speed that was both impressive and terrifying, it began to climb. With the crack of claw on bark and the odd grunt, it was soon in the upper branches, swaying like an overgrown, swarthy koala.

'Not the climb-a-tree-to-escape species, then,' I said. We hastily put our boots on, and as we did so, I told the old joke about two hikers who are being chased by a bear.

One stops and puts on his running shoes. 'You'll never outrun a bear,' says his companion incredulously.

'I don't have to outrun the bear,' comes the reply. 'I just have to outrun *you*.'

Why that triggered a certainty in me, I'm not sure. But I had a strong feeling that I knew what Bojan's first move would be. In fact, that he had already made it before our meeting at *Bacang*.

'Kadek,' I said, 'we've got a bit of time before my flight, yes?'

'Yes, *Ibu*.'

'Turn around.'

'Why?'

'We're going shopping.'

*At last*, said his smile.

I thought they were going to make the move at the airport. I saw the fat cop from the Blue Turtle and *Bacang* hanging around the check-in desks, but he didn't seem interested in me. That could have been an act.

I went straight to the desk that promised they could whisk my luggage to anywhere in the world. I got an accurate weight and a price for shipping to Singapore, but told the clerk I had decided to keep the case with me instead. I then went through the fast-track to the business lounge.

Thanks to the time spent on my shopping spree, I only had to wait ten minutes until boarding. I didn't actually relax until the doors were closed and the engines were warming up. I wasn't sorry to see the back of Bali. On the other hand, I wasn't looking forward to Singapore much either.

And I was right. It was there that they got me.

I was pulled over from the immigration line by two uniformed officers: one young, the second older and greyer. They introduced themselves as being from the Immigration and Checkpoints Authority. They told me I was being detained under Section 8, Paragraph 109 of the Singapore Statutes Customs Act, which apparently covers search, seizure and arrest.

They took me to a secluded area, still airside, closed off from public view by portable screens, guarded by an armed policeman, and the older guy pointed to a table. I put my case on it and they asked me to unlock it. As I did so, they put on blue gloves.

'Don't worry. It's all clean. The underwear,' I said. Not a flicker. *Kill the humour.*

Both had name badges on their blue and gold uniforms. The older man was Pang, the younger, Lee. The latter was a good-looking kid, with skin I would kill for. He looked like he used a lot of product. Pang, on the other hand, had a sickly grey pallor under the strip lights. He looked like he needed more sleep. I sympathised.

'Is that working?' I pointed to the CCTV orb on the ceiling, which had turned its gaze on me.

'Yes,' confirmed Pang.

'Good.'

The young man glanced up as if he had never noticed the CCTV before and then snapped at me, 'What is the purpose of your visit to Singapore?'

Where to start? I am going to trawl all the low-life dens – even Singapore must have them – until I find someone who remembers Matt or Jess. I'm going to kick down doors and bang heads and, hell, I might just chew some gum without a licence while I'm at it. Instead, I said: 'Tourism.'

'What do you want to see?' asked Pang.

Thank God for in-flight magazines. 'I want to eat soft-shell crab and do the night safari at the zoo. The Jurong Bird Park looks interesting.' They looked sceptical at that statement, but I was serious. I just wouldn't be visiting it. 'I also have a relative buried here.' That last part was actually true.

'Kranji?' asked Pang.

'Yes.'

He nodded gravely; a point in my favour. I stood aside and watched them empty the suitcase and check the lining carefully.

Then they did it again.

They looked puzzled. Disappointed, even.

The two men exchanged a few sharp words. 'We will get a female officer to search you,' said the older man.

'On what grounds?'

'Routine check.'

There was nothing routine about shining lights up my various cavities as far as I was concerned.

'I want the case with me at all times.'

'We will give you a receipt.'

That wasn't going to fly. 'I don't want it out of my sight.' I hoped I was being polite, but firm. 'If it does leave my side, then I want it wrapped and sealed in the presence of witnesses.'

'Why?' asked Pang.

'Just so we all know where we stand.' I knew better than to suggest I didn't trust them. But I didn't.

The only corruption story I had been able to find online about Singapore customs was a scam where two officers had refused to give tourists the Goods and Service Tax refunds they were entitled to, then claimed the GST for themselves later. That didn't mean there weren't other bad apples in the ICA I hadn't read about or who hadn't been caught. They might not be above framing some foreign woman in order to get Employee of the Month.

'You have something to hide?' Lee asked.

'No, I'm just making sure nothing gets hidden on me. I also have evidence of how much my luggage weighed in Bali.' I showed them my receipt. 'Just in case.'

I had double-checked and it was 1.5g of crystal meth that was enough to get you fifteen years in prison in Bali. I guessed it was the same in Singapore. It only took 500g of cannabis to qualify for the death penalty.

Exactly what and how much they had put in my case – or where – I wasn't sure. But when my hotel room was searched while I was dropping Noor at the airport, I would put good money on the intruder, or intruders, not having taken anything. Instead, they left a present behind. Something that these officers had been tipped off about.

Which is why I had thrown away my original suit-case and all my clothes and bought replacements. The only things I kept were some quick-fasten restraints and my roll of silver gaffer tape – neither of which was, as far as I knew, prohibited in Singapore. Although, you could never be sure. They might think it was for use in some sort of sex game.

And all the underwear really was clean – it was brand new. As was every stitch of clothing I stood in. I could have done a search of myself to locate the planted material, but I couldn't take the risk I might miss something.

As I said, it doesn't take much to fuck you up in this part of the world.

I didn't put it quite like that. 'I would guess you had a tip-off from Bali police about me. A blue-on-blue friendly word, right? About me being a drugs mule, with something hidden in my case? Let me tell you, the chummy cop who gave you that information is corrupt. I'm being framed. Someone wants to slow me dow—' The end of the word went missing in action.

'Are you all right?' asked the older man.

I could feel sweat prickle on my forehead, as if I was going to be sick. 'Can I have a drink of water?'

The younger one hurried away. I fetched a chair from the wall behind me and sat.

Now I knew what the game was.

Get me arrested for drugs in Singapore, then publicise it. Bali and its notorious Kerobokan prison was a bit of a black hole – people tended to get swallowed by it for weeks on end.

But news would spread very quickly from Singapore.

Newspapers back home would run stories about the unlikely drug mule, journalists would find out about Matt and Jess and they would track them down.

Bojan would use the power of the press and the indignation of the *Daily Mail* to flush them out.

Clever.

I took the water and gulped it down. Perhaps all that was just my febrile imagination. But if that was his scheme, it was a sly ploy worthy of him.

And I would be powerless to stop it.

Hell, knowing Matt, he might just come out and sell his story to someone. 'Can I go now?'

Pang shook his head. 'Not until you're searched and you have a bowel movement.'

'*What*?'

'You ill because packet burst in stomach?'

'I am ill because of . . .' I tamped down on my anger. 'Because someone is messing with my life and playing you to help do it.'

The female officer arrived, all blank-faced brusqueness. Her name badge said she was called Zhang Goh. She looked me up and down like a piece of meat. 'You come with me.'

'Where to?'

'Central Narcotic Bureau has a facility here. You will be monitored. We make sure you not carrying.' It's a job, I suppose, but not one I'd be first in line for: Shit Inspector, First Grade.

'I want to be able to see that case at all times. And I want it weighed to show it hasn't changed since Bali.'

Zhang looked over at the senior man and Pang nodded his permission. Now, I was acting as if I did have something to hide, but better safe than sorry.

I played what I hoped was a trump card. 'I would also like to call my lawyer.'

'You have a lawyer in Singapore?'

The International Bodyguard Association certainly did and I'd made contact before I'd left Bali. 'In fact, she's waiting landside now.'

There was more talk between the three of them that I couldn't follow. 'Your lawyer can visit you at the CNB facility,' Pang announced.

The younger man had repacked my things and now zipped up the case and handed it over to Miss Sunshine. 'Follow me,' she said.

*

234

To reach Kranji cemetery you head for Malaysia. It is about as far north as you can get on the island of Singapore.

After I had been sprung from the CNB's holding tank – and its charming all-Perspex lavatory bowl – I had checked into my hotel and caught a taxi up there. Singapore was a shock after the chaos of Bali, where nobody seemed capable of walking in a straight line thanks to the narrow, crowded streets. Singapore was the exact opposite. You could probably be fined for *not* walking in a straight line.

The city-state had one thing in common with Bali – it was hot and humid. Kranji overlooked the Johor Strait and the meagre wind that managed to stir itself over the water was very welcome.

I walked past some of the 4,500 tombstones and up to the main memorial. It looked like an aeroplane wing, supported by thirteen uprights. Both sides of those verticals were covered in names. This was a record of a further 24,000 men and women with no known grave, who had been captured when Singapore fell and who had perished in Japanese-run work camps, in prisons or on death marches.

I found my relative on one of the inscription panels. My great-grandfather on my mother's side, Herbert Crane. He had been a banker in Singapore and had joined the Singapore Volunteer Force, part of the Straits Settlements Volunteer Force. After the city fell, he had been imprisoned in Changi and had died there.

I felt hot tears roll down my cheeks. All war graves

do that to me. Anyone who has served in a battle zone knows how easy it is to find yourself in the earth a long way from home.

But I also knew that I was pretty exhausted after the past twenty-four hours and my nerves were shot. I needed some proper, dead-to-the-world rest. But sleep no longer seemed to refresh me. If anything, I awoke feeling more tired and tetchy than before.

I also had another thing to worry about: who was watching me? Like the blind violinist, I had no idea who was out there. If I did find a lead in Singapore's underbelly, wouldn't Bojan or his guys be right behind me?

A party of schoolchildren arrived for a visit, respectful, but still noisy. I wiped my eyes, walked back down among the gravestones and looked out over the flat sea, raising my face to the breeze.

What had I hoped to achieve by coming to the cemetery? To put my problems into perspective? Well, that hadn't worked. I wasn't going to abandon my daughter just because it was only one life among thousands. I would throw myself into whatever cesspits the city could offer.

And if I was being followed, well, I'd find a way to deal with that.

*Not much of a plan, Wylde, eh?*

You got anything better? No, I thought not.

So where to begin? Go the lowest levels of society I could find in Singapore and hope for the best.

Orchard Towers was a good place to start, so the lawyer had advised, maybe Clarke Quay, and somewhere called Geylang.

In Geylang, there were alleys called *lorongs*, she explained. The odd-numbered ones were crammed with basic restaurants selling excellent frog porridge or clay-pot rice. The even-numbered ones were where it would be worth showing a photo of Matt around. She also warned me that talking to the girls outside the area's 'nail bars' – many of which did more than simply apply varnish in the evenings – was a waste of time. Most of them were from mainland China and spoke little English.

Get some local knowledge, she had advised.

I might just do that.

But there was another possibility I had to consider: Matt and Jess had never been in Singapore, or at least, not for any length of time. Aja might have been primed by Bojan to tell me – after a little hesitation to sell the story – that they had gone to Singapore. It might have all been a plan to get me caught with drugs at Changi and trigger the media interest. I guess they hadn't figured on me going full psycho on her to get the information.

I had wandered into a hot zone for my phone and it pinged. I looked at the screen and felt a shock as physical as if I'd been plugged into the mains.

It was just two words, but they made my battered heart soar. It was from Freddie.

*Woking. Bingo.*

# TWENTY-NINE

When we were in Iraq, the big fear, of course, was that the opposition would go chemical. Whether the top brass really thought this or it was just to reinforce the propaganda around Weapons of Mass Destruction, I still don't know.

Our medical regiment was issued with NAPS tablets. It stood for Nerve Agent Pre-treatment Set and we were told by the captain who issued them that it would 'pre-coat' our nerves, delaying the effect of any chemical weapon, allowing us extra time to jab ourselves with a combo pen from our Biological Agent Treatment Set (BATS), which contained the antidote to several nerve agents.

The NAPS, we were told, had to be taken three times a day for a whole week. At the end of that time, our nerves would have more insulation than an HT lead. We were then ordered into the Collective Protection tent, which came complete with airlocks.

As the blister packs of twenty-one tablets were handed out for self-administration, Freddie whispered in my ear: 'Don't take it. Keep it under your tongue if you have to.'

'What?' I hissed back. 'And if one of those Scud missiles is full of Tabun?'

'You just make sure you remember your NBC drill. Don't rely on this. Here's the headline, Buster: the people who took this last time around reckon it poisoned them. If nothing else, the tablets give you terrible shits. And yours are pretty bad as it is.'

Nuclear, Biological and Chemical warfare drills were performed daily. The idea was, you were able to get a breathing mask on within nine seconds and then suit up, complete with overboots and thick, black rubber gloves. Next, you would check your buddy to make sure that their gas-tight seals had seated properly. This gear had yet another bloody acronym: IPE (Individual Protection Equipment). Most squaddies preferred to call it the Noddy Suit.

It was a couple of years after the war had ended that I read about the possible side effects of NAPS, which went beyond temporary loose bowels and nausea into long-term confusion and memory loss. The Ministry of Defence insisted that the NAPS pills administered 'would not have had adverse health effects'. But they would say that, wouldn't they?

Anyway, despite frequent false alarms of 'GAS! GAS! GAS!' the nerve agents never actually rained down on us – who would have thought it would eventually rear its toxic head in Salisbury rather than Basra?

I never took the pills; neither did Freddie. Some

other things we saw – and did – in that war might have fucked us up, but we were in the clear for NAPS. I had always been grateful to Freddie for that small mercy.

And when she said 'bingo', I had to believe I had a full house.

I caught a cab to downtown Singapore, but really, even in that suffocating humidity, I could have sprinted it, given the amount of adrenaline I had coursing through me.

Then, just as we were passing signs for the zoo, I realised I was being dicked.

In my brief tour in Afghanistan – being wounded and pregnant cut that one short – if you were ever out on patrol, or picking up a casualty from another base, or scooping up wounded civilians, then young men on motorbikes would be buzzing around, reporting your every move to the Taliban. It was like being harassed by mosquitoes – you wanted to roll up a newspaper and swat them away.

This meant you always had to come back to base via a different route, if possible. Otherwise, a little IED present might be waiting for you on your return trip.

When these guys picked you up, the expression for it was being 'dicked'. And right now, I was being double-dicked.

I didn't think an IED in the middle of Singapore was a likely outcome, but I was definitely on someone's radar.

One of the pair was in a Mazda, the other on a far-too-distinctive Harley-Davidson Street Rod with lurid yellow rear springs. I had seen that bike before on the outward journey – it was the colour that had stuck in my mind.

Now, the Mazda made a point of overtaking and then dropping back, while the Harley had switched with it. BIP, my old instructor used to call it.

Behavioural Indicators of Pursuit.

Even in civilian life I was haunted by acronyms.

I wondered why they bothered putting a tail on me. After all, it was Singapore, not Texas. There were no wide-open spaces to get lost here in the city-state. And sooner or later I'd be back at the hotel. It could only mean they were convinced I was going to jump ship.

Unless ... maybe it was the CNB – Singapore's drug cops – who were following me, still convinced I was Howard Marks.

The traffic thickened and slowed as we approached the towers of downtown and I watched the Harley accelerate away. Perhaps I had been wrong about that one. Just the Mazda behind. Maybe they didn't need two tails – after all, it was a good bet I was heading back to my hotel.

Then the Mazda saw a break in the traffic a couple of lanes over and dived for it. I shook my head as if I could clear it of the obsessive thoughts piling up in there. *Just paranoia*, I thought.

I was wrong, of course.

I got the cabbie to drop me a block from the hotel rather than pull into the drop-off point. Then, I began to wade through the lunchtime crowds on Orchard Road. I realised that Singapore gave you an edge when trying to spot someone following you. It would be the one person not glued to a screen.

Almost everyone in this well-dressed, neatly coiffured and heavily moisturised crowd had their heads down. Yet, they rarely bumped into each other. It was like they had a human anti-collision mechanism, able to break and swerve to avoid any objects ahead.

Those who weren't looking down, who were maybe watching where they were going, stood out. I, of course, was one of them: it worked both ways.

I spotted one guy who seemed off – a tall, broad-shouldered Westerner with a neat military-style haircut – but he ducked into a fast-food restaurant and joined the queue. I glanced over my shoulder a few times but he stayed put.

I turned into the driveway that led up to the reception of the hotel, then stopped halfway.

Nobody appeared from the street behind me, apart from a Japanese couple, laughing and giggling and oblivious to everything outside their bubble-for-two. I waited a minute and then entered the vast marbled lobby, so air-conditioned it felt chilly after the street, already looking forward to a shower and a change of clothes.

There was no message for me at the desk. I grabbed a *Straits Times* and went and sat by the central fountain with a view of the entrance. Water tinkled along with a nearby piano, its player hunched over the keyboard, tensed, as if he were about to explode into *fortississimo*.

I gave the room a 360. Again, everyone around me was focused on their electronic devices. After five minutes of glancing at the same story, I dumped the paper and went to catch the lift, the secondary bank down a corridor, rather than the obvious ones opposite the concierge.

I pressed for my floor and was about to breathe a sigh of relief when a hand grabbed the closing doors and they reluctantly sprang back.

A guy stepped in. Tall, broad, good-looking, with a military-style haircut, and I knew I was in trouble.

Condition: Red.

# THIRTY

'Queue too long, was it?'

He turned to look at me. 'I beg your pardon?'

'At the restaurant. The one I saw you go in while you were following me. Did you change your mind?'

His hand reached for his jacket but I stepped in, grabbed his wrist and yanked it away, going for the ulnar nerve on the pinkie side. Somehow, he managed to slide his arm from my grasp. With his other hand, he got a sharp palm-blow to my elbow that sent me reeling backwards, shock vibrating down through my ribcage.

A strong one, then.

The self-defence experts offer you all sorts of techniques and tips designed to take down a stronger opponent, but believe me, given the choice, you want the guy to be Woody Allen-sized.

This one wasn't.

I went in with a flurry: a kick that connected, an aim for the head that didn't.

A similar blur of limbs came back at me and I lost ground as I raised my elbows to parry him. The only thing that saved me was his rhythm: he came in with a highly practised sequence of moves that was forceful, but predictable. I managed one quick thrust to his head with my fingers, going for his eyes, but he leaned back and I ended up barely brushing him. Then, he used his knees against my thighs, one-two, and my legs decided it was time to lie down.

I got a punch to his neck and used it less to hurt him than to propel myself back, out of his immediate reach.

'Eleventh floor,' cooed the lift and gave its little ding.

The ride from the lobby had seemed to take a Methuselah's age to reach my floor.

As it glided to a halt with barely a shudder, we were on opposite walls of the lift, leaning against the panels that advertised the hotel bar's happy hour on my side and the spa on his.

We were both panting, me more than him.

Not good.

I knew that if the fight continued, unless I got really lucky, I would lose. He had blood on his cheek where one of my nails had caught him under the eye – unlucky for him because I keep my nails short – but I had a throbbing shoulder, sore forearms from blocking his blows and a burning spot of pain on each thigh.

The doors slid open. Standing there was a young, moon-faced woman behind a trolley of dirty room-service trays, most of them reduced to unappetising debris. She pushed in between us and we both stepped out.

The woman giggled. Of course. Two people, sweaty

and panting, who have obviously just unclenched from each other as the doors parted. Lovers. What else could be going on?

The corridor was quiet. The lamps lining it were a modern take on Chinese lanterns and gave my assailant's skin a reddish glow.

There was amusement in his eyes. He was enjoying this.

My room was just a few dozen metres behind me, but I couldn't turn and run. He'd be on me in a second, like a cheetah bringing down a gazelle.

I did the only thing I could: I went into a defensive crouch.

'Rusty,' he said.

'Been a while,' I admitted, keeping my eyes on his limbs, waiting for a tell-tale tightening of muscle or a shift in balance before the move came.

'Even so. He said you were good.'

'Who did?'

'The Colonel.'

He took his time to relax, just in case I did anything dumb. It was a sort of uncoiling from ready-to-strike to stood down. Now it was my turn to enjoy something: watching a professional who had control of his major muscle groups. And from what I could make out, there were plenty of muscles under that suit. Some of them had hurt me, I reminded myself.

I, on the other hand, stayed in my defensive crouch. 'Which Colonel?' I asked.

'Colonel d'Arcy,' he said. I couldn't place the accent.

'Your lawyer contacted him. She was worried about you. Said you were . . .'

'Said I was what?' I asked, tetchier than intended.

'Running solo. No back-up. Which, as you know, is not always the smart way. Not out here. So he asked us to keep an eye on you.'

'Us?'

'Obsidian.'

Now I let some of the air leak out of me, just a little. Obsidian Solutions, to give them their full title. I had the accent now.

'Mossad?'

A non-committal shrug. Mossad was like Fight Club. Ex-agents didn't talk about their time in Mossad; they didn't even confirm they knew what it was. What was Hebrew for *omertà*?

'How many of you on the job?'

'Just me and some local talent. I was reaching for my card when you went chopsocky on me.'

'Krav Maga,' I said. He should know. The self-defence and fighting system was an Israeli invention.

His eyes twinkled as he laughed. When he smiled, only one side of his mouth went up, turning it into a sneer. It wasn't a comforting look. 'As I said, rusty. Look, can we do this over a coffee?'

I held out my hand. 'Give me the card.'

He extracted it slowly and passed it over. It was black, of course, with gold embossed writing. I kept my fingers away from that. It said his name was Nate Segal. Maybe it was.

I took out my phone and called the Swiss number I knew by heart. I kept my eyes on the guy. 'Colonel? Sam. You sent a Mossad gorilla after me?'

'I sent you Obsidian. I was worried—'

'Let's not get into that. Can you give me a heads-up? There's someone here called Nate Segal.'

'That's the guy.'

'Can you give me confirmation?'

'Ask him to do his party piece. You'll never forget it.'

I took the phone away from my ear. 'Do your party piece.'

'Is he sure? Are *you* sure?'

'I'm sure,' I said.

He reached up and did something I couldn't quite believe.

'Sam?' I heard the colonel say.

'Yeah, OK, thanks. I'll speak later.' I clicked the phone off. I probably *would* remember it for the rest of my life.

'Maybe something stronger than coffee?'

'Coffee will be fine.'

I was so distracted I almost forgot to check my room. I gave my luggage a once-over. Nothing disturbed. It all seemed pretty clean, apart from one thing: the chair in front of the desk where I had left the laptop was warm. Barely warm, but still some faint residual radiation brushed my hand. I looked at the position of the window. No sun could have caused it. There was an indentation in the leather, too.

Someone had been sitting there, and quite recently.

'This you?' I asked Segal.

'What?'

'Been sitting here?'

'Not me. First time in your room.' He walked over to the window and looked down over the gardens. 'Nice.'

So who? I thought back to the woman who had entered the lift between us. Maybe it was just a cleaner taking the weight off for a minute.

Maybe.

'I'll do the coffee,' I said.

'Black is fine.'

'You sure this wasn't you?'

Now he came over and examined the work station himself. He pointed at the computer and then ran a finger over his throat. The laptop could have been tampered with by whoever sat in the seat. Something might have been inserted to relay keystrokes to another terminal; the microphone could have been activated and linked to voice-recognition software that would transcribe everything we said. Or, there could be a bug elsewhere in the room.

Without specialist equipment we would probably never find it.

I scooped the computer up off the table, placed it at the bottom of the bathtub and ran the water until it was covered. It might just be paranoia, but once it takes hold, it's hard to stop the spread of suspicion.

What if the laptop was a feint? What if we were meant to find it?

'We have to move,' I said. 'I'll call down and get us a day room.'

We decamped to a room along the corridor on the opposite side. I took my RTG bag, just in case. While I made the coffee, Nate made sure the room was clean – even though nobody had any time to plant anything, it could always have been pre-bugged.

It was one of those pod machines. It took a while for me to figure it out and get two cups. We talked while I did so. After Nate had given the room the once-over, he sat on the edge of the bed and explained how he had become involved.

'So, Jacinta the lawyer called the Colonel who called you to watch my back?' I summarised.

'That's about the size of it. Jacinta said she was worried you might ... well, "go off like a nuke" is how she put it. So, calls were made. Oh, then you attacked me in the lift.'

Well, it was a dumb way to approach a fully loaded and cocked PPO, I wanted to say, but didn't.

'What's Obsidian doing in this part of the world?' I knew the company, of course, but they usually stuck to contracts in the US, the Middle East, some of the 'Stans and South Africa.

'Expanding,' he said. 'Singapore is the head field office for Southeast Asia. We have offices in Bangkok, some of the larger Thai islands, Hong Kong and Kuala Lumpur.'

*Offices* might mean anything from one lonely guy

and a phone, up to the sort of mirrored tower blocks that surrounded us.

Now I remembered what Obsidian was up to. A downpage article in one of the security magazines saying it was recruiting Mandarin speakers, not a skill common among PPOs. 'But the ultimate aim is China?'

He laughed. 'One day, maybe.'

Obsidian Solutions were in the crisis-management business, and China had a whole new raft of entrepreneur billionaires. The sort of people who, one day, would have crises that needed managing, even if they didn't know it yet. As yet, outfits like Obsidian weren't welcome in mainland China. But Hong Kong was a useful foothold.

'So, how much do you know?' I asked.

'About you?'

'About what I am up against.'

'I have a rough idea.'

I smoothed off some of the information. I told him about the two fights with Bojan at the Russian's house in Hampstead; how he ended up with a knife in him that should have meant he bled to death; how he was intent on finding Jess before I did and selling her to some of the arseholes who were out there doing whatever gets arseholes off.

'That's fucked up,' Segal said. 'I'm sorry. About your daughter.'

'Yeah.' I handed him the coffee. It was late afternoon and I felt my stomach rumble. I was forgetting to eat, which was stupid. I also fancied a drink. Even more stupid.

'What happened?' I asked, pointing at my own cheekbone. 'To the face.'

His 'party piece' was to remove an upper half-denture. What came with it appeared to be one side of his face. As he'd removed it, his eye had dropped and his cheek caved in. 'It's called an obturator. Meant to be temporary. They are printing a 3-D version and I'll get a permanent titanium one.'

'That's not what I asked.'

He gave a little smile as he sipped his drink. I could see now that not all the muscles in his face worked correctly. Hence the tendency to sneer.

'Sniper round. In through the zygomatic arch. Bounced around a bit, punctured the sinuses, took out the palate and some teeth and other bits and pieces, came out under here.' He indicated beneath his jawbone.

The coffee soured in my mouth. 'Jesus. Where were you?'

He raised an eyebrow to let me know I shouldn't ask and he wasn't going to answer anyway.

'But that was the end of your Mossad career?'

That smirk again. 'What Mossad career?'

'OK, have it your own way. You hungry?' I asked as my stomach made a plughole gurgle.

'I guess.'

I picked up the cordless phone, found the room-service menu and handed it to him. He put the coffee down and opened it up.

It was then I hit him with my elbow on that zygomatic arch of his.

I felt bad. It must have been like a grenade going off in his head, judging by the noise he made. I followed it up with a blow behind the ear using the handset.

Segal had a thick neck and he didn't go down. But he had lost a bit of fight, and I managed to retrieve the cable tie I had extracted from my luggage when inspecting it for signs of disturbance, and tighten it around his wrists.

He used a double-fisted swing to catch my face and my vision swam. I stabbed with my stiff fingers into his solar plexus as hard as I could. It was pretty hard and the air exploded out of him.

I managed to get a loop of my trusty silver gaffer tape around his feet and I finished the job with various cords from the phone, kettle and TV. By the time I was done, he was hog-tied to the leg of the bed.

'What … what the fuck are you playing at? Is this how you treat your friends?'

'You're not my friend.'

'The Colonel is.'

I shook my head. 'The Colonel doesn't really have friends. Neither do you. Just clients. And right now, I don't know who your client is. I'm going to have to gag you.'

'I can't breathe through my nose,' he said, panic in his voice.

I taped his arms to his side and shoved a pair of tights in his mouth. 'Good a time as any to learn. I won't be long, then we can talk some more. For the moment, I can't have anyone looking over my shoulder. It's nothing personal, OK?'

He tried to say something and I pulled the tights out. 'You fuckin''—' I put the tights back in. He went to bite me.

'Do that again and I'll pull the rest of your teeth out.'

I found a sewing kit in a drawer and punched holes in a length of tape with the seam ripper. I took out the tights and placed the perforated tape across his mouth.

All heart, that's me.

But he'd still have to breathe through his nose some.

Then I went to call the only person I knew I could trust absolutely.

Orchard Tower was a short walk from my hotel. It was apparently known as 'Four Floors of Whores', although that was only true at night when the bars opened. During the day, there were also nail bars – real ones, not like in Geylang – tailors and cobblers and watch repairers doing business.

There was also, according to my phone, an internet café.

How such a quaint institution could survive when the whole population was mainlining into the internet 24/7 baffled me.

The puzzle deepened as I entered. There were eight cubicles, each with a computer terminal and an assortment of printers and copiers, and a guy behind the desk wearing headphones. No customers. A state of affairs that, judging by the dust on some of the keyboards, was not uncommon.

He removed his headphones long enough to give me a log-in code and take my money, and then he went back to his Thai heavy metal, which was fine by me.

It would be close to midnight at home, but I knew Freddie wouldn't mind. I opened up my Skype account and dialled her. I had to assume some of my electronic life was secure. This was a crazed Serbian I was up against, not the FBI. *But you did just turn over an ex-Mossad guy. He'll have friends in low places ...* Yeah, but he wasn't going anywhere for the minute. Although, I hoped I hadn't suffocated him.

Freddie appeared dressed in a baggy T-shirt with faded writing on it and a face scrubbed of make-up, obviously ready for bed. 'You OK, Buster?' she asked.

'I might be. You alone?'

'He ate, shot and left. It's all you want in a man.'

It was only the 'left' part that interested me. 'How are the injuries?'

She held up a still-plastered wrist – at least now she could waggle her fingers – then leaned back and swung a leg on the desk. It landed with a thump that rocked the computer and sent her image haywire for a second. It looked like she was wearing a ski boot. 'It makes the reverse cowboy tricky.'

'I'm sure. Bingo?'

She gave a lazy smile, pleased with herself. 'Bingo.'

'How? And what?'

'The how is Woking, like I thought ...'

'Come on, Freddie, don't be coy.'

She held up her phone, close to the computer's camera. I could see a head and shoulders on the screen. It was someone I had dreamed about giving a good kicking to. And not only in my dreams.

It was Laura, the au pair who had helped engineer the whole kidnap of Jess with my ex-husband.

I couldn't speak for a second or two and I wasn't sure whether I was going to laugh or burst out sobbing. Eventually, I managed to squeak: 'You found Laura?'

'She once said that her dad ran a cab firm in Woking. You remember? So, I reckoned that might have been the truth. Well, back then there were lots of cab firms in Woking. Until Uber came along. Now, it's really easy to narrow it down. But you don't want to talk about Uber to Dad, let me tell you.'

'You found her father?'

'And told him I was an old travelling companion heading back out and would like to hook up with her back in Asia.'

'And he told you where she is?'

'Where she *isn't*. She's not in Asia.'

'Fuck.'

'She's in London. Doing a masters in psychology.'

'So you took that picture?'

'Better. I have video.'

'Of Laura?'

'Yes. To you.'

'Wow,' was all I managed over building excitement.

'She says she's sorry.'

'Fuck her. Did you call the police?'

'No, I didn't. I wanted her to talk. Shall I play you the video?'

'Is that all she does? Apologise?'

'More or less.'

'So where are Matt and Jess?' Christ, if they were back home ...

'Still out there. Laura left him. Apparently, he couldn't keep his eyes off other women.'

That sounded familiar. 'It's not his eyes they need to worry about. Where is he, Fred?'

'Not in Singapore.'

I groaned.

'Never?'

'Laura says not that she knows of. Said a man like Matt would never fit in a place like that. You've been played, Sam.'

'I figured as much. Bojan. Maybe the girl, too. They set me up so I'd be arrested in Singapore for possession of drugs. I think they figured the media furore might flush out Matt and Jess.'

'And I thought you were fucked up.'

'Yeah. Only my suspicious mind saved me.'

'We can't go without suspicious minds,' she said.

'If I am in the wrong place, then where is she, Freddie? Where's Jess?'

'You're not going to do anything stupid?'

'What, more stupid than I've been already?'

'You played out the leads as they came, Sam. That's all. I think you went too far with the funeral pyre. That was fucked up. I'm worried you are going to overstep the mark again. I think you should come home and regroup. Please. You look like shit.'

I growled at her. 'If I have to come home to find out where she is, it won't be to regroup, Fred.'

She shook her head as if I were a petulant child. Perhaps I was.

She held up a piece of paper to the camera. She had written the location down. It took me a while to read it. I realised tears had fogged my vision. 'I'd best book a flight.'

In the end, she played me the video. Laura was contrite, but it didn't assuage my anger at her one iota. She had contrived, with the man she now knew to be a dog's ball sack, to poison my daughter's mind; to turn her against me and let her be taken out of the country. It didn't help that Freddie finished up with this: 'The thing is, she's really well. So Laura claims. Jess is really happy, Sam.'

No, the fuck, she isn't. I didn't want to hear that. I wanted to hear she was missing me; was waiting for the day I'd walk in and take her home. How could she be *happy*? The lying cow.

I did some searches on the internet and then told the desk guy I wanted to buy the hard drive. He looked perplexed. I offered him more than the piece of shit computer was worth and he dismantled it and handed me the drive. Once I was certain I wasn't being tagged, I walked through the crowds and the muggy air to Fort Canning Park and dumped it in the lake.

Back at the hotel, I asked the concierge to search for flights to Hong Kong at around eight or nine o'clock that evening and went back up to the room.

I shouldn't have been surprised, but Nate Segal, the ex-Mossad man, was gone.

# THIRTY-ONE

*You're going mad, woman. What if that Obsidian guy was on the level?*

What if he wasn't?

*I think you could have given him the chance.*

And wait until it was too late?

*He was from the Colonel.*

Who knows the Colonel's motivation? Maybe he blames me for his son's death.

*Unlikely.*

And anyway, all that lot, your Obsidians and the Colonel, they work for whoever pays the most. Guys for hire. What if he got a better offer? From Bojan?

*You overreacted.*

I'm trying to find my fuckin' daughter. I suppose I had promised myself I'd be professional, calm, detached.

I lied.

My inner voice wasn't entirely wrong. I shouldn't have taken Segal down quite so viciously. Moderation had been called for, but I seemed to have lost that setting. I could go from zero to extreme in less than a second. And now I had another guy I'd pissed off out on the streets.

The announcement snapped me back into the world, which was yet another airport.

'Passengers flying to Hong Kong on Cathay Pacific flight 636 . . .'

My flight. I was already at the gate, ready to clock my fellow passengers as they arrived. I had checked in a bag – unusual for me, as I like to move quickly on the other side – and had a small carry-on. I was dressed in light colours for a change: cream cotton trousers, flat shoes and a sleeveless blouse with a blue linen jacket over the top. I had make-up on; had taken some time with my eye concealer. I still looked drawn and tired in the mirror, but I was halfway to being scrubbed-up nice.

*And mentally? How's that looking, girl?*

Fuck you.

The holding pen quickly filled up with a mix of business people catching the last flight home, backpackers and regular holidaymakers. I scanned faces, looked at luggage and watched body language. Nobody so much as glanced my way. But then, the good ones wouldn't be so obvious.

*You're losing it, you know that? Paranoid.*

Now that one, that guy with the grown-out military buzz cut and white shirt and chinos – maybe him. He looked like a younger version of Mr Mossad. Probably still had all his own teeth, though.

He didn't catch my eye, but sat where he had a good

view of me if need be. I stood, went over to the vending machine, got myself a bottle of water and sat back down. Either he was very good or he genuinely wasn't interested in me. It was annoying that I couldn't tell.

An announcement I didn't understand was followed by some of the more smartly dressed passengers striding forward to have their passports checked.

'Ladies and gentlemen, we invite those travelling in our First and Business cabins . . .'

Not me, then. Back of the bus. As the line shortened, they invited Premium Economy passengers to board. Finally, Economy. I watched Mr Buzz Cut. He knew it was pointless rushing through, that you just have to stand in line in the jetway as the passengers bottlenecked.

At least, I hoped that was why he was holding back.

It was down to just three of us now and I was beginning to think that maybe the bearded bloke in the checked shirt was the one. In the end, they both got up and approached the boarding counter. At which point, I stood and briskly walked four gates down and strolled through to my flight to Bangkok, the one I had booked online after talking to Freddie.

It was due to leave ten minutes after the Cathay, so I was cutting it fine. Not that the Hong Kong flight would be on time, not when it was discovered it had a passenger no-show and a suitcase somewhere in the hold belonging to her. Not particularly nice, I know, but checking in luggage is one way of demonstrating to any observer that you are serious about getting on that flight.

And, no, the booking system isn't sophisticated enough – yet – to pick up when someone has made two separate bookings on different airlines using the same passport.

Coming soon, apparently.

They should get a move on. You really can't trust people.

I breezed through onto the Thai Airways flight as the next-to-last passenger, in front of a large American woman who was bellowing down the phone, giving instructions to her son who, I gathered, would be waiting for her at the other end. Nobody else followed me through.

Bingo indeed.

It was early morning by the time I made it to Koh Samui, via Bangkok. The island had one of the cutest airports I had ever seen, like a Disney version of a Thai village. But I was too exhausted to take it in. It didn't help that a sack of eels had burst in my stomach. I knew, could feel, that I was getting nearer to Jess. I hadn't felt it in Bali or in Singapore, but now, on this holiday island, my skin had a life of its own, stretching and itching and squirming.

While I had been on the plane, Freddie had been busy. As I cleared customs, there was a driver waiting for me; a young woman, holding up a card with 'Dust Buster Ltd' written on it. Better than holding up a sign with my name across it.

I went over and said I was from the company, and

she replied: 'My name is Hom. Excuse me, but I need to know what a Hesco is.'

'Blast wall,' I said without thinking, as Freddie knew I would. Hesco barriers were used around Forward Operating Bases in Iraq and Afghanistan. The very name made me shudder. I could smell the vile dust – a mix of sand and shit – that blew through the camps, as fine as ash, insinuating its way into every crevice. It would never leave me.

When I answered correctly, she bowed and tried to take my case. I kept hold of it. She was half my size and as willowy as a twig; there was no way I was going to follow behind while she carried my luggage.

'I need a coffee,' I said. Which was true enough, but I had other reasons for delaying our exit. Never rush out of airports or train stations. They are expecting that. Take your time, look around. Nine times out of ten any tag team will slip up and show themselves if you do something to confound them. Like dawdle.

So, we sat at one of the few tables at a stall selling drinks and snacks, and watched the concourse slowly empty.

I asked Hom about herself. She was not from the island, but the mainland at Surat Thani, where her family still lived in a traditional village with her younger siblings. Her father had cancer and she was working as a guide to pay for his treatment. She made it sound as if she had prostituted herself and admitted she was disillusioned with tourists.

When it looked like I had been overcautious, we

went to the van in the car park. We had a driver, Chai, a sinewy, sour-faced man in his fifties wearing nylon tracksuit bottoms and a Nike top, who wrestled the bag off me. He didn't seem thrilled at having been kept waiting so long after the flight had arrived.

Hom explained that Freddie had hired a villa for me attached to a hotel to the west of Bophut Beach in somewhere called Mae Nam. The borderline-surly Chai would be my driver and there was 24-hour security for the villa.

Koh Samui turned out to be another shop-soiled paradise. From the drive past joyless strips of hostels, massage parlours, moped rentals and fast-food joints, I had the sense I was at least a quarter-century too late to see the island at its best. Perhaps the hinterland would be better, but the section from the airport seemed like an assault on the senses; a riot of naked, gouging capitalism, the tourist hustle made solid.

What was Matt doing in a place like this? One clue was the number of backpackers wandering the streets and riding the rental mopeds, clones of the ones I had seen all over Asia. These weren't the real adventurers or pioneers. Like me, they were way behind the beat.

They were here for Koh Samui, but also the various parties at Koh Phangan, somewhere else that had lost its innocence to mass commercialism and various moon parties. But I reckoned the key to Matt's interest was 'mass'.

All those kids getting out of their heads needed chemicals to do it, even if it was only the local *yaa baa*.

Matt was just the guy to help out a new friend. And he had, according to Laura, got a niche market.

'Where do you hire a boat to Koh Phangan?' I asked.

'Ferry?' asked Hom.

'No, private. Speedboat.'

'Lots of places,' said Chai, suddenly finding his tongue. 'But best is Samui Speedwave. Good price. It not far.'

'I don't want one now,' I said firmly. 'I'm just curious. Maybe we'll have a look later.'

'Yes, boss.'

'There are lots of other speedboats,' Hom said.

Chai glared at her. He clearly had some deal going with Speedwave.

I didn't mind which one I started with. Laura had said Matt was the go-to drugs guy for one of the operators to Koh Phangan. I only had to show Matt's picture to the right racket for them to tell me which stone he was living under. But first, I needed to recharge some very flat batteries.

I felt my head dropping as Chai negotiated the traffic.

I was no good to Jess like this. I needed a shower and at least an hour's sleep. Two would be better.

I closed my eyes and dozed, my rest made choppy by the stink and dust, the thrum of Chinook rotors and the cries of wounded soldiers I could never reach.

The villa was vast – four bedrooms – built in a modern European style. It could have been in Ibiza rather than Thailand, except for the wall art and the heavy teak furniture. It also had a pool where you could put in some serious lengths, if you were so inclined. It overlooked a small section of beach pounded by a rough section of ocean. There were 'No Swimming' signs on the path down to the water's edge. Hence the generous pool, I guessed.

In truth, I didn't care. I wasn't going to be swimming.

I was beat. It might seem that it was procrastination to strip, shower and slide between the sheets, but I knew from my army days what exhaustion could do. I'd been paralysed by indecision when trying to choose between saving a boy with his brains leaking out or another with his legs in tatters.

It's a tough call.

I went with legs, lost the brains. You wonder sometimes if that was the right way round.

Christ, we were losing so many arms and legs at one point that some soldiers went out with tourniquets already in place, one on each limb, so they could tighten them themselves if need be.

Now that's pessimism.

But the IEDs were merciless. You got thirty, forty, fifty wounds per soldier, all filled with dirt and shit from the trenches or culverts where they were laid. It took a long time to sterilise them, let alone try to deal with their massive tissue damage. Give me a nice, clean bullet wound any day.

As the tiredness took hold, you started to hate the army, the war, the government, the locals, the dust, the blood, that smell ... And then, after eight hours of being dead to the world in an accommodation pod, you'd go back out and do it all again. Because you knew if you didn't choose to save the one with the ruined legs – the head injury was too far gone – then maybe nobody would.

And there is one thing that all those amputations and penetrating wounds masked; one thing the media never quite got over to the British public – the medical support worked incredibly well given the conditions.

In any other war, right up to and including the Falklands, many, many soldiers would not have survived the terrible traumas they did in Iraq and Afghanistan.

So, if I was going to work at anything approaching my highest level, I needed to let my brain and body rest. Jess would have to wait. It was logic over emotion. Call me a bad mother.

Then again, what kind of Personal Protection Officer can't protect herself? That's what I felt when I woke up to the smell of cigarettes and the sight of Mr Mossad, dressed in a light-blue tropic-weight suit and striped shirt, sitting at the foot of my bed.

Nate Segal blew smoke into the air as I shuffled to sit up, pulling the sheet to my throat. I didn't ask how he got past hotel security. He was a pro. They weren't.

'That hurt,' he said, pointing at his face. There was some discolouring around his right eye where my elbow had made contact.

'Sorry. But it turns out you *can* breathe through your nose.'

'You didn't know that.'

'Calculated risk.'

'With my life.'

I shrugged. 'How come you got here so fast?'

'The leaving a false trail with the concierge; the last-minute plane switch. Pretty good,' he said. 'For an amateur. But it wasn't hard to access CCTV footage showing what you had actually done. I was on a flight forty-five minutes after you.'

I felt disappointed in myself. I must have been tired. 'I didn't see the tail from the airport this end.'

'There wasn't one.'

I ran through the alternatives. 'The girl? Hom?'

The inclination of his head told me I was right. 'Her dad is very sick. And very poor. Don't blame her. We offered her a lot of money.'

'How did you get to her?' After all, Freddie had booked her.

'You really think we don't know which transport agencies you people use on this island? Your friend went for one of three recommended by IBA. We have someone in each one. It wasn't hard to guess which pick-up you were. Single woman. Code word. But you could have saved me all that trouble just by having a little faith.'

'Look, I said I'm sorry. Sorry I don't – can't – trust anyone. I had no idea if you were for or against me.'

'And the Colonel?'

'Or him. I know it sounds disloyal—'

'Very, after all he has done for you. He was

very disappointed when I told him about the stunt you pulled.'

I didn't have the time or inclination to worry about hurt feelings or sore sinuses. 'Can you get me a robe? I need to get going.'

He shook his head. 'I'm sorry, I can't let you do that.'

And this time, instead of a business card, he pulled a gun out of his jacket.

# THIRTY-TWO

I wasn't bothered about being naked. I had fought naked before. It was part of my training. It had to be, because human beings are conditioned to protect their modesty rather than defend themselves or go on the offensive. The Colonel had insisted we break that inhibition. Hell, I had tackled Bojan in not much more than a bra.

No, it was the whole mechanism of getting out of the bed that bothered me. Throwing back the sheet, swinging off the bed, taking the five or six long strides I would need to reach him. Or, managing to arch my back and do a forward spring – if the mattress was firm enough to let me – which would be quicker, but not by much.

But he did something that made either move redundant.

He threw the gun on the bed so that it landed next to me.

'Sorry,' Segal said again,' I can't let you go out without some back-up.'

I stared at it. I didn't recognise it. An automatic pistol

that looked a little like a Walther PPK that had been put through the hot wash.

'It's a Bersa Thunder,' he said. 'Argentinian. Chambered for the .380.'

'I'd have preferred a nine mil,' I said.

His eyebrows went up in surprise. 'Is that a beggar I hear choosing?'

'Sorry. Just that it's pretty small.'

'Designed for concealed carry. Light, with a rounded trigger guard that won't snag on clothing. There's a manual safety on the slide and a de-cocker, so you won't blow a hole in your hip. I have to ask ... what do you have on the Colonel? I've never known him give second chances.'

Oh, it was a lot more chances than that. 'A winning personality,' I said, picking up the weapon.

It felt too light for me. A .380 cartridge would cause quite the recoil on that frame. Personally, I'd have gone for the Jericho that Mossad use. But that was big and bulky and probably not best suited to carrying around a holiday island.

I dropped the magazine. Eight rounds. Not a lot by modern standards, but enough for my needs. In fact, I hoped to return it unfired. 'Thanks for this.'

'His idea, not mine. And it's not for show. The Colonel says Oktane has been activated.'

'You know there is more than one? Oktane is an assassination franchise.'

'I was aware of that.' He said it as if I had made derogatory remarks about his mother.

'It means a contract has been taken out on someone. Is that me?'

'He doesn't know.'

'When was this?'

'Within the last twenty-four hours.'

'That gives us some time. He would have to travel from Europe to here. Assuming there are no Oktane franchises in this part of the world.'

'I've never heard of one. There's a guy who operates out of Tokyo, but we know where he is. And you've got your Cambodians, but they tend to be domestic, maybe Laos and Vietnam. Plus, the drug people keep them fully occupied. So you're ahead of the game.'

'As long as I'm ahead of Bojan.'

Segal stubbed out his cigarette. 'Speaking of whom.'

He reached down to an item at his feet that I couldn't see because of the bed's teak footboard. I heard the sound of a zip. He tossed a transparent plastic folder over to me containing an official-looking document. 'You should read that. Some old friends sent it over.'

I could well imagine who his old friends were. I wondered how much not being part of Mossad hurt. Being on the outside always did, no matter how ambivalent you felt at the time. Being out in the world, doing security for rich arseholes, was a poor substitute for saving your country. Something I knew only too well.

I was keen to be on my way, especially now I was tooled up and rested, so I said: 'Can you give me the edited highlights?'

He lit a second cigarette without asking. 'What do you know about him? Bojan?'

'He's a Serbian thug.'

'He might be now. But he was one of the Šakali, the Jackals, who operated in Kosovo.'

'The Jackals were arrested and charged.'

'And Bojan was jailed under his real name of Saša Stanic. Press reports say that he, his wife and child were killed in a car accident when he was given compassionate leave for his mother's funeral. They weren't. At least *he* wasn't. You've heard of them? The Jackals? They were like the Scorpions. Paramilitary scum.'

I'd heard of them and about their actions. 'He once boasted to me about the number of women they had raped.'

'The Jackals were hardly the first to weaponise rape over there, but they were very good at it. It was designed to drive the Albanians out of Kosovo. But Bojan likes to play games.'

I knew that. When I first met him, I thought he was just another production-line, boneheaded enforcer.

I was wrong.

After all, it transpired he had contrived a scheme to murder a colleague he suspected was going to sell him out to the International Court of Human Justice in The Hague. He had also, after I had beaten him in a fair fight, engineered a rematch to kick my ass once and for all. Which didn't end well for him.

And now the whole catch-her-if-you-can shtick with Jess.

Yes, he liked to play games.

'He was the Jackals' intelligence officer,' Segal continued. 'They usually put female agent provocateurs into the rape camps who would promise the inmates an escape. They let them get a kilometre or two down the road before they sprung their trap. It crushed the women's resistance. And you've heard of the Yellow House?'

I shook my head. Whatever it was, it didn't sound good.

'The Yellow House was – still is, for all I know – a farmhouse near a place called Burrel in Albania. The story is that ethnic Serbs, captured by Kosovans, were transferred there to have their organs harvested. It was supervised by a Turkish doctor, now believed to be in London. Basically, the fittest young men who had been captured were selected, driven into Albania and had their vital organs sold on the black market. The Yellow House was a farm, all right, but an organ farm.'

'Really?' It sounded like atrocity propaganda to me.

'Really. Well, really, *apparently*. In 2010, a report by Swiss prosecutor Dick Marty to the Council of Europe said there were "credible, convergent indications" of an illegal trade in human organs going back over a decade. Which was true. Except, it was the other way around. The Serbs were harvesting the Kosovans and Albanians, but shouting louder than anyone else that their guys were being butchered for spares. A warm body was worth about forty-five thousand dollars, all in. Anyway, it was Bojan who came up with the decoy plan, sending out false reports, phony documentation, bribing witnesses. Nobody found any evidence at the Yellow House because it was never used for organ harvesting. Classic misdirection – they were looking in the wrong place.'

'So the Albanians were innocent?'

He laughed. 'They were innocent of using the Yellow House. In fact, the KLA and the Albanian mafias decided that, as they were being accused of harvesting and nobody believed their denials, they might as well get in on the act. By the time the war ended, both sides were doing it to their prisoners. Until there was almost a glut of illegal kidneys available in the early noughties.'

'What about the doctors involved?'

'As I said, one of them is believed to be in London. Probably has a practice in Harley Street. The other, from Azerbaijan, was arrested for trial by the special tribunal in Kosovo, but released for lack of evidence. There were probably more medics we didn't know about.'

It occurred to me then that maybe somewhere in there was the answer to how Bojan had survived the nasty knife wound I thought killed him. No NHS hospital for him. He had medical back-up on the ground in London; men who, given their past, wouldn't be in any position to refuse help or ask too many questions.

I flicked the folder. 'Why would Mossad keep notes on a Balkan war?'

'It keeps notes on every war. Any conflict is like throwing acid around – you never know who is going to get splashed and burned. Plus the majority of

Kosovan Albanians are Sunni Muslims. We are always interested in Muslim groups, especially when they make their money from drugs and slavery.'

'So you're telling me this ...?'

'Just so you know what sort of man you are up against. Not just a thug. A clever thug.' He nodded towards the file. 'There's more in there. It's not all an easy read.'

'I'll look at it later. Right now I have to see a man about a powerboat.'

I flipped back the sheets, stood and padded to the bathroom, scooping up some clean underwear as I went.

'The tits could be bigger,' I heard him shout.

I guess I could let him have that one for the assault in the last hotel room we shared. 'Sorry to disappoint. Just trying to bring some beauty into an ugly world.'

He laughed at that, although I wasn't sure whether it was sarcastic or not.

I cleaned my teeth and went back out to finish dressing. Segal was gone. He was making a habit of disappearing from my hotel rooms. But I had a feeling I'd be seeing him again.

I went out with a shoulder bag containing what was left of my restraints, the depleted roll of gaffer tape and the pistol that Segal had given me. I also had a list of the key speedboat operators to Koh Phangan who service the gatherings of the Moon Children on Rin Beach.

There were quite a number running tourist boats.

More than I expected. But, the concierge told me, most who went over now were not the poor hippy *farangs* of old, but rich kids who shunned the ferries and could afford the cost of a private transfer.

Around 10,000 people crossed for each event, more at New Year, and lots were willing to club together to pay the £250 or so each way that the boats charged. There was fierce competition by the runners to relieve the kids of their gap-year funds. So much so that there had been some fatalities on overcrowded boats.

There was no sign of the slippery Hom – she had no doubt gone back to her parents with Nate's cash, which spared her a tongue-lashing from me – so, with Chai driving me, I started at a place down the road known as OK Village. Here, a makeshift metal pier that looked like it was built from a child's construction kit jutted out into the sea. There was no sign of a powerboat, but an illustrated sign showed one skimming over the waves with happy, shiny party people hanging over the sides.

Not a life jacket between them, I noticed.

The owner or operator was equally scarce, the hut next to the pier firmly locked. I took one of the cards from the plastic holder and pocketed it.

The second port of call Chai took me to was in front of a hotel on Chaweng Beach. The boat bobbed offshore, the operator occupying a *sala* on the beach where he sat behind a table covered in a variety of snacks and a Bintang beer. I shucked my shoes before stepping onto the boards of the pavilion, recalling that Thais have a complex relationship with feet and shoes.

He was dressed in a Hawaiian shirt under a loosely tied waffle robe that looked like it had been lifted from a hotel. He gave off a pungent aroma of fish sauce and was big enough to make me think he could overload the boat all by himself. He tried to hustle me for a 'desert-island picnic' until I showed him the picture of Matt.

He shook his head. But his eyes had betrayed him, almost disappearing into his fleshy cheeks with recognition. 'Come on. You know him. He runs boats like you.'

'Not know,' he insisted. 'No *farang* run boats.' He grabbed a handful of rice from a bowl, worked it into a ball and stuffed it into his mouth.

I had chosen my words badly. It wasn't powerboats Matt was running out to Koh Phangan. All those Moondancers needed – *demanded* – stimulants. I could imagine Matt telling himself he was just supplying a need: if he didn't do it, somebody else would ... all the old shit.

I looked out at the prostrate bodies on the sand; the massage women fanning themselves under their umbrellas; the hawkers patrolling the edge of the surf; the sun sparkling off the waves; a kite surfer blasting along parallel to the shoreline, and beyond him a brace of angry-bee jet skis, the thin stream of their watery exhausts making it look like a pissing contest. Beyond them, a couple of gloomy, careworn bulk carriers rode at anchor.

As I scanned the scene, I slipped fifty US dollars on the table.

'He not here,' he said as he palmed the money. 'That one, he hang around Sanam Marina. No run boats. Crew.'

'Where's Sanam Marina?'

'By Big Buddha.'

Close to the airport then, for we came in directly over that temple. Big Buddha was one of the island's prime attractions, although, dating from 1972, it was hardly some ancient relic. But judging by the photographs, it was large and very shiny and very popular, even if it did look like it might have 'Made in China' stamped into its base.

I retrieved my shoes and had begun to walk off the beach when he called me. 'Hey. Lady.'

I turned. He was standing at the edge of the *sala*, his robe flapping open to show his grubby boxers beneath. 'You should stay away from that boy.'

A warning that was about sixteen years too late.

The Sanam Marina was a new development. Billboards advertised berths and the building of a hotel. The approach road was freshly tarmacked, the clapperboard huts clustered around the entrance freshly painted in bright pastels, more Caribbean than Thai. There was the inevitable moped rental place, a boat excursion office and a couple of food shacks. A signpost announced the development of a Miami-style beach club, which appeared, in the illustration at least, to be a clone of a Nikki Beach. It all looked sleepy and underused as yet, peaceful, except for the whine of the Airbuses and Boeings on their final approach to the airport.

There was a uniformed security guard on duty at the barrier, but he hardly looked up from his magazine as I skirted the striped pole. I raised a hand in greeting and he flashed a smile before going back to *Nation Weekend*.

The three piers here were wide, substantial and robust, a trident thrusting out into a newly dredged channel, pointing directly at the green humps of distant islands. There were a couple of decent-sized yachts, three RIBs – rigid inflatable boats – and two powerboats occupying berths. Many more slots awaited custom.

And then, there he was, at the base of the central prong of the trident, talking to two young women, both blonde and in their twenties. Just his type.

*Matt.*

I had imagined seeing him for so many months but, at first, he didn't seem real.

Like I was watching a hologram or a projection.

It was as if he had been Photoshopped in. And my reaction was puzzling.

I thought I'd be overwhelmed by anger or hatred. But a strange numbness crept over me. I had finally caught up with him, yet I was rooted to the spot. My limbs were concrete. Then I heard his laughter float over on the breeze – a lascivious chuckle – and the spell was broken. In that instant, he became solid flesh and bone.

He was dressed in cut-off jeans, flip-flops and a T-shirt with 'Ebola' written on it. I guessed it was the name of a bar or a band, rather than an announcement of an infection. His hair was longer than the last time I'd seen him; tousled, and bleached by the sun. He sported a straggly beard, his skin tone a deep, even brown.

Bastard looked good. It almost reminded me why I married him in the first place.

But that moment of warmth was soon chilled by the thought of what he had done to me. And by the fact that Jess was nowhere to be seen, while he chatted up the local, albeit transitory, talent.

I took a step forward into the hundred metres of clear space that separated us.

The thing about Matt is, he always did have a cockroach's instinct for survival. I had barely taken two more strides when he turned and looked at me, his eyes squinting in disbelief. I could see the cogs turning even from that distance.

And he did what his instincts always told him to do. He ran.

Matt sprinted off towards my right and I did what *my* instincts always told me to do: I took out my gun.

I almost had to rip the words from my throat. This wasn't what I had wanted. 'Matt, stop or I'll shoot.'

Actually, it should have been stop *and* I'll shoot. Because that was the only way I would be able to hit him. It was difficult to clip a running figure, even one in flip-flops, and particularly tricky with the popgun I had. Besides, I didn't want to kill him. Just slow him down.

I let off a warning shot way over his head. It was disappointingly quiet. I could hear Freddie's voice in my skull: *I can fart louder than that.* Indeed she could, and the feeble snap of the bullet was swallowed by sea and sky. The girl's screams were louder.

'Matt, I just want to talk. About Jess.'

But he knew that. Why else would I come halfway across the world?

My eyes followed the path he was on and I saw where he was aiming: a black motorbike in the shadow of one of the new, freshly painted huts.

I started to jog towards it. As I did so, I caught some movement to my right. Nate Segal had emerged from between two of the other empty units. In his hand, he had a long wooden pole, part of a mast perhaps, and it was clear what he intended to do: stop Matt.

Matt didn't slow as Nate took up position, ready to wield the pole like a baseball bat. I considered shooting at the motorbike, then thought better of it. Ricochets, petrol, that sort of thing.

Matt leapt on the bike like John Wayne onto his horse, vaulting over the rear and landing with a thump that would make most men's eyes water. Maybe that would come later.

Segal was only a few metres away from him, closing fast. Matt hit the electric start button.

And that triggered the bomb.

# THIRTY-THREE

I wish I had one of those clocks in my head that told me how long I was out. I don't. But not long, I would reckon. I woke up to find myself pushed into a corner where a wooden wall met concrete. Judging by the pain in my shoulder, I had been flung against one of the huts. I didn't move immediately. I let my vision come into focus, making sure that the reason the scene was fuzzy was because of smoke. My ears buzzed, whistled and popped. I slowly levered myself to sitting and took stock.

The skeletal framework of the motorbike was embedded in the splintered side of a hut, the rest of it spread across the ground before me. Matt had been blown back towards the pier, on the way to where the girls had been standing. No sign of them now. His arms were outstretched, as if he had been crucified. One leg was twitching, but that didn't mean he was alive. I couldn't see Segal from where I was sitting.

I pushed my back against the wall to help me stand upright and found myself keeling over to my left as my knee gave way. I steadied myself and looked down. No visible injury, but something had clumped me good and proper because little squirts of very fine pain – like toothache – were firing out from the joint.

I moved stiff-legged and bent from the waist to pick up my bag. I found the pistol among a tangle of parts that had come from the bike. It was possible one of them had hit my knee. Maybe the wheel. I swung my right arm back and tossed the weapon out to sea. When the cops turned up I could say the girls were imagining things. Gun? What gun? Then slowly, painfully, I hobbled over to Matt.

It was a long time, I realised, since I had seen the injuries a bomb could cause to a human body. No two are alike. An explosion is a strange, capricious thing. You can analyse the physics of them all you like, but no two IEDs were ever identical, in my experience. You couldn't predict who would live and who would die in the vicinity.

Matt hadn't died. At least, not yet.

He had, though, lost a hand.

There was just a stump at the end of his left arm, terminating in a tangle of bone and tendons. Blood was leaking out onto the concrete, although not as much as I expected – it looked like a clean sever, rather than a mangled one caused by blast alone. A piece of metal had excised it, was my guess, acting like a hot knife through butter. I felt like an octogenarian as I knelt down on my good knee and used one of my plastic restraining ties as a tourniquet on his arm. I could smell that desert dust again and I spat to one side, as if that would help.

His face was peppered with small fragments of metal and glass. Nothing I could do about that. His breathing was fast and shallow, but that was shock. Again, I didn't have the gear to deal with it.

The skin on his lower legs, unprotected by jeans, was hanging off in blackened ribbons, showing the glistening connective tissue underneath. One flip-flop had gone, taking a toe with it. The other looked as if it was fused to his foot.

I felt like weeping. I had no morphine, nothing I could help him with. I pushed myself to my feet and went searching for his hand. I found it on the edge of the pier, looking as if it were about to crawl over and drop into the sea of its own accord. I picked it up. The pinkie was missing. I looked down at the water, at the fish darting among the pillars of the jetty. I reckon they'd got it.

I limped back over, rummaged in my bag and gaffer-taped the severed hand into his forearm. When I spoke, my voice was unfamiliar, distorted by the compression blast that had boxed my ears.

'Matt? Matt? Can you hear me?'

He groaned.

'Matt, I need to find Jess. She's in danger. Where is she?'

What came out might have been a word, or maybe a sentence, but not a human one. I tried again and got a low groan. He was beyond answering any of my questions.

'There'll be an ambulance on the way,' I said. Surely the girls or the security guy would have called one? 'You'll be fine.' I took off my jacket and put it under his head. Drops of blood appeared on his forehead. I wiped them away with my sleeve, careful to navigate around two shiny horns of metal that had penetrated his skin.

I heard a babble of voices and looked up. Some of the Thais from the moped shop were peering round the edge of the far hut, too frightened to approach.

'Ambulance!' I shouted in a voice that reminded me of a stroke victim, and then made the international phone sign. There was lots of nodding and they disappeared.

I got back up. It was getting more difficult each time. My limbs felt like they needed lubricating.

I found Segal about twenty metres from the blast. He had skidded on his back, propelled by the explosion. There was a snail's trail of blood along the pristine concrete.

I knelt down next to him. He was breathing, but the sound was wet, bubbly. The headlamp assembly of the bike had flown off and embedded itself in his chest. With its umbilical of wires, he looked as if he were a robot whose ribcage had exploded. The concrete around was sprayed with tubercular crimson globules.

'Nate,' I said.

There was no reply. Just a horrible sucking sound from his chest. It was followed by a whistle, then a bubbling noise.

I leaned over his face. It was relatively unmarked.

'Nate. Ambulance on the way. *Fuck*. Bojan, eh? You said he liked to play games.' His eyes moved under closed lids, but his lips stayed still.

I examined him to see if there was anything I could do, albeit with no drugs and no trauma kit. His trousers were ripped to shreds, the skin beneath cut and grazed. But nothing I could see compared to that chest wound. The chances were he had internal injuries too.

If I were in Iraq I knew what I would do. I'd give him morphine, write the dose administered on his forehead and go on to treat someone I might actually have a chance of saving.

I leaned over him again, hoping he could hear me. 'Nate, I'm sorry.' Just as with Matt, small blooms of blood appeared on his face. It was then I realised it wasn't Nate's blood, just as it hadn't been Matt's.

It was mine.

I managed to pull back from him, to avoid collapsing on his chest wound, the second before I fainted.

There are several hospitals on Samui, more than you would expect for an island of that size. All have one speciality: putting together foreigners who have fallen off motorbikes. We were a little more serious than that. The two ambulances took us to the green-roofed, low-rise Thai International Hospital.

I was sick in the ambulance and, upon arrival, was taken to a private room, where I was stripped, washed, treated and put into bed by two nurses. All my questions were met with a polite smile.

Thailand: Land of Smiles, even when what you really want is an answer to your fucking questions.

I was visited by a man in a smart suit who asked me about insurance. I handed over a credit card and he seemed satisfied. I was insured – nearly all PPOs have an annual policy in case last-minute work abroad comes up – but I would worry about that later.

The blood that had dripped on Matt and Nate's faces came from a gash on my forehead. It wasn't bad, but all injuries up there bled a lot – it's just skin, blood vessels and bone, with no meat. It had been closed by the nurses with butterfly strips. My knee had swollen and was throbbing – it would need an X-ray. I'd been given painkillers and they had filled my head with Fuzzy Felt.

After an hour of sitting up and trying not to sleep – they were worried about concussion – someone finally came to answer my questions. But not a doctor. A policeman. Well, they were always going to show up some time.

Captain Sarit Sangkamantorn was in his thirties, well turned out in his uniform, with thick black hair and the whitest of smiles, which suggested excessive tooth bleaching. His English was excellent, albeit inflected with an American twang.

He introduced himself and asked if he could sit. I said yes, and he positioned himself in a chair to the right of my bed, down towards the foot, as if he wanted to be out of my reach. Or perhaps he thought whatever I had was infectious.

'How are you feeling, Miss Wylde?'

Blurred around the edges was the real answer. 'A little banged up. How is Matt? The one who lost a hand.'

'He has been transferred.'

'To where?'

'To the Government Hospital. There is a specialist micro-surgery unit there.' He held up his hand and examined it. 'Apparently, they are one of the best in Thailand. We have a long history of *farangs* losing limbs ... but not in this way. A bomb. Unusual for Westerners to be involved with bombs here.'

'And Nate Segal? The other one?'

'Being operated on as we speak.' I analysed his words for any hidden meaning, but there was none. I knew Segal had been injured the most, even though he hadn't been on the bike. 'I assume he was not the target.'

'No. I can explain ...' I gave him an edited account of Matt, Jess and the role of Bojan. I realised it came across scrambled and not a little deranged. Perhaps I *was* concussed.

He frowned the whole way through my speech. 'You know this man Bojan is on Koh Samui then?'

'Well, no,' I admitted. 'Not for certain.'

'You last saw him where?'

'Bali.'

'His full name?' he asked, flipping open his notebook.

'I don't know,' I said, feeling foolish. I tried to recall if Segal had mentioned it. I didn't think so. And I hadn't read the files he had left me. But I did recall one thing from our conversation. 'It was Saša Stanic originally. But he'll have changed that ... sorry.'

'You think the bomb was planted by this man who is after your daughter?'

'Yes. Which is why I need to talk to Matt.'

He closed his notebook. 'You are mistaken, Miss Wylde.'

'About what?'

'About who is responsible for this situation. This is not the first assassination attempt by rival gangs.'

'What do you mean?'

'Forget this Serbian nonsense.' He bent forward, an intense look on his face. 'This is what you call a turf war. Drugs. Always drugs or sex. There is a battle for who supplies drugs across this island as well as Koh Phangan and Koh Tao. Your husband fell in with some Australians and their Thai partners. But he chose the wrong side. The newcomers. The original guys, Chai Po, objected.'

I shook my head to try to clear it. That only got me a little hammer whacking at my left temple. 'Chai Po?'

'You say, perhaps, godfathers. From Han, originally. Some Burmese. Most start in Koh Tao working for the Five Families, and they send some here. They run protection, gambling, motorbike scams. And drugs. The Five Families control all here, Koh Phangan, as well as Koh Tao. They don't want a sixth family. There have been shootings, stabbings. Last week a restaurant was firebombed. I think what happened to your husband was in response. Tit-for-tit,' he said.

'Tat,' I corrected. 'But it could still be Bojan. Your turf wars aren't the only possible explanation.'

He shook his head. 'But the most likely. Drugs are mainly behind all incidents like this. I do not know your Bojan. And you do not even know his full name. And to me, this fits a pattern of the Five Families.' I felt something like relief. A local gangster hit I could handle. It meant it wasn't Bojan's work.

And Jess? What about her? Where was she in this turf war? The thought of her being mixed up in this made me furious, and I raised my voice a little more than was prudent. 'And you don't do anything? Even though you know who runs the drugs gangs? What kind of police force do you have here?'

He looked irritated at that. 'The Narcotics Suppression Bureau do a good job. We arrest men like Moorby. You know him?' I shook my head and it hurt. 'Jonathon Moorby. Big drug lord in the UK. We arrested him here. We arrest Russian, Thai, Vietnamese, Burmese. We put *farangs* in jail as a warning to others. Ten, twenty years. And then the next lot of dealers come. You know why?' He didn't wait for a reply this time. 'Because your children come here and expect drugs. Come to Thailand, get high, dance. It is supply and demand. And where there is easy money, you get war. We have war now. Thanks to your husband.'

''Ex-husband. You'll arrest him?'

'For being blown up? Is that a crime? Not even here. We'll arrest him when we catch him red-handed.' He hesitated. 'Sorry. That sounded like a sick joke.'

'Will they be able to fix his hand?'

'Doctors say maybe, yes.'

'And Nate?' I asked again.

'We shall see.'

'I have to find my daughter. Jess. She'll be alone. Somewhere on the island.'

'You have to make a formal statement before you can go anywhere. Police. NSB.'

'So, can you pick her up and bring her here?'

'Where is she?'

'I don't know,' I snapped. 'Matt knows. And I need to know she's safe from ... from this shit.'

'I see. I can make a telephone call to his police guard. See if he can speak. But he might be in the operating theatre.'

'If you could, please, I'd be grateful.'

He didn't move. Oh, for fuck's sake. Five Families plus corrupt police. That made six mafia clans on the islands.

'Very grateful.' I reached off the bed to my bag, found my purse and, once my head had stopped doing its merry-go-round number, pulled out a hundred US. 'I'm sure those trunk calls are expensive.'

'I think you have the wrong idea about the Royal Thai Police,' he said, waving the money away. 'I am just trying to decide whether I believe your story.'

'Look in the bag.' I couldn't risk that journey over the side of the bed again. The room was still spinning.

He did so, and found the pictures of Jess, Jess with me, Jess with me and Matt, and the ones Jess had sent from Bali to her friends, the set that had been dredged from the internet for me. His expression softened. 'Very well. I'll see what we can do.'

He left the room. I don't know how long he was gone, but I closed my eyes and tried to ignore the thump coming from behind the dressing on my forehead, and that little hammer in my temple.

I snapped my eyes open when he returned. He looked grave. 'I have some bad news. About your friend.'

'Segal?'

A nod. 'I'm afraid he died on the operating table.'

I slumped back and closed my eyes. More collateral damage. I doubt you could call Nate Segal an innocent bystander. Anyone who had been in Mossad was hardly that. But it was my fault that he had died.

'And something else.'

I sat up again.

'I spoke to your husband just before he was put under. Your daughter is not on Koh Samui.'

That was good, at least she wasn't caught in drug-war crossfire. But, of course, it was bad because I was in the wrong place. 'What? Then where the fuck is she?' I saw the look of distaste on his face at my profanity and naked anger. I had lost face. 'I'm sorry. Where is she?'

'At the International School in Bangkok. She boards there.'

I felt a wave of relief. Matt had done something sensible for once. Parked her out of harm's way.

'I put in a call to the school,' the captain continued. 'And I spoke to the headmistress.'

'She's OK?'

'Jess was picked up by a friend of her father's earlier today. He had a letter of authority.'

There is something called a ketamine hole, or K-hole; a pit of horror and despair that opens up and swallows the unfortunate drug-dabbler when they overindulge. It is a cruel, frightening and dark place, and comes with a side order of out-of-body experiences and hallucinations, and something much like that gaped beneath as I processed his words. 'Friend of her father's', my arse. I knew who had Jess.

Bojan.

# PART THREE

*'Endure and persist. This pain
will turn to good by and by'*

# THIRTY-FOUR

'She tried to tear his hand off, apparently,' said Freddie as she eased the cork out of a bottle of wine. She and Nina were in the kitchen of Freddie's place in North London, the bi-fold doors pulled open even though there was an autumnal chill in the air and the leaves on the trees were brittle and quivering, ready for the fall.

'Isn't it a little early for that?' Nina asked as Freddie moved over to the central island, dragging her boot slightly along the slate floor. It was four in the afternoon. Nina had left the newspaper early – she had been writing a feature on why women should adopt men's multi-watch habit. It made her want to pluck her eyes out. She would have come anyway once Freddie had told her Sam was home. But the added incentive of passing over the puff piece to someone else gave her extra wings.

'I need this,' Freddie said as she put her lips to the glass.

'Anyway, you were saying. Sam attacked Matt?'

Freddie nodded while she swallowed. 'Snuck out

the hospital, took a cab to the one where he had been treated, jumped on his bed and tried to pull off the hand they had just sewn back on. Broke his nose as well.'

'Jesus,' said Nina.

'At least he was in hospital where they could fix it.'

'Is that meant to be funny?' Nina asked.

'None of this is funny. I wish it was.'

'I wish it *were*.'

'Fuck off.'

'Sorry. And then what?'

Freddie poured out a generous measure of wine and slid the glass to Nina, who, despite her earlier protestations, took a sip. 'And then they arrested her for assault. But even they realised that she was not a well woman. She was put in a secure wing of the hospital, pending psychiatric reports.'

Now Nina took a larger mouthful of wine. 'Oh, sweet Lord. It gets better. So how did you get her home?'

'Letter from a private doctor saying she will receive treatment. I sent Tom out to fetch her.'

'Tom?' Nina said witheringly. 'I thought she and Tom had parted. After the rape business.'

'Well, we don't know that Leka was telling the truth about that, do we? For some reason, Sam chose to believe the word of an Albanian people-trafficker over her friend. Look, it needed to be a familiar face and . . .'

'Ach, I would have gone,' said Nina, her Scottish accent suddenly stronger.

'And I would have gone but for this boot. But, sadly, even in this day and age, I think it had to be a man.

They have more authority out there. Yes, yes, I know it sucks, but this wasn't the time to take a feminist stand. He did well to get her out.'

'Where is he now?'

'Tom? He's staying in a Premier Inn. We're still not sure whether Leka, or the wife, are out to get him.'

'I thought you had taken care of that?'

Freddie shrugged. 'Fuck knows. Unlike Sam, I don't buy anything Leka says.'

Nina worked on the wine some more. 'She's not been well for a while, has she? Sam, I mean.'

Freddie gave a thin smile at the understatement. It was wiped off by the dash of vitriol that followed.

'But still you let her run off to Albania, Bali, God knows where . . .'

That stung. 'Hold on. Nobody *lets* Sam do anything. My role was to act as wing woman, to have her back . . .' Freddie stopped. While she was with her in Albania and France, Freddie had felt she had a degree of control. That what they were doing at least had a certain logic. And justification. Doubts about Sam only crept in when she told her what she had done to Aja. And how she had treated Nate Segal when he was on her side. But by that point, Freddie was powerless to help. Finding Matt and still losing Jess had been the final crack in Sam's mental firewall.

Certainly, the woman she had picked up at the airport was a husk of the old Sam. She had suffered some sort of mental implosion. Tom had got the full story from a police captain in Koh Samui. Bojan, or his representative, had picked up Jess from her school and disappeared. A police alert was put out once it became clear it was a kidnap, but to no avail.

Sam's breakdown was probably triggered by this realisation: if Sam had left well alone, Jess would still be fine. She only came on Bojan's radar when she hired Oktane to intimidate Leka. It was Sam's actions that had led Bojan to Jess. She could blame Matt all she wanted, but the truth was that stubborn, impetuous Sam had pushed the dominos that resulted in Bojan having Jess.

'You thought about sectioning her?' asked Nina.

'If she was violent or a danger to herself, the doctor said the police could give her a Section 136, which would restrict her to a place of safety, like here, until a mental assessment is carried out. As it is, he thought, you know, time is the great healer. Maybe we wouldn't need a Section 136, or a 135, which is more drac-whatsit, apparently. Draconian?' Nina nodded. 'He reckoned we should wait and see. Although, I don't think the doc quite grasped what was likely to happen to Jess.'

'And what do you think will happen?' Nina asked.

'I think Bojan is the kind of guy who will let us know exactly what happens to her.' She shivered at the thought and crossed the room to close the bi-folds, even though it wasn't the breeze causing the chill. 'He is a right cunt. The worst.'

'I'm sure. But I meant with Sam.'

'Oh. As I said, she's sedated and sleeping. Christ,

I think she would prefer to stay like that. Otherwise she'll have to face up to what's happened.' What might have happened and what probably will happen.

'Shit.'

Freddie topped up the glasses. 'Never mind shit, Nina. We have to do something.'

'Like what?'

'I was hoping you'd have some ideas.'

'Me? You're the action woman.'

'And you're the shit-hot investigative journalist.'

'Not any longer. Wristwatches, puppies and celebs, me. I think I've forgotten everything I knew.'

'Learn again,' snapped Freddie.

'What about all your contacts in the bodyguarding business? I thought you had the SAS on speed dial.'

Freddie ignored the jibe. 'I spoke to the Colonel. The Israeli who died in the explosion was the son of a close friend. I don't think he feels like sending any more sacrificial lambs.'

Even though Sam couldn't have known about the drug feuds or the bomb in the bike, the Colonel still blamed her erratic behaviour for Nate Segal's death. It was hard to argue with his assessment.

'He won't help at all?' asked Nina.

'He said something like: If Bojan has the girl it is game over. Close the file and move on.'

'He sounds like a nice bloke.'

'He has, or *had*, a soft spot for Sam. But that only goes so far. There's been a lot of fallout. Some of the things she's done ...' Freddie shook her head slowly.

'I know she's been under a lot of pressure. Christ, it doesn't bear thinking about. We'd all buckle, I reckon. But Jesus, there's buckling and there's *buckling*.'

Nina, as always, cut to the chase. 'You think she's lost it?'

Freddie gave a shrug that might have been a yes.

'So what can we do?'

The answer was croaky and slow. 'F ... O ... T ... B.'

They both turned. Sam was in the kitchen doorway, leaning her weight against the frame, hair tousled, wearing a long T-shirt but otherwise naked. Her eyes were straining to find focus.

'Fucksake, Sam, you're meant to be resting,' said Freddie, crossing to her.

'Hello, Sam,' said Nina in a does-she-take-sugar voice. 'How are you?'

Sam's answer was almost a snarl. 'How the fuck do you think I am, Nina?'

'Sit down, Sam,' said Freddie.

She didn't move, just mumbled four letters to herself once more. 'F-O-T-B.'

Freddie tried to take Sam's arm, but she shrugged her off and swayed further into the kitchen, taking small, fast steps until she could support herself on the central island. 'F ... O ... T ... B. What does it mean?' she asked nobody in particular.

'I don't know,' said Nina.

'Neither do I,' snapped Sam. 'But it's something Bojan said to me in Bali. FOTB. At the time, I didn't ask what it meant. Just assumed it was like BDM and S, or whatever it is.'

'BDSM,' said Freddie.

'Yes. So I thought it was an acro-whatsit, like that. You know, fucking, oral ... dunno. But what if it's not? What if it's something to do with where Jess is?' She banged the table in frustration and tears started to film her eyes.

Nina looked at Freddie. 'Any thoughts?'

Freddie reluctantly shook her head.

There was just a trace of triumph in Nina's voice when she spoke. 'Then it's a good job I have.'

The Anthony Quayle book was not going well. In fact, Adam had to be honest, it wasn't *going* at all. He hated the term 'writer's block'. He wasn't blocked, he was stymied. Distracted. He *could* write the Quayle book. The problem was he didn't *want* to.

Every time he sat down and typed the word Albania, he thought about driving down the mountain with those two women, and the piece he wrote that was spiked. He could see the shattered bodies on the roadside, smell the coppery blood as it seeped into the gravel, and the acrid stench of discharged weapons.

That was the story he should write, not the adventures of a Hollywood actor that barely anyone under the age of forty remembered. And if they did, it was for Zorba the fuckin' Greek, which starred Anthony *Quinn*.

Who were those women? Were they really body-guards? How did they know each other? Army medics, they had said. They certainly knew their weapons. And what an intriguing relationship. The blonde, Sam, apparently made most of the decisions, while Freddie was the tougher cookie, he thought. With Sam, though, there was something else, a recklessness underneath her cool, clinical exterior. Like she had nothing to lose. Not exactly a death wish, but brittleness of spirit. Freddie didn't have that. But there was a bond between them he couldn't help but admire. Like they would go to the ends of the earth for each other. Rural Albania, for instance.

He looked at the screen again. Chapter Ten. There was no Chapter Ten. But there ought to be. Time was ticking by. He had been given a three-month sabbatical from the paper to complete the book. Would there be a job for him when he returned?

*Commercialisation* was the word now. What it meant was advertorials. There used to be a firewall, as solid as medieval battlements, between the editorial and advertising departments. But that was scaled and breached, and now the flag of the advertising bods flew from the top of the castle keep.

Actually, not even advertising. Synergetic revenue opportunities. Editorial, apart from the hard news, was increasingly predicated on finding a way to drive readers to the website and getting them clicking like demented lab rats hoping for a lick of cocaine. There was a band he remembered called Pop Will Eat Itself. It described perfectly what the print media was doing.

Adam glanced down at *The Times* crossword next to

the keyboard, still mostly white spaces. No, he had to resist. That was just another procrastination. He stared over the computer, out of the window at Kath, who was clearing leaves from the garden. She was raking them into a pile and would then suck them up with one of those giant ridiculous leaf blower/vacs, deafening birds for miles around. That would be the signal for him to make coffee and seek silence elsewhere.

Kath sensed someone looking at her, turned and waved to him. He raised a hand back. Why was she greeting him as if they hadn't spoken but ten minutes previously?

He was puzzled by many aspects of Kath of late. On his return from Albania, she was incredibly attentive and thoughtful. Nothing was too much trouble for the Hero of Tirana, as she mockingly called him – Tirana being the only town or city over there she could name. She could even say the word Albania without spitting it. And Roza was never mentioned.

Now, though, he felt as if Kath's attention was elsewhere. He often caught her staring over a mug of tea as it cooled, as if she had forgotten she was meant to drink it. Wistful was the word. He supposed that he did the same thing when he mused about Sam and Freddie. She often said something like, 'Penny for your thoughts', and he realised he had been back in that Dacia plunging down a mountainside.

The memory was simultaneously terrifying and electrifying. It made his current life seem pale and enervated in comparison.

But what would cause Kath to be quite so detached? She hadn't been caught in a gunfight between professional bodyguards and Albanian gangsters. It was probably something to do with Conor. Kath had discovered a packet of white powder in his trousers and he had claimed it was crushed aspirin before snatching it off her. They all do drugs, he had told her. We did drugs. Yes, but what they have out there are Frankenstein drugs, she had said. Well, there was certainly more choice.

But what if it wasn't Conor causing her distraction?

He let out a long, weary breath just as his phone rang and he picked it up without checking the caller ID. 'Hello?'

He half-expected to be asked whether he'd had an accident that wasn't his fault. 'Adam?'

'Yes.'

'It's Nina.'

'Oh.' She was hardly what he would consider a friend, prone to casual calls. Pushy rival was more like it. Nina had shown a steel core and a thick skin when she first arrived on the magazine, carving out a niche for herself. Like all of them, she was fighting against having to write the journalistic equivalent of clickbait. 'Everything all right?'

'No. Not really. I think we need you, Adam.' Not, he thought, words he heard often enough these days.

'Who is "we"?' he asked.

Five minutes later, he was in the garden, signalling that Kath should turn off the infernal racket of the blower. 'I've got to go to London. Immediately.'

Kath brushed hair from her face, leaving a streak of mud across her forehead. 'Really? Why?'

'Research.'

'Bit late in the day, isn't it? What's the hurry?'

'It's someone who knew Anthony Quayle in the war – must be well into his nineties – in town for one night only. I'll buy him dinner. Might be the breakthrough I need. I'll put up at the Nadler.' At least one part of that was true.

The truth was, he could have told Nina all she wanted to know over the phone. But the chance to see his two saviours again was too good to pass up. He arrived early evening. Nina and Freddie were in the kitchen, two empty bottles of wine on the marble top between them. Once he had sat down, Freddie opened a third. There was another man there, too, with a glass of water in front of him. He was introduced as Tom, a friend of Sam's.

The 'friend' was in slightly strained inverted commas. Adam found himself a little disappointed that there was a boyfriend. Mind you, he was a good-looking specimen, and gym-buffed. He had the sort of arms Adam knew he would never acquire even with a year of personal training. They had the shape of hams hanging in a Spanish deli.

'Where's Sam?' Adam asked. Tom's eyes flicked to stare over his shoulder.

'In bed. She got up for a while,' said Freddie, 'but she's exhausted.'

'Does she need to see a doctor?'

'She's seen a doctor,' answered Nina. 'It's a psych ward next unless we sort this out.'

'Which is where you come in,' said Freddie, who gave him a run-down of the story so far. Including the term FOTB.

After she had finished, Adam went back into the hall and fetched his overnight bag. From it, he took out a sheaf of loose papers and three notebooks. He placed it all on the table and then moved them aside for the wine glass that Freddie placed before him.

'OK, I didn't have time to look through this before I left. But I *have* heard that phrase before, when I was doing the Romanian work. Cam girls, you know?' He looked from one to the other. 'The two biggest centres for live sex streaming are Romania and the Philippines.'

'So?' prompted Freddie.

Adam flicked through one of the notebooks, then looked up. 'It makes for grim reading. You ready?'

'Go ahead,' said Freddie, 'you don't need to treat us with kid gloves.'

'FOTB is Fresh Off The Boat. Originally, it was just a phrase. A code word for virgins. Young girls, anyway. But there is also an organisation of the same name, which is run out of Amsterdam ...'

'Of course it is ...' said Tom, the first words he had spoken after 'hello'.

'This lot act like a Christie's or a Sotheby's of the sex-trafficking world. It caters to what we call High Net Worth Individuals.'

'The sort we bodyguard for,' said Freddie, but mostly to herself.

'Basically, it runs online auctions. You can view the merchandise beforehand and attend in person if you wish. But for obvious reasons, most buyers prefer to do it online. Through very secure closed and encrypted links.'

It was dark outside now and Freddie got up to lower the blinds.

'So you think Jess might have been fed into this?' asked Nina.

Freddie said nothing. Just sat back down and chewed her lip.

'The only positive spin I can give you is that these are not weekly events. She could be slated to go into the next one. Which might be months away.'

'And till then?' Nina asked.

'She will probably be reasonably well looked after, physically at least. FOTB is all about undamaged goods.'

Freddie mumbled to herself. Nobody could make out the words, but they all got the gist. Then she said, 'So how do we get in touch with FOTB? Find out when the next auction is?

'Not easy. They used to be in onionland—'

'In what?' Tom asked.

'The regular dark web network called Tor. It has a dot-onion domain name. But the FBI's Violent Crimes Against Children unit started infecting the site with malware to trace the users. Then, when they arrested

Matthew Falder, the police broke some of the encryption. So, of course, they moved on.'

Nina took a drink of wine. 'Where?'

'Darker and deeper. I don't actually know.' He flicked his notebook shut. 'I didn't stay on top of this once I'd finished the piece. You can't stay in that world for very long. It's like freediving through shit. You hold your breath and you know you have a limited time available.'

'Can't we go searching?' asked Freddie.

A shake of the head. 'Not you and me. Amateurs, I mean. Plus, unless you know what you are doing, you'll have Europol and the FBI breaking down your door. I'm not sure "I was just doing research" will wash with those guys.'

Freddie drummed her fingers on the worktop. For the first time, Adam noticed a slight slur to her words when she spoke. 'The Colonel had a computer expert. He helped find the images of Jess on the net.' She considered what she had just suggested. 'But again, I think maybe those bridges have been burned.'

'What about the car man with the kid who's an expert? Worth a try?' suggested Nina.

'One-eyed Jack? Fuck, no. The last time he got involved with Sam, his son got threatened. Can you imagine if we ask his boy to go into this cesspit?' She shook her head firmly. 'No. Too much to ask.'

'Freddie? Can I have a word? In private.'

Tom didn't wait for an answer, just got up and walked out of the kitchen. Freddie shot the other two a puzzled look and followed. She found him in the room at the front of the house that Freddie mainly used to watch TV. He sat in one of the armchairs and Freddie took the sofa. 'What is it?'

'I know a way to get to these guys.'

'You?' Freddie asked. 'What have you ever had to do with that crap?'

'I haven't. But you can bet Leka has. Anyone whose job is trafficking—'

'Leka? I'm not going to waltz to that tune again, thanks. Sam nearly got us both killed when she went to see Leka. We were lucky to get out alive. We only did because—'

'Because Leka wanted Sam to confront me with his version of events,' said Tom. 'Look, I don't know what Sam told you about what they said ...'

'All of it, of course,' said Freddie. 'No secrets.'

'It isn't true.'

'Well, something is off,' she said.

'Yes, it is,' he admitted. 'The story I told Sam. Well, it was one I believed too. Over the years, I told myself it was what happened. But it wasn't. Yes, we saw the girl with the goats, and a couple of the lads went up to talk to her. They gave her some chocolate, just messing about. Just banter.' Freddie rolled her eyes. 'Leka and his family turned up and reckoned we were going to ... that we were out to rape her. And they began to take the lead. That's when it became ugly. In the girl's mind, maybe in Leka's, they thought we were there first and had first dibs. That's why the firefight started. But it wasn't like she said. Our boys didn't start it.'

Freddie said nothing.

'It's false memory syndrome or whatever they call it. You have to believe me.'

'I don't know what to believe,' Freddie said at last. 'It was a long time ago and it was a nasty little war and I'm prepared to believe almost anything of anyone. Wars do that. I don't believe you are a bad bloke, Tom. But I do know one thing – if you go to see Leka, he'll kill you.'

'Maybe not.'

Freddie laughed. 'Maybe? I'd want a damn sight more than maybe.'

'Have you got a better idea? Like I said, this guy traffics people. Women, no doubt. And what happens to a significant number of those women? Of course he'll know about FOTB. Maybe where, what, when, who. Sam told me there was a possible hit still out on me. I mean, how long can I go on ducking and diving like this? I have to do it for Sam. For Jess, for Christ's sake. The last time I tried to help Sam, she clobbered me. Remember? Knocked me out cold so she could face Bojan alone. I'm army trained. Yet she thought she could do better than me. And don't tell me she's as good as me. You were fuckin' medics.'

'Oh, come on, she's pretty good at taking care of herself.'

'Not as good as she thinks. The thing is, she's been manic since Jess went. "Oh, I'm fine," she says, when we all know she isn't. Can't be. She thinks she's super-woman. Or wants us to think she is, anyway. But she's not. She's damaged. Like you said, she's just been lucky, that's all. Lucky she's alive. I have to try this. And you can't stop me.'

Freddie laughed and ran her eyes over his torso. 'You have beefed up. I don't think I'd give you too much trouble. Slow you down a little, perhaps.'

'Well, maybe I knew in my heart that something like this was coming. That's why I stayed match fit.'

'Walking into the lion's den isn't much of a plan.'

'It's the only plan we've got. I love her, Freddie. I can't bear to see her like this. It hurts. Right here.' He punched his own stomach with a force that made Freddie wince. 'Let me do this for her. Please.'

Freddie was taken aback by such a raw admission. 'Like you said. I can't stop you. But I can help. What do you need?'

# THIRTY-FIVE

Sam Wylde is in hell. A strange, aquatic sort of hell, with real life refracted and blurred by the waves above her head. She tries to swim upwards, but the surface never gets any closer. She is aware that someone is feeding her, offering her drinks, and she takes them. There is no conversation with these visitors. When she tries to speak, the sound starts in her head. It is not screaming exactly. More a rushing, tumbling roar, like a waterfall as it plunges down onto rocks.

But she knows what it really is: white noise, designed to blank out reality. She doesn't want it blanked out. She wants to stare straight at it, in all its bright, cruel heartlessness.

But something won't let her. Some kind of coping mechanism, like a limiter on a powerful car, is preventing her confronting what has happened.

She is broken.

Or some part of her is. Shattered.

Her insides are liquefying. She can feel them. Dissolving into sludge. Her once-taut muscles are the same, without any substance or texture. The flesh yields beneath her fingers. If she pushes hard enough, it feels as if they might go right through the skin, as if her body were rotting flesh.

She can barely lift her arms. She has tried getting up, out of the bed, but when she swings her legs off she is trapped in a whirlpool that spins faster and faster until she is forced to flop back down. And then she is sick, retching up bile.

The worst thing is, she can't think. Her neural connections are down. There is a grey fuzz settled in her brain. Sam has always thought of a way out of every situation. But this one has no roadmap, not so much as a signpost. She is lost in a featureless, watery wilderness.

'What can I do?'

*Haven't you done enough?*

She is aware that there are people talking, and talking about her. Occasionally, her name floats up the stairs. And then, perhaps, laughter, quickly stifled. A doctor has been in, too, who checked her pulse and shone a light in her eyes and listened to her heart and asked her some stupid questions. Did he give her drugs? Is that why the limiter is in place? She can't tell.

Doors slam. Cars start up. She hears kids going to school, the local yappy dog, apparently called Bella, judging by the owner's frustrated shouts. The world turns. But not hers. Apart from when it spins.

She has a song stuck in her head. An earworm. No, an ear cancer. It is some piece of shit from the 1980s.

'The Final Countdown'. She wants it to stop. When it does, it is replaced by 'Living on a Prayer'. It is like being trapped in Capital Gold. Not good at all.

She is aware of the door opening. Footsteps. Freddie again, perhaps. With chicken noodle soup or the equivalent. Or maybe the doctor, with some more sly medication. Chemical cosh. But the footsteps stop. Now Sam can hear breathing.

Using those rubber limbs, she pushes herself up in the bed. There is a little girl standing there. Eight, nine. Whose child is that? The film on her eyes clears. It is my child, she thinks. Jess, not as she is now, but as she was seven or eight years ago. Innocent. Unharmed.

'Jess?' she asks.

A smile spreads over the girl's face, showing the gaps in her upper teeth. She holds out her hand.

'Why didn't you come and get me, Mummy?'

There is the sound of water receding, sucked away from the shore, as if a tsunami is coming. A synapse fizzes in her brain. Cataracts fall from her eyes, the tiny bones in her ear, long frozen in spasm, begin to move freely again. She can taste the staleness in her mouth. She can smell coffee. And her own body odour. She blinks. The child is still there, fading now like an old Polaroid.

'Why didn't you come and get me, Mummy?' Jess asks one last time, before she dissolves completely.

Sam swings her legs off the bed, waiting for the nausea to hit. It doesn't come. She holds out a hand. It doesn't shake. She can feel muscle and tendon holding it there, steady. Ready. Sam looks at the space once occupied by Jess. There is an after-image on her retina.

'Of course I'm coming, darling. Just hold on. Just stay alive till I get there.'

# THIRTY-SIX

Freddie was alone when the call came through; Adam had gone back home, Nina was at work. She thought she heard Sam moving around, but just as she went to investigate, her mobile rang. It was Tom, so she took it.

'Tom? Where are you?'

'I'm here.'

'Fuck. You OK?'

'So far.' He gave an unconvincing laugh. 'Still alive, anyway. I have a meeting. With the girl. To sort this out. She's a woman now, of course.'

That was for some other time as far as Freddie was concerned. 'And you have seen Leka?'

'He's here in the room with me.'

Freddie felt a wave of admiration, sympathy and gratitude for him that almost made her cry. It was incredibly stupid and incredibly brave what he was doing. Mostly stupid, though. 'And you've asked him?'

'He wants to speak to you.'

'OK.'

Leka started without preamble. 'I can't say I am sorry for your friend. She is a fucking nuisance.'

'I've told her that a lot.'

'And reckless.'

'I hate to agree with you, but yes, that too.'

'Still, I have to admire her. And I hear she is in a bad way.'

There was a thump from above and Freddie looked at the ceiling. 'You could say that.'

'OK, listen carefully. I do not work with these FOTB. They are sons of bitches. I am not saying I am Medicins Sans Frontières, you understand. But the men they deal with – their *clients* ...' He made a disgusted noise in his throat. 'So, I cannot tell you too much. They sometimes come to me, asking if I have any candidates for them. They used to patrol the Jungle, you know? Looking for girls, till we drove them out. Then they sent some Kurds, as front men, and we dealt with them, too.'

Freddie wasn't sure what sort of bullshit this was, but it was pretty ripe. She didn't think a man like Leka worried about how others made a buck. If he drove them out of 'his' camps it was simply getting rid of a business rival. 'OK. You aren't bosom buddies with FOTB. Can you give me anything?'

'I know someone with such tastes. Not a friend, you understand. I told him I needed a young girl, a virgin, FOTB, where could I get one? He said, there is an auction coming up in a week, ten days at the most. In The Void.'

'The Void?'

'The exact location is secret until you pay the entry fee. Which, by the way, includes a live stream of the event and ... the follow-up.' A red mist began to cloud Freddie's brain, like hill fog rolling down into a valley. She blanked out the implications of what he just said about live feeds. It wouldn't help. 'It is usually a port, many of these people like to arrive by boat to collect their winning bids. It avoids any embarrassment at airports. But, to join is expensive, and you aren't worth that to me.'

'How do I enrol?'

He gave a laugh. 'You can't. Not you, your friends, not the police. Absolute personal recommendations only. Tighter than a duck's arse. Ask the FBI.'

'For God's sake, man, have a heart here. If I gave you the money—'

'You deal in bitcoin, do you? Forget it. I have done my part. The Void. Make of it what you will.'

'Hold on, hold on. Leka? What about Tom?'

There was a lengthy pause and she thought for a minute he had broken the connection. 'That remains to be seen,' he said eventually, and the line went dead.

The Void?

Still turning the word over in her head, Freddie went upstairs, cursing the damned boot she still had two weeks left of wearing, to see what all the racket was. She pushed the door to Sam's room open with her foot. The bed covers had been thrown back. The wardrobe was open, clothes on the floor.

And Sam was gone.

*

'What do you mean, she's gone?' Nina asked, a mix of alarm and disapproval layered through her words.

'She was fuckin' comatose last time I looked in. How was I to know she was just playing Snow White?'

'Have you called the police?'

'What will they do?' asked Freddie. 'She's a grown woman.'

'She's a *sick* grown woman. Christ. Maybe you should have sectioned her.'

Freddie clenched her jaws tight for a second before she spoke. 'Not helpful.'

'Sorry. You've looked outside?'

'Yes, but I can't exactly run in this fuckin' boot. I've called her flat. No answer.'

'How long has she been gone?'

Freddie glanced at the wall clock. 'Probably only twenty or thirty minutes.' It seemed far longer.

'I'll come over,' said Nina.

'No point. What can you do?'

'I can move faster than you with that bloody boot on.'

'There's statues in the park that can move faster than me. Listen, just before I realised she had gone, Tom called.'

'Lord. And?'

'Well, he's OK. He put me on to Leka. He said that the auction is due to take place at something called The Void.'

'Where's that?'

'Leka claims he doesn't know.'

'I find that hard to believe.'

323

'I agree. But if he does, he's not telling.'

'The Void. Anything else?'

'It'll most likely be at a port. That's what he said. For fast, untraceable getaways by sea.'

'Have you asked Adam if it means anything?'

'No,' said Freddie. 'It went out of my head once I realised the patient had gone.'

'Christ knows what is going through her mind. Can you imagine?'

'I'm trying not to.' A deep booming sound bounced down the hallway. Someone was hammering with the brass door-knocker. It was followed by the shriller tones of the bell. 'Hold on.'

Freddie hobbled down to the front door and opened it. Sam was leaning against the brickwork, her forehead covered in sweat, breath ragged. 'Why didn't you tell me my knee was fucked?' she said as she barged by. 'It went from under me. It's taken me half an hour to hobble about a hundred yards back here.'

'It's Sam,' Freddie said down the phone. 'Or someone who looks like Sam.'

'Where's she been?'

'I think she's been out for a run.'

When she followed Sam to the kitchen, Freddie found her sitting on a stool with one foot propped up on the seat opposite her. She was massaging her knee.

'You knew it was hurt. Your knee. The explosion.'

'Oh, yes,' said Sam distractedly, as if almost being

blown to bits was the sort of thing that could easily slip your mind. 'How is Matt? Do you know?'

'No.' Matt wasn't her concern. He had probably crawled under another rock.

'I should get in touch,' said Sam.

Freddie took another perch. 'What's going on, Sam?'

A shrug. 'You tell me.'

'I think we should go to see a doctor.'

'I'm fine. I was … somewhere else for a bit. Now I'm back.' She felt like her body had put itself into an induced coma to give it time to rest, recuperate and recover. And when it was sure it was the right time, it – some part of her subconscious, anyway – sent Jess to tell her to get off her lazy arse and come looking. She didn't need to be asked twice. 'Anyway, you've had doctors round. I remember.'

'Yes. But you were like a fish on a slab. They wanted to take you to hospital for observation. I still think we should.'

Sam stared at her, as if she were seeing a human for the first time. 'You have to be kidding me.'

'No. I'm not. You have suffered some sort of collapse. I dunno, Buster, back when we were in the medical business it's what we would have called completely losing your shit.'

'And now I've found it again.'

Freddie looked into Sam's eyes. She didn't like what she could see in there. 'I'll just get you checked over.'

Freddie reached for the phone, but Sam snatched it off the marble top. 'First things first. What have you discovered?'

'About what?'

'About Jess. Don't tell me you haven't tried to find out where she is?'

Freddie felt anger rush through her like a flash-fire. 'Of course we have. Me, Nina, Tom, Adam—'

'Adam?'

'From Albania.'

'Oh ... The writer. Why him?'

'He did some work on trafficking. Remember?'

'Of course,' she said, in a tone that suggested she didn't. 'And? Tell me everything, Freddie. And I mean everything. I can take it. I won't go into ... into that place again. Promise.'

So Freddie did, watching Sam carefully as she digested the information about Tom going to confront Leka and the phone call that gave them The Void. As the tale unfolded, Sam's expression became more and more grim.

'And you don't know what happened to Tom?'

'No, I've tried calling ... straight to voicemail.'

'I wish we could go over and help him ...'

'It might be too late, Buster. We were in good shape when we took on Leka last time. Look at us now: barely one pair of good legs between us.'

'I can strap this knee. But you're right. And Tom knew what he was doing. He might be OK.' She didn't sound too sure about that statement. 'Did you believe him? About the rape?'

'I think if he was lying, he's just committed suicide by going over there.'

Sam nodded. She closed her eyes and squeezed the lids. 'Can I have a drink of water?'

Freddie fetched one. After she had sat back down she released the straps on the boot and scratched under the hard shell. She couldn't wait to get it off. Meanwhile, Sam gulped down the water.

Nina's words came back to Freddie. About sectioning. 'I'd still like you to see a doctor, Sam.'

'Doctor or shrink?'

'Both?'

Sam made a dismissive noise. 'I'll tell you what I need. Really need.'

'Go on.'

'A good curry. I'm starved. What the fuck have you been feeding me?'

'Whatever you wouldn't dribble down your front or spit all over me.' Freddie didn't try to hide her irritation at the ingratitude.

'Sorry. But a curry would hit the spot. There's Monsoon.'

'Give me the phone and I'll call the order.'

'And some cigarettes.'

Freddie sighed. 'Really?'

'I could really do with one. And there's fifteen per cent off if you collect your order at Monsoon.'

Freddie put her hands on her hips and tilted her head to one side. A quizzical eyebrow went up. 'Do I look like a dick? Or just act like one?'

'What?' Sam asked. 'Neither. Of course.'

'Then why are you treating me like one?'

'Fred . . .'

'You are up to something, aren't you?'

'Yes, trying to get a plate of curry and rice.'

'I don't believe you.'

'Trust me.'

'I don't do that, either. You're trying to get rid of me. I know you, Sam Wylde.'

Sam put her hands up in surrender. 'I just want to make some calls. I'll phone Adam while you get the grub.' That much was true. 'Hyderabad chicken for me and the usual gubbins.'

'Jesus Christ.' Freddie re-strapped the boot. 'It's a good job I love you.'

'Thank you.'

She flashed a smile. 'And you'll be here when I get back?'

'Of course.'

She looked doubtful. 'I must need my head testing as well as the rest of me.'

Once Freddie had dragged her bad leg out to visit the local Indian takeaway and the convenience store, Sam dialled Adam. Freddie would be gone at least thirty minutes at the speed she moved. Sam calculated that she had plenty of time to do what she needed to and get out of there. She shivered when she heard the words in her skull: clear as if Jess was standing at her shoulder.

'Why didn't you come and get me, Mummy?'

Shame she would miss the curry.

# PART FOUR

*'There's no place left where I
can be dealt fresh wounds'*

# THIRTY-SEVEN

It was a woman who answered the phone. The wife, I assumed.

'Hello?'

'Hi. Is Adam there?'

'Yes ...' Suspicion stretched out the word. 'Who is calling?'

'Sam Wylde.'

'Sam ...?'

'Wylde. Tell him it's one of the women from Albania.'

He took a long time to come to the phone. I could sense the tension at the other end of the line. Eventually, he came on. 'Sam?'

'Yes.'

'Good God. How are you?'

'If I said tickety-boo, would you believe me?'

'No.'

'I'm as well as could be expected.'

'Good, I'm glad. You had us frightened. Listen, I am so sorry about—'

I cut him off. I didn't need platitudes about Jess. 'We

331

all are, Adam. But I need to ask you something. Ever heard of The Void?'

'Confused poet faces vast emptiness.'

'What?' I asked.

'Sorry, crossword clue. Force of habit. Confused poet – Void is an anagram of Ovid. Emptiness is a void.'

'Congratulations.'

'I'm sorry. How is that relevant? Void, I mean, not Ovid.'

'Freddie spoke to Leka—'

'Christ almighty. I knew Tom was going over. Is he OK?'

'I hope so. I don't know. He said that Jess will probably end up at somewhere called The Void. Some sort of auction room. It'll be at a port. A lot of these people have boats.'

A whistle, forced between clenched teeth, came down the line. 'That's a tall order. Could be anywhere. Nothing else?'

'Not that Freddie told me. But let's assume, given Bojan's background, that this is happening in Eastern Europe . . .'

'Look, it happens all over the world, Sam.'

'But Bojan isn't from all over the world. He's from Serbia.'

'Serbia is landlocked. Most sea traffic goes through Montenegro.'

'I *know* Serbia is landlocked,' I said, annoyed he was missing the point. 'What I mean is, he's more likely to be operating there than in the Philippines or Mexico.'

'So, where then?'

'Albania, Croatia, Romania ...'

'Romania, yes, a possibility. Given the cam-girl racket.' A little laugh came down the line. 'You know that ...' Then, silence.

'Adam?'

'Wait. I'm thinking.'

'Then think faster.'

'This is ... well, it sounds ridiculous.'

'Try me with ridiculous,' I said. 'No sensible offer refused.'

'What do you know about Ovid? The poet?'

'Roughly about as much as Melvyn Bragg knows about field-stripping an SA80.'

'You are feeling better.'

'Come on, Adam, I haven't got much time.'

'Ovid was exiled from Rome by the Emperor Augustus to somewhere called Tomis.'

I tried to place it but failed. 'Never heard of it.'

'Neither had Ovid. He was thoroughly miserable there. It was the end of the civilised world, a remote part of Thrace, where the locals spoke a sort of pidgin Greek.'

'Melvyn,' I reprimanded.

'OK, OK. He died there. There's a statue. It's now part of Romania.'

My heart quickened a little. 'Go on.'

'Does this seem likely? An anagram?'

*He likes to play games.*

'Yes, it does,' I prompted. 'Go on.'

333

'Tomis is now called Constanta. It's a port on the Black Sea.'

I limped over to the work surface where Freddie had left her laptop. I flipped it open and typed in the password. I opened Google Earth and entered the modern name. There was a marina and a proper port, a beach area. It looked like a holiday town.

'Listen, Adam, I'm going it alone.'

'What do you mean?'

'I'm ditching Freddie. She would only slow me down.'

'This is a job for the police, surely.'

I didn't answer.

'Sam?'

'If Freddie remembers to call you, tell her that Void means nothing, OK? Don't tell her about Ovid or Constanta.'

'Sam.'

'I know it's an unreasonable request, but consider this: if you do tell her I will break both your fucking legs. Clear?'

'Sam ...'

'OK, how about this: You tell Freddie where I have gone, Freddie, the loyal friend, follows me out, but that boot means she isn't as nimble as she might be. I have to keep one eye watching her back. In having to look after her, I lose my chance to get Jess. In which case, the fuck-up is your fault, because I wanted Freddie kept out of it. You think I'd stop at your legs?'

His voice was much smaller. 'I would imagine not. But what are you going to do?'

I was going to go home, grab my RTG bag and spare passport – I didn't have time to find where Freddie had put mine – my cash reserve, activate a new credit card and head out. I was just about to close the page, delete history and log out when something on screen caught my eye.

*He likes to play games ... Place your bets, ladies and gentlemen ...*

And I knew where Bojan was, or where he was going to be, and where I just might find Jess.

'Sam?'

'Sorry. Thank you, Adam. I really do hope I don't have to carry out that threat.'

'Me too, Sam. Of course, there is always a chance Freddie will find out I wasn't entirely honest with her and do it to me anyway.' That was very, very true, but I kept quiet. 'In which case, it's lose-lose for me, isn't it? Good luck.'

'Thanks.'

Already my mind was on the logistics and I missed his next question.

'What? Sorry?'

'So you're going to Constanta?' Adam repeated.

'No,' I said. 'I'm going to Bratislava.'

I felt guilty about ditching Freddie. And lying to her, of course. It was breaking up the team once more, but it had to be done. Anyway, she *knew*. Even as she left to fetch me a curry, she knew I had something up my sleeve. She was not, after all, as she so succinctly put it, a dick. Freddie just couldn't think of how to stop me. Or whether she should. But I owed her an explanation.

So I'd left a message for her explaining my reasons for doing what I had done. The explanation lay in the trail of the damaged and the dead: Matt, with a new hand, but other injuries; Nate Segal, blown to pieces; an innocent delivery driver murdered in Normandy; the Colonel's son driven to suicide, or murdered; Tom, walking with misplaced nobility into the jaws of Leka's hell, hoping he could talk his way out of a bullet to the head. Or worse. And Jess. Poor Jess.

'Why didn't you come and get—?'

I had to suppress those words. I couldn't operate with my stomach in knots, my brain boiled with anger and pain, my heart almost bursting in my chest. I'd let it overwhelm me once. My breakdown was both physical and mental. I'd watched it happen to soldiers in the field. Men and women who had seen friends and colleagues blown to pieces, eviscerated by machine-gun fire, hacked to death by machetes. Soldiers who found their limit; their breaking point.

'There's no shame in it,' I told them.

But I was lying.

As far as I was concerned, my body and brain had betrayed me, delayed me, and I found that hard to forgive.

But the self-loathing could wait. And there was always the possibility that my body had been right. I needed a time-out, a breath, a chance to get match fit.

A calm before the storm.

If that were so, the storm was certainly coming now. A shitstorm.

It was snowing as I drove over the bridge crossing the Danube, the water close to the river's banks already mushy and opaque with ice. I was pointing east, leaving the drab outskirts of Bratislava behind. I was heading for the town of Smolenice, all castellated manor houses, cobbled squares and red roofs. It sat at the foothills of the Little Carpathians. In fact, I would stop short of that picturesque town, diverting to a farm on the outskirts I had first visited more than a decade ago. I hoped the welcome was still warm.

The snow began to thicken so I turned on the wipers. Traffic was light and I kept the speed down. I was fairly sure nobody had tailed me from the airport. Why would they? I reckoned they knew where I was going. Not this stop, perhaps, but eventually.

All roads led to Jess.

A truck overtook me with a blast of its horn and the car became skittish in its wash as the tyres struggled for grip. I wondered if I should have insisted on winter ones. There were chains in the boot, but I didn't want to waste time fitting them. I decided it would be OK.

The peaks of the mountain range were on my left and, although I was climbing, I reckoned I would avoid the deeper drifts that dotted the higher slopes. To my right was flat farmland, dusted with the snow. The blots on the windscreen seemed less substantial now. It was turning to sleet. I'd manage without the chains.

I drove through a series of utilitarian hamlets, houses

that were neat, freshly painted but with no memorable features apart from tree-lined pavements and window boxes. A couple of bars on the edge of one town had lights on, and through the window of one I saw a huge open fire flickering invitingly.

I kept my foot down. Twenty minutes to go.

What had happened to me in Thailand? Was it a retreat from what I had done? In my selfishness to get my daughter – to have her as mine, to hold her again, to feel that love – I had put her in harm's way. There, I could say it now. It was me, me, me – selfish me.

Jess was in Bojan's hands because of me.

This helplessness, this despair, worse than any physical pain, was what he wanted me to feel. I knew that, but I could use that knowledge to ameliorate the pain I was feeling. For now, anyway.

All I knew is the promise I made to myself as I was rising from those depths, back to life. I said: *If I get Jess back, I'm done. No more bodyguarding. No more pampered rich people. No more guns, knives, fast cars. Give me domestic, give me boring. Give me Jess.*

I almost missed the turning. It was the same sign I remembered, small and insignificant, as if it were a test to see if you were paying attention. All it said was 'SSA', with an arrow to the right. I took to the track at low speed, the car bouncing over the same potholes I recalled from before. I reached smoother asphalt and pointed the bonnet towards the cluster of farm buildings made indistinct by the curtain of sleet.

I drove past the agricultural buildings – a cow

shed, a stable and a freshly erected barn for some new machinery – to the second complex: three windowless buildings, all with SSA stencilled on them in white letters. As I pulled into the empty parking apron, a door opened in the largest building and a man stepped out. He was dressed in a US Army arctic parka, hood up. He came over to me and, when he was within three metres, pulled the hood back.

I lowered the window. 'You still look like Dolph Lundgren.'

He grinned. He sort of did, given all the angles in his face and a buzz cut, but a better-preserved one. Not surprising, because he was a good dozen years younger than the actor.

He grabbed the door handle and hesitated. 'Hello, Sam,' Pavol said. 'Your email was a surprise.'

'I never thought I'd be back here either.'

He opened the door for me and I stepped out. I am pretty tall, but Pavol towered over me like one of the Carpathian peaks behind me. 'Well, welcome. What would you like? Coffee? Drink? Food?'

'I'd like a coffee, then I'd like to do some shooting.'

'OK.'

'And then I'd like you to fuck me.'

Pavol burst out laughing and shook his head. 'Sounds like a perfect day.'

Maybe not perfect, but necessary. In the largest building, which was the training range of Shield Security Associates, I put three magazines each through a Glock, a Browning and a Sig. Then I used an H&K

MP25 to wreak destruction on a series of dummies. That was followed by more coffee, and then we adjourned to the small wood-lined apartment above the SSA office where Pavol undressed me and did just what I had asked.

He didn't make love to me, just as he hadn't when we got together the first time around. I lay back and he climbed on top and thrust away until I couldn't hold on any longer. My friend Freddie says that sometimes a girl just needs ... well, that. No foreplay, no strings, nothing fancy; just a man with a body that's taut in all the right places, and more than taut where it counts; just a release that is like a resetting of the buttons. It had been quite a while.

Afterwards, I lit one of my cigarettes and he refused one. I felt soft inside, but not like I had at Freddie's. Not weak. This was a warm and cotton-woolly feeling, like a stuffed toy. Right at that moment, I couldn't have fought off Pingu. But that wouldn't last.

Through the circular window opposite the foot of the bed I could see snow was falling once more. The place, with its comforting scents of cedar and pine, could have been a cosy ski lodge. I was about to ruin that illusion.

He lay on one elbow and studied me. I pulled the sheet up to my throat. My current body wasn't the one I had brought along as a young trainee bodyguard to get my weapons training certificate. 'Don't.'

'What?'

'Stare.'

'You are still beautiful, Sam Wylde.'

'"Still" kind of suggests my days are numbered.'

'I'm sorry. My English is not subtle.'

'Nothing about you is subtle,' I said, touching his cheek.

Pavol frowned, trying to divine if that meant he had been clumsy or inconsiderate.

'That's what I love about you,' I added.

'Love?' There was a touch of panic in his voice, as if I were about to demand a house in the suburbs and a couple of kids. And a horse.

'Like? I don't know, somewhere between the two.'

Pavol sighed. 'I'm sorry. I shouldn't have done that, Sam. We shouldn't have done that.'

'Why?'

'I am engaged.' He lay back, put his hands behind his head and examined the knots in the wooden ceiling.

I let out a stream of smoke. 'Congratulations. And that means it's me who should be sorry. I shouldn't have. Neither should you. Do you feel bad?'

He turned and looked at me. 'Do you?'

'I feel great,' I said, truthfully.

He smiled. 'Good. I am sure Adriana will understand.'

It took me a second to understand who he meant. The fiancée. 'No, she won't,' I said carefully. 'Don't you dare tell her.'

'We have no secrets from each other.'

'Bollocks.'

He looked hurt. 'We don't.'

341

'Do you tell her every time you have a wank?'

'No, but that's different.'

I reached down for the glass of water I had left at the side of the bed and dropped the cigarette in it. It hissed in the centimetre of liquid in the bottom. 'It's not really. Just think of this like that. Functional. Like before. Best kept to yourself.'

'We were not, what did you say ... *functional* before?'

Bad choice of words, Sam. 'No, but I had someone I liked back home ... and you and I were never going to go anywhere. It did its job. Which was to allow us both a good time in between blowing cardboard cut-outs to smithereens.'

He gave a little chuckle. 'You are a strange woman, Sam Wylde.'

And about to get stranger, I thought. 'Pavol, the sex was a bonus for me. I honestly threw it into the mix at the last minute. I just saw you and remembered you weren't just good at hitting bulls. I didn't come here for that. But I do need your help.'

He might have bristled a little. I couldn't tell whether it was play-acting or not. 'Oh. Have you been softening me up? Is this what this is about?'

'Pavol, you aren't getting this. That was for me. Not you. If I was trying to soften you up I'd have sucked your cock or let you fuck me up the arse.'

His eyebrows shot up. 'Would you?'

I squashed that thought before it took wing. 'With that thing? No. Fuck off.'

He laughed. 'Only kidding.'

Yeah, guys always kid about that sort of thing.

'Besides, now we've mentioned Adriana I am not sure I can.'

'Good on you. Look, I need some weapons. I need them delivered to Bucharest to a safe house where I can pick them up. It's quite a list.'

'Are you in trouble?'

'Someone is. It might be me. It's certainly my daughter.' I gave him the short version of what had happened with Jess and Bojan.

After I had finished he puffed out his chest. 'I will come with you. Back-up.'

'No, you won't. What would Andrea say?'

'Adriana. She knows I was soldier.'

'*Was* a soldier. I've caused too much pain, Pavol. You come with me, and the odds of you coming back aren't great. I think aircrews bombing Germany in the war had a better survival rate than my friends. And the last thing I need is Anthea coming after me to avenge her fiancé.'

He poked me with a stiff finger, which made a change. 'Adriana.'

'I know, Adriana. This is a solo show, Pavol.'

'I have some contacts in Bucharest.'

'You do know what solo means?'

'Like having a wank.'

It was my turn to laugh. 'Yes. Like having a wank. A one-man, or one-woman job.'

'I give you some names. For local knowledge: hotel, a cab company you can trust, safe house, where to eat, how to avoid police. Advice only.'

'OK. Advice only.'

'So, more coffee?'

'Yes, thank you.'

He slid out of bed and pulled on his boxers and a T-shirt. Most men don't like making coffee naked. Too vulnerable. Too much steam. He set to work at the small kitchenette that occupied one end of the room. 'What sort of weapons do you need?'

'A small machine gun I can use with one hand. An Uzi?'

'You fired an Uzi?'

'When I was here, yes.'

He turned and mimed shooting the sky. 'You don't remember? How they pull? Semi-auto OK, but on full auto the recoil is too much for one hand. I know what you need. Leave it to me.'

'And at least one automatic pistol. That Glock was fine. Maybe a back-up.'

'Two Glocks, then. Don't mix your guns too much. You want to be able to swap mags.'

'OK, you're the boss. Then, a knife with a retractable blade. So I don't stab myself putting it down my trousers.'

'A Benchmade or a Kershaw. Perhaps the Gerber. Or I could get you a local copy of any of them. Cheaper.'

'Money isn't the issue. Get me the best.'

'Is there much more? I don't like the sound of this.'

He certainly wasn't going to enjoy what was to come. I still had quite the shopping list. I thought I'd get the one that would make his jaw drop out of the way first. 'Can you get me a TED?'

'A TED.'

'A Tactical—'

'Sam, I know what a TED is.' He sounded hurt. He came over with the coffee. 'I am just ... do you want to start a war?'

'I want two.'

'Oh, it's a *world* war.' He shook his head, like I was Kim Jong-un.

'It's a local skirmish. I just want weaponry on my side.'

He thought it over. Then shrugged. 'Maybe I can get you a TED. Or two. And a VAD. Not from people I enjoy dealing with, you understand.'

'Thank you.' I put my mug on a side table and extracted the phone from my trousers at the foot of the bed. I pulled up and showed him a photo on the screen. 'And I need the plans for this building.'

He sipped his coffee and his face creased in concern, as if he had just realised investments can go down as well as up. 'You know, Sam, I think I sold myself too cheap.'

# THIRTY-EIGHT

*How far would you go to save a loved one? Your own flesh and blood?*

This far, I thought, as I eased open one of the art nouveau panelled doors and stepped inside the ruined casino. There were no guards to stop me. That was one of the things I had used Pavol's people for. They had bundled the three uniformed security guards into a van and would keep them in a remote location overnight, then let them go. Minus their phones, of course, and with a long trudge along snow-covered roads.

Nothing too cruel.

Now, some of Pavol's chums wearing the guards' uniforms stood at the entrance, just in case anyone got curious about the lack of security for the 'private function' taking place. I had until the shift change – six hours – to do my work and get out. I really wouldn't need that long.

I closed the door behind me, guiding it into place with no more than a soft click. The interior, lit by fake, flickering electric candles, reminded me of a cathedral:

a great soaring dome, supported by once-gilded ribs, now cracked and denuded of decoration. At some point, this house of cards would have rivalled the great casinos of Europe in grandeur. In fact, it would have made Monte Carlo look like a branch of Betfred. I could almost hear the laughter and chink of glasses of the *fin de siècle beau monde*.

Almost.

I listened for any disturbance in the air. Apart from the drip of water from a breach in the roof and the occasional hiss of waves on the promenade outside, there was nothing. The Black Sea has no tidal range to speak of, so the rhythmic thud of waves against the exterior stone walls was a constant.

Wherever they were, the men I was looking for weren't in the building. At least, not this part. Why would they be? It might have been out of season, but the roof leaked and there was always the chance of an idle tourist wandering in. A tourist who would find themselves with a hole in the skull quicker than they could think, 'Oops, wrong turn!'

No, if I had read the plans correctly, the auction would be below my feet, in the cellars – *catacombs*? – of this derelict building.

The Void.

I had to go down there. I could hear Freddie's voice in my head: *Wait for back-up*.

But there was no back-up. My back-up was either dead or damaged.

I was on my own.

I placed the holdall I had been carrying onto the floor and crouched next to it. With gloved hands I pulled the zip. From within, I took out the submachine gun that Pavol had recommended. It was the kind of gun that would get me a hefty prison sentence if I were to even possess it in the UK. If they knew what I intended to do with it, what hate was eating up my heart, they'd lock me up and throw away the key.

I stood and checked it over in the thin light that penetrated the centre of the hall. It was a weird-looking weapon, all right. Made of polymer, the FN P-90 could pass for a ray gun in a 1950s science-fiction film. Or a device for vacuuming the interior of a car. But, as requested, it could be fired one-handed, could punch through body armour at one hundred metres and its magazine could carry an impressive fifty rounds.

But even fifty rounds wouldn't last long on full automatic.

I stuffed two extra mags behind my own body armour and switched on the P-90's laser-dot system. As I moved the weapon, the glowing spot danced on the far wall, over the scabrous rococo plasterwork. I imagined it exploding into dust. I made sure the safety was on, just in case my imagination translated into an involuntary pull of the trigger.

I looked up and scanned the higher floors. There was a circular space where perhaps an internal window once sat. It was empty now. I drew the laser over it but the dot danced in empty space. Nobody was up there getting a bead on me.

I killed the laser, took out a Glock and put it in my belt, tucked down against my arse. I couldn't feel its polymer body against my skin because I was wearing a thin neoprene wetsuit under my body armour and clothes. I had a few other bits and pieces that I put around my body, but most of the items were in the small black rucksack that I threaded my arms through.

I put on a head torch, but left it switched off. Same with the throat mic assembly. I inserted an ear-pro capsule into each side of my head and flipped the retaining clip behind the lobe. Even these US-made earplugs were not as good as full defender headphones, but they were better than nothing.

Satisfied I was done, I slid the holdall into a corner, then checked everything was tight, from bootlaces to bra straps.

It was. I was ready to go.

As I headed for the stairs, limping to ease the pain in my left knee, I tried to recall how all this started; how I'd ended up looking for men to kill. The answer was always the same.

Albania.

It seemed like a lifetime ago now, that mountain. How did I know it was a hit?

I just did. It's what I do.

I found the stairwell that would take me down to the basement. I cocked an ear.

I could hear voices.

It had been difficult to monitor the comings and goings through the sleet and fog that had surrounded the casino over the past couple of days. Trucks had backed up to the loading bay, boats had tied up at the pier. I hadn't been able to mount a full watch, so I wasn't sure how many people were down there. Or if Jess was even in the building.

I would find out soon enough.

I padded down the stone steps, feeling the cold air wrap itself around my face. My body was warm; I was sweating under the rubber and the Kevlar that coated me. But my breath was steaming in the chill coming up from the basement.

I switched on the laser and it traced patterns on the thick black curtain that blanked off the bottom of the staircase.

I paused at the foot of the stairs.

The curtain was velvet and new. It was the only thing I had seen so far that wasn't threadbare or careworn or cracked. Still, the voices from beyond penetrated slightly, past the barrier and my ear protection, enough for me to know that *someone* was on the other side. I decided on a hard entry. Hell, who was I kidding? It was always going to be a hard entry.

I unclipped the two ACS flash grenades from the sides of my backpack. These would explode with the light of 400,000 candlepower and a noise of up to 170 decibels.

It was disorientating without damaging. That was the theory.

I flipped back the fuse protector and pulled the pin on the first, lifted the curtain and rolled it under. I repeated the action with the second, but I pulled the curtain aside for this one and threw. Then I ducked away, closed my eyes and put my fingers over the ear defenders.

I saw the light from the magnesium and mercury powder even through the curtains and my closed lids, as if a sun had been born, flared and died. The pressure wave created by the bang element of the charge billowed the velvet all around me. As soon as I felt that die away I charged through the curtain, the FN sub ready to go.

Then I stopped dead.

I had burst through into an empty room.

# THIRTY-NINE

'Room' was an inadequate description of the space. It was brick-built – although said bricks were weathered – ancient and, in places, water-damaged. The arched and ribbed ceiling was also made of old, uneven brick. The subterranean areas were much older than the casino above, elements of it Roman and Byzantine, with some medieval additions, such as the roof above me.

The main area was subdivided by two rows of pillars, which flanked a central, nave-like corridor. The floor was made of enormous stone flags, some of them containing rusted metal rings, as if to secure ropes. It was possible this had once been a dry dock of some description.

There were no windows, just a large circular metal plate high on one wall, where it looked as though a rose window had been sealed up. I knew from the plans it wasn't a window, never had been. Every second pillar was equipped with a lamp holder with a bare bulb, apart from at the far end, where the darkness shimmered. Smoke from the grenades curled around the lights, and the air was gritty and choking, grabbing the back of my throat, like a forty-a-day fag habit.

I took all this in within a second.

My attention was mostly held by a white cinema-style screen hanging at the black end of the nave. Projected onto it was a series of faces, head-and-shoulder shots of various people, mostly male, fifty or older, I would guess. It was like a geriatric Benetton ad or a Michael Jackson video.

Each person mouthed a single phrase that was relayed, slightly out of sync with the image, over speakers I couldn't see. I pulled out the earplugs. The words were in a polyglot of languages, but even I knew what they were saying.

*Thank you.*

No buyers. No auction. No girls. No Jess.

*He likes to play games.*

A red dot scurried along the stone flags like a glowing cockroach, then up my leg until it came to rest on my chest. I could see sections of its beam picked out here and there in the smoke from the grenades. It was coming from just to the side of the projection screen, originating somewhere in the blackness beyond it. I thought about the Kevlar armour I had strapped across my torso. Maybe the gunman did, too, because the dot slowly crawled to my throat. Not an easy shot, but certainly a vulnerable one.

The speakers went quiet. The faces continued to rotate, six of them in all, still silently mouthing their gratitude. I looked at the nearest pillar. Three, maybe four paces.

He read my thoughts. 'Just remember, Sam, Oktane never misses.'

It was Bojan's disembodied voice. And this was what Oktane had been activated for.

Me.

'Stay exactly where you are. You will never make it. And just in case you think you'll get me, be aware that I am not stupid enough to be in the building, Sam. Neither is Jess actually in here.'

'The Void? The auction?' I asked. 'All a ruse?'

He laughed, a metallic sound over the speakers. 'All a little game.'

'How could you know I'd find this place?' It was, after all, more by luck than any skill I'd found out about The Void.

'I couldn't be sure. But the spike of activity of people in London searching for FOTB told me it was very likely you had. I was impressed. I had some other clues ready to feed you if you hadn't taken the bait. So I knew I'd get you here one way or another.'

What kind of target would I make, turned sideways, crouched, running? Small. How good could he be, this man?

'Put your weapon down. Now.'

'Where's Jess?'

'All in good time. Do as I say. Or he'll shoot you where you stand and then you'll never see your daughter again. Not in this life.'

I did as he said.

'Kick it away.'

354

I kicked it away. It skidded over the flags like a curling kettle. It travelled further than I had hoped.

'Turn around.'

I did so.

'There's a pistol in the small of your back, take it out.' I complied. 'Throw it after the other one.'

It clattered onto the floor. That was the sum total of guns about my body. The spare Glock was in the backpack. Not an easy extraction, but possible ...

He read my mind. Again.

'Now, if you want to know about your daughter, take off your backpack.' I shrugged it. 'Place it at your feet. If I know you, Sam Wylde, there'll be a second weapon in there. Maybe even a third. Very slowly, take it off.'

Again, I did as I was told.

'You'll have some restraining straps in there. Yes? I want you, again *very* slowly, to take one out.'

Four paces to the pillar. Maybe five.

But I unzipped the bag and brought out one of the straps. Four paces was a long way, after all. Five, far too many.

'Take out the gun. Slowly.'

I was very measured in my movements.

'Throw it away.'

I complied with his instructions.

'And rucksack.'

It, too, ended up beyond my reach.

'Now, using the restraining strap, tie your hands together. Tighten with your teeth. You know how it's done.'

I knew how it was done. I had made people do it myself. It took a few moments, but eventually my wrists were bound.

'Tighter.'

I put the free end of the strap in my mouth and pulled. As I did so, I touched my throat.

'Good. Well done.'

There was a crackle on the speaker. Then the faces on screen found their voices again. *Thank you, danke, shukran, xiè xie nǐ.*

After two rotations of the cast, they went silent once more. I waited. I killed the time by counting the number and memorising the positions of the rings set into the floor. Easy to trip over those things.

'You know who they are thanking?'

I didn't want to play his game. I kept quiet.

'Jess.'

I swallowed hard. It was best I didn't speak. Were these the 'buyers'? Had I missed the sale?

'And you know what they have to thank her for?'

*You're going to tell me, aren't you, you sick fuck?* But I said nothing.

'Life.'

'What?'

'Life. That one has Jess's heart. A fine young heart. The Chinese guy, the liver; the Saudi, new eyes, all thanks to Jess. You know what the old name of this place was? Of Constanta? It was Tomis. It means "to cut". Ironic, eh?'

The noise began in my head again, the sizzling short

356

circuit. My vision began to darken at the periphery. I took a step forward.

'And that's what we have done. Cut her. A young body like your daughter's is worth more as spare parts than any sex trafficker could get. Of course, we could have sold her on and used the organs when FOTB was finished with her. But there would be a chance of infection then – AIDS, herpes, hepatitis. But how much more could we charge if she was unsullied? A lot. Heart, lungs, liver, corneas, kidneys ...'

I forced the sounds in my head back to where they had come from, deep, deep into my brain. I spoke loudly, clearly, as if my partner could actually hear me. 'Freddie. Activate ... Vesuvius. *Vesuvius.*'

My words crossed the ether and arrived at a radio receiver in the VAD – Voice Activated Detonator. The explosion from the two TEDs was muffled, but there was nothing subdued about the boom of the metal disc from the 'window' as it spun through the air and bounced off one of the pillars, nor about the throaty gurgle and roar of the sea as it rushed in after it.

Tactical Entry Devices were designed to blow down a terrorist's or a drug dealer's steel doors and allow the entry of law enforcement. But they had done an equally good job of letting the Black Sea into this old building via the rose-window-style panel, which was actually a sea door.

The plume of water shot across the cellar, slicing through the laser beam, and I made my move to the pillar, scooping up my backpack. There was a crack of a round, fired blindly, but I had no idea where it went. By the time I made it to cover, the gurgling, swirling water was a foot deep and rising, cold and black around me.

I reached into the backpack and pulled out the Snorka cylinder and, hands still tied together, clamped my teeth and lips over the mouthpiece.

Up to my knees now, the sea a torrent of white streaks as it spewed from the aperture, frothing where it hit the surface of the newly created lake, and glistening like ink as it flowed into the far reaches of the room. There was a loud bang followed by a crackle and some of the lights went out.

I found the knife Pavol had bought for me, hit the blade release, and spent a few precious seconds sawing through the ties, cutting the base of my thumb through the glove as I did so. But I couldn't feel the pain.

I hit the quick-release buttons on the side straps and shed the skin of the Kevlar body armour. It would only get in the way. The spare mags I had hidden behind it plopped into the water.

The incoming sea had seeped into my wetsuit now. It should have kept me warm, but this was winter sea. Plus, my gloves weren't up to the job. I had selected them for flexibility, not warmth. You can't flick off a safety and fire a gun with sausage-like fingers.

But that might have been a mistake.

My teeth wanted to chatter. Hypothermia was looming. I turned on the Snorka's oxygen valve and felt the gas flow brush against my tongue.

The sea was creeping over my hips to my waist. I crouched down and let myself tumble forward and underwater. With no hood, my ears began to hum with pain. And I was blind. Hardly any of what was left of the light penetrated beneath the surface. I could just make out the dark column of one of the brick pillars. Using it as a way marker, I pushed myself down to the floor and began to swim, feeling myself lift towards the surface as I did so. I was too buoyant. My fingers found the first of the metal rings and I yanked, pulling myself down, until I was parallel to the floor. I hadn't factored these in. I was happy they were there, though. They would act as my weight belt, keeping me submerged.

*Worth more as spare parts . . .*

Not now. Please, God, not now.

I pushed off and kicked over to the next ring, right where I thought the submachine gun would be. I groped around on the floor, but couldn't find it. How useful would it be after a submersion? I had no idea. Or the Glocks? The latter were rated for full saltwater immersion, but I had never heard that tested. Besides, I couldn't find either of the damned things anyway.

I moved to my right, fingertips outstretched for my next handhold. I found it. Six more, I reckoned, and I would be at the entrance to the staircase, where the curtain was. That would be where he would head, too. Oktane. For the exit. I had to get there before him.

I kicked hard, hoping not to break the surface. The

Snorka produced a thin stream of bubbles, but I reckoned my opponent or opponents would hardly notice them in the turmoil above. Snorkas were used as an emergency air reserve by scuba divers. This model gave me ten minutes, at most. It would be enough. If I didn't freeze to death first.

Two more handholds were achieved. I was having trouble moving, though. I was heavy, but not in a good way. My limbs felt like wax, making my movements ponderous. My eyes were burning and I should have thought of a nose clip. I was probably consuming the oxygen in the tiny cylinder far faster than I should.

*Heart, lungs, liver.*

I tried not to scream into the mouthpiece as I swam on, colliding with the base of a pillar. I scrabbled for grip on the floor, but there was no ring. I grabbed the corner of the column for purchase and thrust myself forward. But still no rings. I was in danger of floating up to the surface.

Just then, somebody stood on my hand.

Whether they knew it was a hand, I don't know, but it slithered off. I could see the shape of the man's legs and the boots that were trying to find purchase on the floor. The water must be up to his chest, at least, I estimated.

What I did next was instinctive.

I stabbed the back of his knee with my knife and saw something darker than the water squirt out, like a cloud of squid ink. Then I spiked the back of the thigh. Once, twice. And then I stood.

It was up to my chest, maybe a bit lower for him. He had on a sodden balaclava, just his eyes showing. And in those, surprise and pain.

Oktane still had the rifle in his hands, but I was too close for him to bring it to bear. He swung the barrel at me and it caught my freezing cheek, setting off pixels of pain across the side of my head.

As I turned, the front sight of the weapon caught the Snorka, ripping it from my mouth. I slashed at his arm as it came past, and I must have hit something because the rifle flew from his hands and was swallowed by the water.

I sucked in fresh air, stepped in close and sank the blade into his neck and twisted, enjoying the warmth of the blood that penetrated the gloves to my cold fingers. He didn't move. The shock had petrified him. I extracted the blade, changed hands and did the other side.

Then, as if the spell had been broken, this frozen man came to life and lunged at me. A terrible gurgling sound came out of Oktane's mouth as he leapt and, with the strength of a madman, wrapped his arms around my upper body and squeezed. I felt a rib pop. I still had my arms free and I carried on stabbing, but he had me in a grip and was dragging me under. His entire weight was on top of me now, and I couldn't shake him. He screamed again and blood spattered over my face. I raised the knife and brought it down on his back, but it skidded off his ribs, twisting from my grip.

I pushed his head back, gouged the eyes, tore at the mouth, almost ripped off an ear, but I knew he was dead. He was just doing his damnedest to make sure I went with him.

# FORTY

I don't remember the hands that pulled me to the surface or unpeeled me from Oktane's death grip. It wasn't Freddie. After all, Freddie wasn't even in the country. I had simply used a familiar name as a radio trigger.

The first contact I remembered was a young, female medic standing over me, wrapping a dressing around my upper arm. I tried to take in my surroundings, but she forced my head back down. I was on a stretcher, but raised off the ground, so probably a wheeled medical trolley of some description. I was mostly wrapped in a light, shiny metal blanket. I was cold, bloodless, the hand that I could see marbled with blue veins.

'What happened to my arm?' I asked through blubbery lips.

'Bullet wound.'

*Bullet wound*? Then I remembered the shot as I dashed for the pillar. I thought he'd been firing blind. Maybe not. Or maybe the inrush of water, the disturbance of the air, had affected the flight of the round.

Oktane never misses.

Except when someone has blown a sea door nearby. Even so, why hadn't I felt it?

I looked up at the dome above my head and the restless pigeons, unsettled by all this activity. I was on the ground floor of the casino. I was aware of other bodies moving around, and in my peripheral vision I could see men in combat gear with serious weaponry held at waist height. Well, I always guessed, no matter what had happened, the cops would turn up, most likely elite ones like these. What I didn't expect was Tom.

He knelt next to my trolley and touched my face. 'Hi.'

'Hi,' I said. And I began to cry; great sobs that caused the medic to tut. Tom hugged me as best he could and waited until the worst of it had gone. 'How ...?'

'Bratislava,' he said. 'You told Adam you were going there, remember?'

I didn't remember. It must have been a slip of the tongue. Careless. It was one of the gaps in my memory of recent events. There seemed to be quite a number of them.

'Adam, in his own sweet time, told Freddie, Freddie put two and two together. Weapons training. She figured you went there to get tooled up and get your eye back in. So, she sent me out to see your chum Pavol. Who was very worried about you. Very.'

There was a lot of weight to that 'very'. I kept quiet.

'He told me about the weapons and that you had

asked to see the plans for this building. I told Europol that there was a sex-slave auction here. They contacted the FBI ...'

I sighed. My words came slow, deliberate so the chatter of my teeth didn't distort them. 'The FBI? Jesus. There's no auction. It was all a ... it was all a sick game. A ruse to draw me in.'

'We know that now. The FBI has cyber-forensics on it. It was all a front: the auction, FOTB. He knew you'd come if he laid out the breadcrumbs properly.'

There was a question I was afraid to ask, but it came out anyway, escaping like a greyhound out of the traps. 'Is there a body down there?'

'Yes.'

My throat caught before I realised: of course there was a body down there. I created it. 'No, no. Jess, I mean. Is Jess there?'

He squeezed my good arm through the blanket. 'Not that they've found.'

The tears came again, hot, but as salty as that sea. 'Oh, God. What have I done, Tom? To Jess. And he's not here. Bojan. He was using a remote set-up. He got away.' And I had to find him. I had to know whether Bojan was telling the truth about Jess or whether it was another of his psychological tortures. His *games*.

'Shush. We're taking you to hospital. You need to rest. Get checked out.' Where had I heard that before?

The medic finished. Suddenly, after feeling like I was entombed in an iceberg, I was warm, but the sort of warmth you get from an electric blanket. Artificial. Not quite right. I'd been given drugs. I felt my head drop to one side. Bollocks, not now.

My words slurred, as if I was half a bottle of vodka down. I struggled to keep it slow and deliberate. 'I need something. From downstairs. When they . . . when they pump the water out.'

'What?'

'There's a projector or a computer. Something rigged up to show a short film. I need it. Don't let the police take it. Don't.'

'It's the FBI. They know what they are doing.'

'The FBI means it'll disappear for years. I need it now.'

'Why? It'll be water-damaged anyway.'

'I want you to get it,' I said with as much feeling as I could muster. I could feel a veil coming down. 'Get it. Steal it if you have to. Bribe someone. Please.'

There was a commotion of clanging and groaning as another trolley was manhandled up the stairs. I swivelled on one elbow.

There was a body strapped to it. A body with a balaclava on his face.

One of the cops stepped forward and pulled it off. With a final push, I raised myself up further to see the face of Oktane.

Except it wasn't Oktane.

Or maybe it was all along, and there had only been one of them from the get-go. Perhaps all that bullshit about the Phantom had been just that. Either way, the man I was looking at, as pallid as a dead fish on a slab, his neck disfigured by vicious sawing wounds, was Bojan.

I'd killed the one man who could tell me what had really happened to my daughter.

# EPILOGUE

I can see Freddie, her face illuminated by the light from the TV screen in her living room. Lovely, loyal Freddie. She deserves a better friend than me.

She is sipping a glass of wine. Of course she is. I am smoking another cigarette. Well, not smoking. Holding. Last one for a long time, I promise myself.

Spring is almost here and the trees in her road are ready to unveil their new foliage. It is dusk and the street-lamps have flickered on. New, sterile white ones that remind me of an operating theatre. I miss the yellow of sodium. It was less clinical, the tones of my childhood; warm and safe.

Although, that's nostalgia talking. Childhood is rarely warm and safe. Mine certainly wasn't. Jess's . . .

I watch a worm of pulsing light crawl around the periphery of my retina. Inside it are tiny blue and silver fragments of cubic zirconium. The events at the casino have left me prone to the visual disturbances of migraines, although not the headaches. No doctor can tell me why that should be. So now I just live with the light show they provide. It fades after ten minutes.

I should get out of the car and ring Freddie's bell, but I am hesitating. I have been hesitating for almost an hour.

Many weeks have passed since I was released by the police in Romania without charge. Self-defence, they decided. Especially when it transpired that I had killed Oktane, the well-known international assassin.

Or one of them.

I denied having anything to do with the TED device that detonated and blew out the circular sea door. Why the throat mic? they asked.

Well, it was a voice-activation device for the explosives. Like Siri or Alexa. Except, my electronic helper was called Freddie – saying her name, coupled with Vesuvius, triggered the explosion. But I didn't tell the police about that. Play dumb, my lawyer said. There was no *playing* in it. Numb and dumb, that was me. I told them it was just part of the body-armour kit, designed to communicate with partners. But I had no partners. I had acted alone. Charge me or discharge me. They chose the latter.

After they had let me go, I went back with Tom. He nursed me as best he could. I wasn't an easy patient. Over time, some sort of equilibrium was re-established between us. Not like the old days. It could never be like that. But someone to hold me when I cried, that was often more than enough for me.

But he is gone now. Back to France. He cut some sort of deal with Leka. He wouldn't tell me what. But it was like he had a penance to serve or he was an indentured servant. My guess is he's bodyguarding Elona and her kids. That would be ironic. Tom gets my old job, while I ... I what? How do you describe what I have become, what I am about to do?

Best not give it a name.

I spoke to Freddie on the phone several times while I was up north. She is disappointed in me. She has two good legs now. She wants to move ahead with Winter & Wylde, the all-female PPO agency. I told her I have much to do before then. And I don't have much time to do it. Although, at that point I didn't know just how little.

She told me that Adam had separated from his wife Kath. She had been having an affair with his boss, apparently. He quit the paper and is writing a book set in Albania. No, not about the war and that actor, Anthony someone. About two freelance bodyguards. Inspired by actual events, he says.

And what about me? I have work to do, too. On the seat next to me is a folder containing photographs of six people. I don't really need the pictures. Their faces are burned into my cerebral cortex, branded there by hot irons. *Lungs, heart, liver, kidneys ...*

But my mental images can't be processed through facial-recognition technology. If these people are out there in cyberspace, I can find them. That's why I need the photographs.

If what Bojan said was true, these six have pieces of my Jess in them. Pieces they didn't deserve. Parts they acquired illegally.

And now, they'll have to pay.

And there is at least one doctor involved. Someone had to harvest those body parts. So, he or she or they will have to be struck off. Permanently. It is getting to be quite the to-do list.

Of course, I only have Bojan's word for what happened to Jess, and his word wasn't worth much. Almost everything he told me was all smoke and mirrors. It might be I am mistaken. Jess might be alive.

I relish that word. *Alive.*

And if she is, then tracking down those people on the film might lead me to her. It is worth the effort, no matter what the outcome.

And there is still this question: how did Bojan beat me to the punch? How did he get to Jess at her school first? So, at some point, I'll be talking to Matt. A drug dealer with a Frankenstein hand couldn't be that hard to track down. And if the answers aren't there, I will pay a house call on Dieter. And maybe I'd say hi to Aja again. I suspect the answer to Bojan's success lies somewhere in that trio.

And then there is Leka. He had told Tom about The Void. Had he been instrumental in setting me up to go to Constanta and find what Bojan had done? After all, Leka and Bojan could easily have known each other. Especially if Bojan really was an Oktane. Or if Bojan went back after we left Calais and struck a sick deal with him. Had I been suckered into the whole encounter in Constanta?

There are lots of questions to be asking. I suspect the answer to the last one, though, is a resounding yes.

Truth will out eventually. Even if you have to drag it into the light kicking and screaming.

But first I will find them, these six people from The Void, and use them to find out exactly what happened to my daughter.

'Why didn't you come and get me, Mummy?'

I am, my love. I am. This time for real.

I look across to Freddie once more. I suspect I won't be seeing her for a while and it hurts. But she doesn't understand what I have to do. How could she? How could anyone?

I came here tonight with big news. But I don't know how she will take it. I run my hand over the bump of my belly the way I do dozens of times a day now, as if I can't quite believe there is something growing in there. *Someone*, I correct myself.

I haven't told Freddie yet. Hell, I haven't even told the father. But the little he or she inside me won't change anything. I have a baby growing in me, it's true. But I still have another child, out there in the world.

I drop the unsmoked cigarette out of the window, raise the glass up, start the car and move off, glad it has begun at last.

# AUTHOR'S NOTE

There is a rather spectacular derelict casino on the seafront at Constanta. But it's not like the one in this book. It just looks a bit like it. Ovid *was* exiled to the town, though, and there is a statue of him there. He hated the place. The quotes at the opening of Parts 1–4 are from Ovid.

Actor Anthony Quayle really was in Albania for SOE during the Second World War. We have been there too, and it isn't full of people-trafficking gangsters. We put them there. The stories about organ harvesting at the Yellow House persist, even though solid evidence is hard to pin down.

We would like to thank the Four Seasons and Coco Shambala on Bali and the Belmond Napasi on Koh Samui for advice and hospitality. All the members of staff and various characters depicted here are fictitious and bear no resemblance to any actual persons. Bella Ryan and Jessica Masterson did our 'location scouting' elsewhere in Asia.

Also, thank you to our editors Jo Dickinson and

Rebecca Farrell, and to Sue Stephens, Justine Gold, Richard Vlietstra, Jess Barratt, Dawn Burnett and all at Simon & Schuster for supporting the series.

Once again, our gratitude goes to Lisa Baldwin, the PPO who kick-started Sam Wylde into action. A piece we did for *The Times* on the reality behind PPOs is included as an appendix.

There are, of course, unanswered questions at the end of *Winner Kills All* – about how Bojan got Jess and whether Bojan and Leka were in cahoots. And, of course, about who is the father of Sam's child. They will be addressed in Sam Wylde IV.

# THE REAL SAM WYLDES

How much of Sam Wylde's background/training is based on the reality of the bodyguarding business? Are there really that many female Personal Protection Officers? At a book event in 2017, an editor at *The Times* asked both these questions. We had explained what the series was about and she had assumed that Sam's role was completely fictitious. When we insisted that Sam is inspired by actual PPOs – although she does tend to go off-piste more than your average PPO – and that, as a female, she can command higher fees than males, the editor asked us to research and write a piece to prove it. This is the resulting article, which was published in T2 of *The Times* in 2017.

*

Our instructions were simple. Fly to Dublin. Catch a bus to a shopping mall on the outskirts of the city. Go to a particular coffee shop. We would meet there.

'How will I recognise you?' we asked.

'Don't worry,' came the reply from my contact. 'I'll spot you.'

I am about to enter the world of the Circuit, the slang term used for the international brotherhood and, increasingly, sisterhood of what is variously known as Close Protection, Personal Protection or Executive Protection Officers (CPO/PPO/EPO). Or, in everyday vernacular, bodyguards, a term that most on the Circuit dislike, believing it has misleading associations (many involving Kevin Costner).

Our journey to the coffee shop began a few months previously, with an arresting advert on the Gumtree website. 'We are looking for an experienced female CPO/PPO/driver OR an experienced driver with a knowledge of security for our clients in Westminster. You will be driving the new Rolls-Royce Ghost and MUST have previous experience driving luxury cars . . . 2-3 months during the summer may be spent in Monte Carlo with possible short trips in the winter months to St Moritz.'

As novelists always on the lookout for an interesting protagonist, we were intrigued. Apart from it sounding like quite a gig, why did it specify a female? 'Cultural reasons' was the explanation when we asked. And did many women bodyguards exist? Yes they did – it turned out I had stumbled upon an aspect of the security industry that was in the midst of a boom.

It didn't take long to discover evidence of many female bodyguards. The Duchess of Cambridge has been pictured with her female Protection Officer.

David Cameron regularly took his along for a jog. A woman made up part of Tony Blair's post-PM protection – although unfortunately this came to light only when she left her Glock pistol in the lavatory of a Starbucks – and there is at least one female in Theresa May's security team.

These individuals, of course, are firearms-trained members of the Met's elite Protection Command. However, I was also interested in the 'executive' protection business, those PPOs used by Rihanna, J.K. Rowling or Beyoncé, as well as high-net-worth individuals who are worried about kidnap, especially of their children. It is a commercial PPO called Lisa Baldwin, who is willing to talk on the record, who we have flown to Dublin to meet.

As soon as we walk into the coffee shop, she clocks us (having positioned herself so she had sight lines of both entrances) and raises a hand in greeting. Our first impression as we sit – and she shifts slightly to preserve her view of the room – is: she's so small.

We were expecting someone who could compete with the usual brick outhouses with earphones that you see acting as bodyguards to the stars – but although Baldwin, thirty-three, is fit and gym-toned, she is certainly no heavyweight.

'That ex-military look can sometimes be a disadvantage, for a woman anyway,' she says. 'I remember the first job interview I had, when I was twenty, I was up against another candidate who looked like G.I. Jane, all muscles and shaved head. And I got the job. They were more interested in whether I had protective driving skills, which I had, and a firearms cert, which I also had. In fact, they didn't want me to carry a firearm, but to show I had training in that field.'

Like most PPOs who have to learn to handle a gun, Baldwin had to do it in Slovenia because handguns are illegal in the UK. Has she ever had to be armed, given that training? 'No, I've mostly worked in Ireland and Great Britain. Some people like going to high-risk areas where they will be carrying weapons as a matter of course, but those tend to be ex-military, ex-SAS, who make a fortune running convoys in Afghanistan, say. That's not for me.

'Nine times out of ten, the people I work for want someone who can blend in. They don't want obvious security, like the kind used by Madonna or Britney Spears. Those bodyguards, the big guys, actually draw attention to the clients and put them at more stress and risk. In a playground, I just look like a friend or a nanny, especially if I dress down, which I prefer to the black trouser suit. With the bulkier guys, people will think, "Why have those kids got a bodyguard?" And I'd like to see those big guys run. They are fine if you are just keeping fans back, but I am dealing with things like kidnap threats and might have to get out of a situation very quickly. Pure muscle isn't enough.'

How does a normal person without an army or police background find themselves on the Circuit?

'To be honest, I was looking for a job that wasn't in an office,' says Baldwin. 'I'd realised I wasn't going to make money from my swimming. And someone suggested I try an International Bodyguard Association course. The timing was good. When I started thirteen years ago, there were very few female PPOs. Then suddenly they were being requested all over the place, especially for Muslim families who might not want the women mixing too closely with men. And then there are the bathrooms – if you have a male bodyguard and a female client, that's going to be an issue.'

Neil Davis, a former army officer, confirms this. He runs Horizon, a Glasgow-based security company that offers training in close protection, field medicine and Krav Maga, an Israeli self-defence system favoured by PPOs. 'There is a very high demand for female PPOs right now,' he says. 'Especially as there still aren't that many on the Circuit. Clients who might not want their children looked after by a man often specify a woman. These days, the good female PPOs can work all year round while men struggle to find jobs, especially as there has been an influx from Eastern Europe competing for work. Such is the demand for women, they get paid more than the men at the moment.'

A PPO with the Met's Protection Command can earn up to £100,000 a year with overtime; out in the commercial world it might be 'a healthy five-figure sum', according to Davis. 'The women have to have the right package, though,' he adds. 'Proper training, the ability to speak an extra language or two, maybe a scuba-diving or skiing qualification, so they can always go out with the kids. That all helps.'

Why would you use a female CPO when the client is male, as with Cameron or Blair?

'They have certain advantages,' says Davis. 'If I was putting together a security team of eight, I'd like at least two, maybe three, women in the mix. Do that and the group dynamic instantly changes. Women lower the testosterone level.' He gives an example: 'If it kicks off in bar and some drunk is causing problems for your client, if a man steps up to confront him then the situation can escalate. If a woman does it, the aggression levels drop because, no matter how drunk they are, most men are conditioned to know it is wrong to hit a woman. A female PPO tends to be better at conflict resolution rather than making the situation worse.'

Davis also thinks that a 'civilian' such as Baldwin sometimes has advantages over the usual ex-military or police recruits. 'The people who come from a military background, you sometimes have to retrain them to dial it down. They often come with the wrong attitude. The army teaches you to be aggressive and that's not always the best response for the client when things get noisy. Those from other walks of life tend to have better interpersonal skills.'

At the moment, Horizon has two civilians on a CPO course, one a male deputy head teacher and the other a twenty-three-year-old woman with a degree in criminal investigation. Scottish-born, Horizon-trained Kerry Riddock, twenty-eight, however, is one of those who came to the Circuit from the military. 'I joined the army at sixteen, did eight years as a communication specialist and, when I came out, everything else seemed boring,' she says. 'If you are ex-army I think you see the world differently. Whenever I am shopping or out with friends, the first thing I do is check where the nearest exit is. You are always security conscious. You never lose that. And close protection is one job where you can make use of those skills.'

Would she recommend it as a career choice? 'If you are single, yes. It's terrible on relationships, especially if your partner is a civilian who doesn't understand. And there's also a lot of waiting about. You have to be 'on' 24/7, but things tend to happen at the last minute and then it's all go, go, go. The army prepares you for that, though.'

Baldwin agrees: 'It's better if you are unattached, because the hours . . . you have no life at all. You can be working from crack of dawn to late at night. If you have a client who likes nightclubs, God knows when you'll get to bed. It does mean you have no time to spend the money you are making, though; it's a great way to save up. I know some people who would earn enough for a year just by working the summer season when many Middle Eastern families come over to London.'

What about relationships with clients: is it ever just like *The Bodyguard*?

'It's great if the client will talk to you, discuss things, take advice,' says Baldwin, 'but you don't want to get too close. It's business. I mean, romantic attachments do happen, but it's not as common as Hollywood would have you believe.'

The downside of working for the very rich or very famous is that they can make for very demanding bosses. Baldwin and Riddock have stories – but neither will name names. 'One of our girls got a dream job with a big R&B star,' says Baldwin, 'but they were such a nightmare to work for, she walked away. And I heard some terrible things about a footballer a PPO friend of mine worked for.'

Riddock, meanwhile, worked for six months as part of a large security team for a wealthy family where the two children had a male and a female bodyguard each. 'I looked after a boy of four who was heir to the business and was treated like a prince,' says Riddock. 'What he said went. Yet I was responsible for his safety and security. At one point he decided he didn't want his seat belt on, so I refused to move the vehicle until he was strapped in. I was the one who was told off by the mother for not doing as I was told.' Riddock says she didn't renew her contract, but wouldn't go into any more detail.

In fact, most PPOs are scathing about bodyguards who guard 'n' tell and end up exposing their celebrity clients' sex lives or the standard of their parenting. 'Discretion is an essential part of the job,' says Baldwin. And anyway, gossiping about clients is a good way to make sure you don't work in the industry again. 'After all, who is going to employ a bodyguard with a big mouth?'

Have you read the first fast-paced, unputdownable
thriller featuring Sam Wylde?

# SAFE
# FROM
# HARM

### YOU CAN RUN

Sam Wylde is a Close Protection Officer to the rich
and powerful. In a world dominated by men, being a
woman has been an advantage. And she is the best in the
business at what she does.

### YOU CAN HIDE

She takes a job protecting the daughter of the Sharifs –
Pakistani textile tycoons – but she realises that there
is more to their organisation than meets the eye and
suddenly she finds herself in danger.

### BUT ONLY ONE PERSON WILL KEEP YOU
### SAFE FROM HARM

Now she is trapped underground, with no light, no
signal and no escape. Dangerous men are coming to hurt
her and the young charge she is meant to be protecting.
With time running out, can she channel everything she
knows to keep them alive?

SIMON &
SCHUSTER

Like most people on The Circuit – the ad-hoc and often fractious fellowship of Personal Protection Officers worldwide – I am very good at packing. I take a modular approach, with the commonest essentials already encased in plastic sleeves in my wardrobe to be laid into the suitcase in the appropriate order. And there is always a Ready To Go pack, too, filled with the tools of my trade – spare batteries, travel plug, solar charger, camera, lightweight jacket, wash kit, broad-spectrum antibiotics, a supply of various currencies, tampons and a first-aid kit with haemostatic packs. This time, though, the packing seemed to be getting away from me.

When I had first tossed the Tumi suitcase on the bed and unzipped it, the inside had seemed cavernous. Now, after placing in the jeans, day and evening dresses and the one-piece Chloe jumpsuit (what Paul called my *Mission Impossible To Get Into* outfit), it seemed to be imploding like something out of Stephen Hawking's imagination. The black hole of the interior was definitely shrinking.

'I'm going to need a bigger suitcase,' I shouted, looking at the pile of clothes still on the bed. I don't usually bother with hold luggage when I'm flying and working, but at least two of the travelling party were putting suitcases in the belly of the beast and that removed any advantage of carry-on.

'What have you got?'

I turned to look at Paul, my husband, who was pulling on a waxed cotton jacket over a shirt and jeans.

'What's this? Dress-down Tuesday?' I asked.

He shrugged and smiled, his eyes crinkling. On me, those lines just looked like age. On him, they looked cute. He was more than ten years older than me – he could see the forces of fifty massing on the hills for an attack and his hair was now evenly balanced between dark and grey – but I couldn't help feeling that, by some freak of nature, I was busy catching up with him.

'How much have you got on?' he repeated.

'One reception, one lunch, two dinners,' I recited. 'Two cocktail parties and a fundraiser. Plus two TV shows and a radio. Dressy was the word that came down from on high.'

'I hear they have shops in America,' he said, snaking his arms around my waist.

'I hear that too,' I said, unwrapping his hands. 'It's

time I won't have.' I gave a sigh, thinking about the next five days and the plans that had crumbled to dust before our very eyes when the work call came for me. 'I can't believe we managed to lose Jess for a whole week and Elena for five days of those and here I am packing for the States.'

Elena was our au pair, who was heading home to Estonia to see her family. Paul turned me, stepped in close and gave me a quick darting kiss on the cheek before leaning back. I caught a hint of the Tom Ford I had bought him for Christmas. 'We could always . . .'

I knew that look. Paul was no different from every other man.

'Let's be clear, dear,' I said quickly. 'There's no chance of one last fuck in case my plane goes down so you can always remember me that way. Have a wank on me.' That didn't come out quite like I intended, so I put a finger to his lips.

Those eyes crinkled again. 'Shields up already?'

He was referring to my psychological barriers, which come down to block out all extraneous emotions when I'm working. Nothing, apart from the job in hand, gets through to me. I'm hardly alone in that. How can a nurse work with dying people all day long and still function? How do firemen face the next day after carrying an asphyxiated child from a house? What about the cops who have to trawl through some depraved bastard's computer looking at . . .

We all have shields. And Paul was right. Mine were already clicking into place.

'Yup.'

I disentangled myself with a slight reluctance and looked at the case again.

'Do you really need three pairs of shoes?' he offered.

'Trainers and two flats.' I'm lucky to be tall enough to get away with flats, even at the formal dinners. I have colleagues on The Circuit who swear by heels with scored soles for grip. Not me. If I have to run, I want something on my feet that won't snap and that sticks to the floor like octopus suckers. It's why I tend to favour floor-length clothes for formal events, just in case someone wonders why I'm not in needle-heeled Louboutins like everyone else. 'And if that's the best you've got, I'll figure this out myself. Get going.' I looked him up and down. 'Where you off to anyway?'

He wouldn't be wearing such a casual outfit if he were heading for the Civil Nuclear Constabulary HQ near Oxford. He'd be in either a dark suit and tie or full CNC uniform, depending on the occasion.

'A few house calls to make. And I've got to pop in at St John's Wood on the way.'

He said it matter-of-factly, but I knew what St John's Wood meant. A weapon was to be drawn. It was my turn to step in close. 'Is there trouble?'

Paul shook his head. 'Just routine, ma'am. Then I'm off for the rest of the week, remember? All on my lonesome.' He gave me a kiss on the forehead – I might be tall but he was taller still. It was one of the things I liked about him straight away – no more hunched shoulders and cricked necks stooping down to be at the same level as men of average height.

'Look, I'll call you, let you know I got there safely, eh?'

'WhatsApp me. It's free.' Paul was always bang on the pulse of technology, whereas I definitely dragged behind the beat.

'Of course. You'll be all right?' I asked, feeling a wave of affection for him crash over the shields and take me by surprise.

'It will be a feast of China Garden and the Tiffin Hut.' Paul was a good cook, but he drew the line at preparing meals for one when both Jess and I were away. When I returned there would be a forest's-worth of takeaway leaflets on the fridge, neat circles around the numbers of his favourites. 'And I'll be here when Jess gets back from her sleep-over, for sure,' he added. 'So don't worry.'

'I won't. Love you,' I said, hoping he knew I meant it, despite my next comment. 'Now fuck off and leave me alone.'

I pretended to fuss over my packing until I heard the sound of Paul's car starting and then let out a long, slow breath. In truth, part of me didn't like travelling, didn't enjoy leaving home, hated those bloody barriers

I had to put between us. But I knew it was the wrench of closing the door behind me that was the hardest part. Once I was in that car on the way to Heathrow, I began looking only forward, to doing my job and doing it well, the shields locked solid.

But there was a craving to hear Jess's voice before I put her aside for a few days. I punched in her number but it came up busy. Of course it would be. Chatting shit, as Paul put it. I'd already had to have words about the size of her bill. Her response? Well, apparently all her friends have unlimited-minutes contracts. *What cruel, cruel parents we are*, I thought. But I smiled inwardly at those big imploring eyes of hers and the round, as-yet-unformed face, due to change as womanhood began to exert its influence. It had started already. The rocky shores of adolescence were ahead, the treacherous shoals of Hormonal Bay. I hoped we wouldn't get wrecked on them. I tried her one more time, sent a text, and let the shields click fully into place.

I pulled out the trouser suit and put it to one side. I could always double up on one of the outfits. After all, it was unlikely I'd end up in *Mail Online* with a split picture: 'Unknown Woman Wears Same Outfit Twice'. And besides, Paul was right. They did have shops over there.

Then my mobile rang. It was Jess, panic and shame laced through her voice.

*It had begun.*

The second action-packed thriller featuring
Sam Wylde …

# NOBODY GETS HURT

Bodyguard Sam Wylde has had her British licence
revoked. She is now operating in Europe, running
security on a swanky motor yacht during the Historic
Grand Prix race. And at the same time she trawls for
news of her ex-husband and daughter.

In fact, the owner of the boat is bankrupt and the bank
wants the multi-million-dollar vessel back. Sam is in
the middle of a very dangerous situation that is rapidly
escalating out of control.

Alongside her partner Konrad, Sam has to fight enemies
on all fronts. But will they too find themselves on
opposite sides when it comes to the final showdown?

**Nobody Gets Hurt. If only that were true.**

SIMON &
SCHUSTER